THE WEEKEND WEDDING ASSISTANT

The Weekend Wedding Assistant

A Novel

Rachel Gladstone

TURNER PUBLISHING COMPANY

Turner Publishing Company
Nashville, Tennessee
www.turnerpublishing.com

The Weekend Wedding Assistant
Copyright © 2019 Rachel Gladstone

This is a work of fiction. All the characters and events portrayed in this book are either products of the author's imagination or are used fictitiously.

Cover Design: Kerri Resnick
Book design: Meg Reid
Author Photo: Lori B. Toth Photography

Library of Congress Cataloging-in-Publication Data

Names: Gladstone, Rachel, 1953- author.
Title: The weekend wedding assistant : a novel / by Rachel Gladstone. Description: [Nashville] : [Turner Publishing Company], [2020] | Summary:

"As she ushers four brides a weekend down the aisle she was supposed to walk down herself, Julia tries to understand why she said "I Do" to a job she never set out to get, in a place she'd only meant to occupy for an afternoon and wonders if she'll ever find true love again"—Provided by publisher.

Identifiers: LCCN 2019025089 (print) | LCCN 2019025090 (ebook)
 ISBN 9781684423774 (paperback) | ISBN 9781684423781 (hardcover)
 ISBN 9781684423798 (ebook)
Subjects: GSAFD: Love stories.
Classification: LCC PS3607.L3434 W44 2020 (print) | LCC PS3607.L3434 (ebook) | DDC 813/.6--dc23

LC record available at https://lccn.loc.gov/2019025089
LC ebook record available at https://lccn.loc.gov/2019025090

Printed in the United States of America
19 20 10 9 8 7 6 5 4 3 2 1

This book is dedicated to my mother Ruthe Gladstone, writer, poet and self-appointed sage. You taught me the power and beauty of the English language and to believe that I could do anything I set my mind to. I miss you mightily every day.

chapter one

'm in the wrong life, and I don't know how I got here. I blame
the whole thing on his bucket list.

That damn list! He was obsessed with it, to tell you the
truth, and ticking things off of it was something he lived for.
And died for. That's right—my fiancé, Aaron DeMinthe, kicked
the bucket doing something on his bucket list. Granted, it was a
big item, I'll give him that. But why he had to tick this particular
thing off his list right before our wedding is something I'll never
understand.

Aaron was an athlete. I, unfortunately, am not. Breaking a
sweat makes me break out in a rash. But I never begrudged his
weekends spent playing soccer and basketball, skiing or rock
climbing. On the contrary, his athleticism was one of his most
attractive qualities and one of the things that made me fall in love
with him.

A few years before we met, Aaron had decided to conquer the Appalachian Trail, all 2,184 miles of it. Beginning in Georgia and ending in Maine, the Appalachian Trail rambles across the Eastern Seaboard of the United States like a wilderness river of never-ending hills and valleys, mountains and meadows. And seeing as how the darn thing stretches from here to eternity, most people choose to hike the trail in sections, which is just what Aaron did. Thousands of people have devoted themselves to conquering the AT (as it's commonly known), which is something I simply could not understand. This devotion smacked of cultlike behavior, if you ask me. But cult or not, I had to respect Aaron's pact with the infernal trail and the fact that he'd vowed to complete the entire journey before we got married. He figured that he'd never get around to finishing it once we tied the knot, especially in light of the fact that I hated hiking. But I think it was a rite of passage for him, a coming-of-age kind of thing. Honestly, that's just my best guess. We never discussed it in any depth, and now that he's dead, I'll never know. I wish I'd asked more questions—so many more—because the not knowing fills me with regret. But what I do know is that Aaron's decision was carved in stone and there was nothing I could have done to stop him.

The winter had been unusually harsh, which made for many canceled trips to the AT. As our wedding date drew near, Aaron tried to make up for lost time. He hiked longer stretches of the trail, added extra days when he could, and as far as I knew, he was right on schedule. But I was so caught up in planning our perfect wedding I didn't notice the fact that he hadn't finished yet. And Aaron, bless his heart, decided he'd spring that news on me just six weeks before the big day.

Now, I must tell you that I am not a morning person. As a matter of fact, the rising sun and I are barely on speaking terms.

So, naturally, Aaron decided to make his move at dawn. There I was, fighting my morning stupor and trying my best to be patient as the glacially slow coffee maker drip, drip, dripped my precious elixir into the pot. I won't say who, but someone had forgotten to set the damn timer the night before and I was kind of pissed off about it. But the minute I heard the offending party's footsteps coming down the stairs and rounding into the kitchen my breath caught in my throat, as it always did when he approached, and all my murderous thoughts evaporated. I can't deny it—I was a sucker for that man.

As he slid his arms around my waist from behind, I dipped back into the full six foot two of his muscled frame and let myself get lost in the salty, lemony scent of him. The feel of his freshly pressed suit jacket, solid and steady as a prayer, stretched beneath my palms. As I slid my fingers against the grain of the fabric and closed them around his wrists, I felt as I always did in his arms: safe and protected.

Taking full advantage of my somnambulistic state and the fact that not a drop of caffeine had permeated my weakened brain, Aaron chose that moment to break the news that he hadn't actually finished hiking the AT and that he intended to do so before he made me his wife.

"I have to do this." Aaron released me and backed up a couple of steps, burning a hole in the back of my head with those limpid brown eyes of his.

"Why now?" I cried in the most obnoxious, high-pitched whine I could muster as I turned to face him. "Couldn't you have found a way to fit this in at an earlier time? Like, before we met?" I pouted, turning back to the coffee maker and filling my cup to the brim.

But Aaron would not be cowed. He knew what he had to do. He would see my whiny voice and raise me one by being the grown-up in the room. "Julia, you know how important you are to me," he began, as he always did when he was trying to get his way. Reaching for another mug and filling it, he took a moment to add cream and sugar, stirring slowly for effect. "And you know how much this trip means to me," he said, leaning his shoulder into mine. "Are you actually saying you want me to choose?"

"Of course that's not what I'm saying!" I looked up into his rugged, angular face. "I don't want you to choose—I want you to agree with me!"

Usually, all I had to do was cajole him like this until I got my way. But this time he stood his ground. "I'll be gone for only two days." He raked his fingers through a tangled knot of my stubborn red curls. "You'll barely even miss me. And besides, this will be the last time I hike the AT. I'll be done, and I'll never have to leave you again," he promised.

True to form, I was a sucker for this reasonable approach of his. It always worked on me, especially if I was moody and unreasonable or if it was before noon. And Lord help me I caved. But in my defense, Aaron's reasonableness was another of the things that I loved about him. I mean, you've just got to love a reasonable man; in my experience, they're difficult to find.

Still, I had my pride and wasn't about to cave in without a few caveats of my own. I stepped back dramatically, sloshing coffee all over myself in the process, and began listing my demands while madly blotting at the stains with a dampened tea towel. "All of the errand running for the wedding would have to be done by the time you leave," I told him. "And you have to help me with that blasted seating chart and make sure you and your groomsmen have your final tux fittings." I waved the tea towel in his general direction.

"Done, done, and done." He sliced the air with an imaginary pen. "Anything else I can do?"

Honestly, I had nothing. I had everything firmly under control (or so I thought). And I frowned because, for the first time in my life, I was sorry that I was so organized. Part of me just wanted to make him work for this a little harder.

Taking the towel out of my hand, he set it on the counter, took me in his arms, and caught me up in a lingering kiss. He tasted like coffee ice cream with a note of peppermint toothpaste, and I smiled up at him, brushing his cheek with the back of my hand and then winding it around his neck. "So we're good then?" He smiled. I nodded.

Two weeks later, just one month before our wedding day, off he went. Ostensibly, he would be gone for just a long weekend. Accompanying Aaron on his trek was his best friend and soon-to-be best man, Lincoln Douglas, who was more like a brother than a friend. They'd grown up together, gone to Vanderbilt together, and when Aaron's parents had been killed in a freak car accident right after graduation, Linc had moved into their rambling old bungalow with Aaron and helped him get back to the business of living. Since they'd taken their virgin steps on the Appalachian Trail together, it seemed fitting that it was the two of them that headed off on that fateful day in May. I suppose it was a blessing that Aaron wasn't alone at the end, although I'm sure Linc didn't see it that way.

It was supposed to be the bridal shower to end all bridal showers. Everything was planned around Aaron's trek into the wild, and I, for one, intended to have a wild time of my own. I knew I would not be alone in that pursuit.

To say that I have the greatest girlfriends in the world would be an understatement because nobody knows me better or loves me more. Chief among my beautiful brood is Lili Sinclair, my dearest friend. Physically, we are polar opposites; she's a petite, curvy blonde with large, doelike brown eyes while I am a tall, lanky redhead with baby blues. But in all other ways, we are of a singular mind—willful, funny, and loyal to a fault. Very rarely does a day go by when we don't sign off with a good-night phone call.

Then there's my other bestie, Harper Ray Dyson, a Chinese Southern belle and tiny firecracker of a woman who sports the most beautiful, long, shiny black mane imaginable. Adopted from China as a baby, Harper was raised by a couple in Belle Meade, where the denizens of Old Nashville society reside. Married to the incomparable Jeff Dyson—a math professor and fabulous dad to their twin five-year-old boys—she's always at the top of her game, perfectly composed and annoyingly well coiffed despite the fact that she's always doing fifty million things at once. If I didn't love her so much, I'd hate her guts.

Anyway, the weekend Aaron and Linc took their trek into the wild, Lili and Harper threw me a shower to end all showers at Lili's charming Victorian in Sylvan Park. They planned every detail, from the decorations to the DJ. They had decided we would drink champagne and dance our hearts out while eating lots and lots of fattening food. Twenty other women were invited. Once the party was in full swing, the place bore a striking resemblance to the inside of a very well-decorated chicken coop as we screamed, whooped, and laughed our way into the shank of the night at top volume.

I was in the middle of opening scads of boxes, each one containing a smaller and frillier undergarment than the last, when the doorbell rang. Of course, it was hard to hear it over the plaintive wail of Bryan Adams singing "Heaven." But after the bell had rung repeatedly, we finally picked up on the fact that someone new had turned up to join in the fun. I couldn't imagine who could be calling, as everyone was present and accounted for, so I raced to the door to see what exciting gift-giving guest was here to surprise me. Trailed by a gaggle of champagne-laden, out-of-control women who had thrown all congenial behavior to the wind (in other words, they were shit-faced), I was anything but quiet.

"Maybe I've won the Publishers Clearing House sweepstakes!" I shrieked as I fiddled hopelessly with the dead bolt that stood between me and my mystery guest.

"Lili, did you get a stripper?" one of my friends shouted as I continued to struggle with the locks.

"Lili! You didn't!" I scolded her in mock horror as I pulled at the door, which was still locked fast.

She pushed me gently, but firmly, aside and took over. Lili easily opened the door (apparently it's easy if you live there) to reveal Linc standing in the shadows, looking like he'd just seen a ghost (which, for all intents and purposes, he had).

"You're not a stripper!" I guffawed. This was met with hysterical laughter from my throng of drunken counterparts.

But as I began to take him in, my revelry melted. He was supposed to be at the top of some godforsaken mountain in Maine with Aaron. And if he was here, why was he alone? Where was Aaron? Had they finished their hike early and come to crash my bachelorette party?

Linc walked toward me, holding out his arms and then grabbing me in a fierce bear hug. "Oh, Julia—I'm so sorry! I'm so sorry!" he repeated over and over, his face plowing into my hair, his hands gripping me so tightly I could barely breathe.

What did he mean, he was sorry? "Where's Aaron?" I looked about wildly, up and down the porch as if I'd missed something and Aaron was standing just behind Linc in the bushes or hobbling up the driveway. "Was he hurt? Where is he?" I heard my voice coming from outside of my body, as if I had no connection to it at all.

"He had a terrible accident, Jules," Linc said in a deep, husky whisper.

"An accident?" I screeched.

Linc looked down at his feet and then back at me, the blood drained completely from his face. "Aaron's dead. I'm so sorry!" Linc's eyes bore into mine, his head shaking in disbelief.

My heart felt like it had burst into a thousand tiny pieces. The earth was off its axis, and nothing would ever right it.

Nothing sobers up a crowd faster than the news of a sudden death. And nothing can empty a room as effectively. I remember everyone hugging me and murmuring tearful condolences. And I remember my parents arriving after Linc broke the unimaginable news and them rushing in at his heels to comfort me. But other than that, I have little recollection of what happened in the immediate aftermath. All I knew was that I wanted more than anything to stop time or, better yet, reverse it.

It was down to Lili, Harper, Linc, and me when the imperturbable Jeff arrived with words of wisdom and comfort. He was always good in a crisis. Soon thereafter, he took Harper home. My parents had retreated to the guest room by then. Lili, Linc, and I hunkered down on her mammoth sofa, wrapped around each other like a tangled chain of half-dead daisies, too delicate to unwind lest it break apart.

I made Linc tell us every detail of Aaron's accident, from the final moments of his life to the seconds after his death. The words fell like lead from his lips, each and every syllable weighing on me like an unrelenting anchor, pulling me down, down, down to a place where all I could feel was numb. It occurred to me that although Linc was traumatized because he'd been with Aaron at the end, I was traumatized because I hadn't been. And the deep and unrelenting pain that undulated with the territory bonded us like accidental tourists on a derailed train.

I flashed on the last words Aaron had said to me: "I'll be back before you know it! Don't get too wild tomorrow night." He'd laughed lightly, kissed me, and then hopped into the Uber that he and Linc were taking to the airport. They'd booked an insanely early flight. I, ever the sleepyhead, had opted out of driving them, a regret that ripped through me suddenly. Those would be the last words he'd ever say to me; his last kiss, last laugh, last glance. I said as much to Linc and Lili through a curtain of tears.

"He who laughs last, laughs best," Linc volunteered, passing me a bottle of tequila. "That's what Aaron would have said."

Grabbing for a Kleenex from the dwindling box, I wiped my face dry, blew my nose, and took a generous swig of the proffered bottle. "I need you to tell me what happened…again," I said, looking Linc dead in the eye, passing the bottle back.

It had been an unusually cold and rainy morning as the pair made their ascent to the tallest peak on Mount Katahdin. Aaron was carrying a flag with our picture on it, which he intended to plant at the summit. There we would be, emblazoned on a square of water-repellent cloth, our arms wrapped tight around each other, heads tilted together, our mouths stretched in the biggest, goofiest grins we could manage. He'd wanted me to be there with him, and since I had no intention of ever scaling a mountain, this was the next best thing.

Aaron slid the flag from its protected spot inside his backpack and stood ready to brave the wind and march out to the spot at the top of Mount Katahdin where he'd plant it, a testament to our love and the completion of his big bucket list item. But just then, gale-force winds came screaming up, seemingly out of nowhere, followed by a bank of angry clouds that were rapidly descending all around them.

Linc had a bad feeling about proceeding and tried reasoning with Aaron. "I grabbed his arm and tried to stop him," he remembered. "I kept yelling it was time to head back, that we could return once the weather passed."

But Aaron wouldn't be deterred. With that shit-eating grin he liked to whip out in the toughest of moments, he'd told Linc he hadn't come this far to back out now. They argued back and forth, but in the end Aaron made it clear he was going to have his way. Linc felt like he had no choice but to back him.

Then like a deluge out of the blue, the rain began to come down—a hard, driving rain accompanied by earth-shattering rumbles of thunder and lightning strikes so fierce, it made them jump back. They grabbed on to each other to steady themselves and keep from rolling down the enormous cliffside trail they had just traversed. Reluctantly, Aaron agreed they should find cover until the worst had passed. Wedging themselves under an outcropping of rock, they'd hunkered down to wait out the worst of the storm. A few minutes later, Aaron spotted a patch of blue sky off in the distance. His and Linc's spirits lifted. They figured they wouldn't have long to wait.

As the rain slowed to a light drizzle, Aaron decided it was safe enough for the flag-planting ceremony. It looked like the sun might just come out from behind the bank of clouds that were retreating to the west. A few errant rays caught the mist up in a rainbow of light. But quickly, a new bank of gunmetal-gray clouds came rushing up behind the first, once again obliterating the sun and threatening another downpour. Aaron yelled to Linc amid the building wind that he was going to make a run for the summit. Up he went, the final five hundred feet of his journey, with Linc hot on his trail.

Aaron and Linc scrambled over the slick, rocky terrain. As Aaron came to a halt by the cliffside, he planted the flag with a mighty shove. He stood shooting his arms toward the sky. He arched his back and, face to the clouds, began to do a ceremonial jig, whooping triumphantly.

And then, out of nowhere, it came. A stray bolt of lightning shot from the heavens and struck Aaron dead center, like it had been meant for him. Before he knew what hit him, Aaron had been knocked off his feet and had fallen backward. And with one long, resounding cry, he'd tumbled over the edge of the cliff, disappearing from view as he fell into oblivion.

"He never saw it coming." Linc began to sob, curling his arms around his legs and hugging himself into a ball. Lili and I surrounded him, held on tight, and let him ride out the waves of misery and hysteria that overtook him, until he finally gave into his exhaustion, like a spent two-year-old, and passed out there between us.

The house was silent as a tomb save for Linc's deep, steady breathing, which was annoyingly out of sync with the ticktock of the grandfather clock in the foyer. I felt swallowed up by the heft of the sudden stillness that pressed in around me like a cloying and sodden blanket. Lili, who'd been fighting to stay awake, had slid off the couch just after Linc passed out and then headed to her room. My mind was still racing way too fast to sleep. Curling up next to Linc, I tried to close my eyes, thinking that if I could match my breathing with his, maybe I could slow my brain down. But it was no use. Because the one thing I couldn't stop thinking about, the picture I couldn't erase from my mind, was how the last thing Aaron ever saw was our smiling faces plastered on that blasted flag, planted on top of the mountain, whipping wildly in the wind.

chapter two

At some point, I stumbled to Lili's bed and collapsed beside her. But it wasn't long before the sound of her gently rolling snores woke me out of a troubled sleep. It took me a few seconds to remember where I was. Once I did, I longed for those blissfully fuzzy seconds that had held me in the shelter of their protective cocoon, because they were all that stood between me and utter madness.

I sat bolt upright as a searing pain cut me in half like an ax, sure and true. Uncertain if my skin could take the pressure that was building inside, I had the urge to break free of my body and run, run, run for my life, away from the truth that echoed mercilessly inside my head. "Aaron is dead!" I shrieked. "Aaron, Aaron!" Wailing, I clutched at the sheets and bunched them between my fingers, pulling them up to my chin like I was holding on to them for dear life.

"Jules, Jules, it's OK. It's OK," Lili murmured from underneath my cries, which were practically drowning her out. I felt her arm tighten around my shoulder, solid and alive. Her voice, pulling me back down to earth, repeated the mantra over and over. "It's gonna be OK. It's gonna be OK."

"Who the fuck are you kidding?" I spat at her, snot keeping pace with my tears, which streamed down my face and spilled over onto my wrinkled dress. I hadn't even thought to change into something more comfortable before sinking down beside her. "Nothing will ever be OK again!"

Lili reached behind me and pulled a few tissues from a bedside box, shoving them into my hand. "Is that any way to speak to the woman who has tissues at the ready when you fucking need them?" she asked incredulously.

I blew my nose and burst out laughing mid-blow, drenching my hands with the thick, dribbling mess as I continued to laugh uncontrollably. And then I was sobbing again.

Stumbling to the bathroom, which was just a few steps away, I turned on the faucet and bathed my hands in the warm water spouting from the tap. Mercifully, the bathroom was dark save for a night-light that illuminated the space with a grayish-green hue, enabling me to see the sink while not allowing me to get a clear view of my face in the mirror.

Staggering back to bed, I glanced at the clock, which read 5:45. Although I'd slept no more than an hour, I was wide awake. My nerve endings were buzzing like they were connected to a series of live wires that pumped my overamped brain with ceaseless jolts of electricity. All I wanted in that moment was the oblivion of unconsciousness that eluded me. Glancing down at Lili, I noticed she had fallen back to sleep and was dead to the world, so to speak. I stood and stared at her, jealous of the fact that she was floating out in dreamland while I was awake and standing in the first circle of hell for what, I was sure, would be the rest of eternity. She looked so peaceful lying there, like a cherub with sleep apnea. Not wanting to disturb her again, I tiptoed out of the room and headed toward the kitchen.

Slumped down at the kitchen table, I was nursing my second cup of coffee when dawn broke through the kitchen windows in a glorious explosion of pink light and lavender clouds. I tried to make sense of this unnecessary display of joy and beauty that filled the early morning skies as my eyes strained against the brilliant illumination. The whole thing felt so wrong! How could the sun just rise like that? Didn't it know that Aaron was dead and the world had stopped spinning? This outrageously perfect sunrise struck me as a total affront to all that was decent.

I jumped up from my seat to pull down the blinds against the unwanted sight and heard Linc making his way to the kitchen. I headed back to the coffee maker for a much-needed refill and pulled a cup from the cabinet for him.

"Did you get any sleep?" he inquired in a crackly voice, stepping up beside me and filling his cup all the way.

"A little," I muttered as I sat at the kitchen table, Linc sinking into a chair beside me.

It wasn't long before my parents came in. My father paused to grab me by the shoulders, kissing the top of my head and gracing me with a knowing smile that was sturdy and resolute. My mother, on the other hand—ever the emotional one—rushed in for a deeper hug and, in the process, sloshed the hot brew from my cup all over my lap.

"Well, this dress is obviously finished," I halfheartedly joked. It had been one of my favorites. And as my mother jumped in quickly with a tea towel, I flashed to the morning just two weeks before, when Aaron had announced his plans to scale the mountain that would ultimately kill him. A fresh wave of hysteria rushed over me, covering me up.

"Let's get you into the shower and some fresh clothes." My mother took me by the hand and led me to the guest room. As I stood under the steamy water, my mind began to race with the list of people I needed to call and the arrangements that needed to be made. And for a moment I felt like I could breathe again. As numb as I was, at least there was work to be done, and I knew that the array of tasks ahead would take my mind off of Aaron and the way he had fallen off the edge of the world.

Order has always been my friend. From the moment I could understand what a rule was, I've followed each and every one that's been presented, without question and without fail. For instance, I've always driven at the speed limit and silenced my phone when sitting in a movie theatre. I send thank-you notes promptly and never wear white after Labor Day. I know better than to show up to a dinner party empty-handed, and I've always yielded to the car on my left when coming to a four-way stop. But that morning, as I emerged from the shower and began to towel off, I realized that everything was going to be different now. The rules of life that had always seen me through had been smashed to hell. Because surely when you meet the man of your dreams you're supposed to live happily ever after. And when you plan the perfect wedding, down to the very last flower petal and bridesmaid's dress, it's supposed to go off without a hitch. Isn't it? The answer should have been yes! But that was no longer the case. It was then and there I realized I was going to be playing by a whole new set of rules, for which I was wholly unprepared. Despite the fact that this freaked me out, I knew one thing: I'd have to take the new rules as they came. And the more I thought about it, the more I understood that the first new rule of my life had already been set in place.

RULE #1: *Don't let your fiancé die a month before your wedding. It sucks balls.*

chapter three

The things you say can hurt, but it's the things you don't say that might kill you—like "Don't go, Aaron!" and "What the hell are you thinking?" These words bounced off the walls of my sleep-deprived brain, nonstop, like a kid on a sugar high. My thoughts slapped me around. *Why didn't you stop him? If you'd gotten your ass out of bed and driven him to the airport you would have had an extra twenty minutes with him!* It was like having the inside of my brain wallpapered with dog shit.

It had been four days since Aaron had died, but it might have been four hundred for all I knew; time had lost all meaning. All I could do was crawl from one minute to the next. But four days or four hundred, there I was—sitting in my church, wearing black, surrounded by scores of mourners, all of whom were there to bid farewell to the love of my life. It was unreal.

Propped up in the front pew like a semiconscious rag doll, I fought to banish the self-flagellating thoughts that would not shut the fuck up! The more I fought them, the louder they got. I was surprised that the entire congregation couldn't hear them. I struggled to turn my attention to Reverend Hayes, who had the other mourners in the palm of his hand as he eulogized his ass off from the pulpit. But try as I might, I couldn't make sense of a single word.

Had I told Aaron often enough just how much I loved him? That he meant the world to me? I'd wanted to be his wife more than anything! But instead of making our wedding about our future together and the life we would surely build, I'd fussed at him about seating charts and save-the-date cards like an old schoolmarm. Suddenly, all the hours I'd spent planning my perfect day looked like a foolish waste of time—time I'd never get back. A wave of nausea began its rise from the pit of my stomach to the base of my throat. I lowered my head, taking in a few slow, deep breaths in order to hold the wave in place.

I regret every fight we had, every cross word, every slight, I thought as I stared at my shoes. We hadn't fought often, but still, the angry words I'd spat at him on more than one occasion, which had long ago been forgiven, were words that I'd never be able to take back. I cringed at the thought that time might never lessen this unwieldy burden.

The days leading up to this moment had lumbered by in a fog of condolence calls and funeral arrangements, lukewarm casseroles and spurts of unrelenting tears. I'd alternately binged on coffee and booze with sleep running a distant third, and this left me looking ragged around the edges. This routine could also have been part of the cause for the running voices in my head. But this morning, after emptying the entire contents of my closet while trying to get dressed, I had truly lost it when I'd come to the devastating conclusion that I didn't have a thing to wear.

"I have nothing black," I moaned as I paced back and forth like a caged animal clad only in a lacy black bra and matching panties.

OK, I did have something black, but it was hardly church-appropriate attire.

"What about this?" Harper asked innocently, proffering the little black cocktail dress that was the only item left hanging in my closet.

Lili visibly cringed as I began to pace a bit faster. "That's the dress she was wearing the night she met Aaron."

"I looked so good in it." I continued to sniffle.

"Go ahead. Try it on," Harper urged. Nothing cowed that woman!

Reluctantly, I slipped the dress off the hanger and over my head, pulling it down over my torso. It fit like a glove—a really formfitting, sexy kind of glove. I glowered at my reflection in the mirror. This would never do! Although, I had to admit, I'd never looked thinner. Yeah, I thought, that "Too-Sick-to-Eat-Because-Your-Fiancé-Died Diet" is really the way to go!

I pivoted to the right and then the left, glancing over my shoulder so I could get a good look at my tightly sheathed derriere. "I can't go to the church dressed like this!"

"We could go shopping," Lili suggested.

"I can't go shopping!" I wailed, throwing myself down dramatically atop the pile of rejected outfits that covered the bed. "Look at me! I could barely make it from here to the shower this morning. Besides, I hate shopping! You know that."

"All she needs is a jacket," Harper told Lili as if I weren't in the room.

"You're right." Lili brightened, continuing the conversation as if I truly wasn't there. Sinking down on the bed beside me, she laid a consoling hand on my shoulder as I turned to face her. "I have tons of black jackets! What kind of real estate agent would I be if I didn't have a closet full of jackets?" She stood and headed for the door.

"You run and get a few for her to choose from. I'll deal with the makeup and hair." Harper yanked me to my feet as if I were one of her unruly twins.

And now, here I sat, dressed to the nines in a church-appropriate jacket that hid my tightly sheathed behind, fixated on the larger-than-life photo of Aaron that stared out at me from the center of the stage. He was smiling—beaming actually. He looked like he was keeping a secret he was dying to share, like he'd just discovered the key to happiness or something. Maybe he was smiling because he knew we'd always remember him in the prime of life while we, the ones he'd abandoned, would go on living without him. We'd get older and lose our youthful glow, while he would always remain as he was: strong, exuberant, and full of life. He would forever be young in our eyes. The joke was definitely on us, and he knew it.

I thought about his parents and how lucky they were to have died before he had. Were they waiting for him on the other side? Were they all together again?

Aaron was a planner, something we definitely had in common. If he'd been a Boy Scout, he'd easily have earned the merit badge for funeral planning. Everything was laid out in his wills—both living and final—including the details for disposal of his remains. He'd preferred cremation to burial. The thought of spending the rest of eternity in the cold, dark ground had held little attraction for him; he had been a bit claustrophobic (which explained his need to be out conquering the wide-open spaces all the damn time!). So in true Boy Scout fashion, Aaron had chosen the crematorium, prepaid for their services (they had one of those forever-stamp kind of deals), and he'd even chosen the urn into which he wanted to be poured. It was a platinum affair, intricately embossed with a Celtic design that wound its way around the urn's circumference like an errant breeze. And sitting beside the large urn was an exact replica of the first urn in miniature, which contained a single serving of Aaron's ashes.

That would fit nicely in my purse, I mused silently, eyeing the tiny urn. I could just carry it around with me like a fun accessory. I found this thought strangely comforting, and I smiled to myself as I pictured the tiny urn keeping me company at breakfast or in the shower.

We stood to sing the final hymn. Aaron had been a sucker for a good hymn. I missed his throaty baritone, which had ricocheted off the walls of this church on many a Sunday morning. And in my head I could hear him even now, singing like a man possessed.

And then it was over and we were filing down the aisle. How strange, I thought, that I'm walking down an aisle just a few weeks before my wedding, leaving behind the remnants of my one true love and facing a future without him. This was definitely not the walk I'd always dreamed of.

Every single person who'd attended Aaron's funeral appeared at the reception afterward, which was both flattering and a bit overwhelming. They filled every nook and cranny of our redbrick Craftsman bungalow and spilled out onto the screened-in back porch, which boasted a large collection of overstuffed wicker furniture, and onto the large front porch, which was furnished much the same. There wasn't an inch of breathing room to be had.

My mother and the church ladies staffed command central, a.k.a. the kitchen, where dozens of fresh casseroles, salads, and desserts sat, waiting for their marching orders. While Lili and Linc capably manned the bar, Harper stood at my side in the foyer as I personally greeted every single mourner that filed through the oversized front door. To say that my heart wasn't in it, let alone the rest of my body, would have been an understatement. I ached with exhaustion and grief. It was only my training as a polite Southern woman that kept me from splitting apart at the seams in front of everyone assembled there.

RULE #5: *Be true to your breeding, and it will serve you well when you are barely able to stand in your shoes.*

"I'm so sorry for your loss." "I don't know what to say." "I'm here if I can do anything." These were the phrases that escaped the lips of each and every person who offered sympathies to me. I'd never hugged so many people on one occasion in my life!

But despite the never-ending stream of well-wishers who took up every inch of physical and emotional real estate, the place felt eerily empty. Aaron's electric energy had had a way of filling this house from the cellar to the attic. There was something bone-chillingly real about his absence. A world without him in it felt like a complete impossibility. He was everywhere, yet he was nowhere to be seen, and the impact of his absence made me feel like I was being swallowed up by quicksand. I had no idea how I was going to make it through one more minute of this day, let alone this life.

I couldn't remember how to breathe or carry on a conversation, and I thought I might pass out on the spot. I quickly signaled my distress to Harper, who could handle the crowd from here on out, and then turned from the tearful well-wisher who was mid-condolence and fled.

The afternoon sun slanted through the large, multipaned windows, casting a soft golden light across the living room as I squeezed through the crush of humanity that jammed the space to full capacity. They were chattering and drinking, swapping priceless Aaron stories, tearing up, and laughing through their tears. I felt like a lone grape pushing my way through a sea of partly congealed lemon Jell-O. And as I wove through the well-meaning mob of people who continued to hug me at every turn, I instinctively headed for the staircase. I needed to get out of there before I totally lost my shit.

The timeworn mahogany banister beckoned to me: "This way to paradise!" And as I picked my way through the mourners who lined the stairs, large plates of funeral food balanced on their laps, condolences sprang from their lips like an out-of-control garden hose. This only hastened my rush to higher ground.

More than anything, I longed to run to my room, pull the shades, sink into my bed, and yank the covers over my head until this whole ridiculous nightmare had passed. I rounded the corner and leaned against the doorframe, staring with longing at the smooth, padded contours of my bed. But the old rules, the ones that dictated certain behaviors—like not retreating to your bed when your house is full of guests—forced me away from the comfort of the doorway and down the hall. I still needed a place to hide, and I knew just where to go.

Opening the door to Aaron's walk-in closet, which was located down the hall in the guest room, I was greeted by a rush of quiet mingled with the aroma of his clothes, which hit me like an oncoming train. This was the perfect spot! No one would think to look for me here. I snapped on the light and quickly closed the door behind me, lest I let an iota of his scent escape into the ether. Grabbing his well-worn brown leather bomber jacket from its hook on the door, I buried my nose in the lining and sank to the floor in defeat.

"Aaron! How could you leave me like this?" I cried out to the familiar sea of garments. I surveyed the little room, everything hanging just so, orderly and neat—so like my Aaron. A place for everything and everything in its place; that had been his motto and had gotten him through many of the major hurdles in his life. When his parents had left him—an only child of twenty-two—the thing that had kept him sane, he'd told me, was keeping his possessions and their house, where we now lived, ordered and accounted for. I'd always marveled at the fact that he could have such a regimented philosophy about life while simultaneously keeping a great sense of humor and spontaneity in the mix. For all his attention to detail, he'd maintained the ability to embrace life as it came. He'd explained that his parents had been much the same and that, although he missed them every day, he knew they'd wanted to pass that legacy on to their son. They would have wanted him to find joy in life despite the deep sorrow their early departure had brought. And for the first time, I realized how truly brave Aaron had been in the face of unspeakable heartbreak. I wondered if I would ever measure up.

I hadn't been alone for more than sixty seconds when the door behind me opened and Lili burst into the closet, ruining my quiet moment. She closed the door behind her as quickly as she'd opened it and plopped down beside me.

"There goes my solitude." I pouted in her general direction.

"Solitude is overrated," she retorted.

RULE #12: *You can't hide from your best friend, so don't even try. She always knows right where to find you.*

Pulling a flask from the pocket of her jacket, Lili offered it to me. "Wiancées first," she added, handing it over to me with a flourish.

"Is that what I am?" I queried as I unscrewed the cap. "A wiancée? Really?"

"It seems like the most appropriate title for you," Lili answered matter-of-factly. "You are a widowed-fiancée." She had a penchant for calling things as she saw them.

"It does have a ring to it." I nodded thoughtfully and tipped back a shot. The smooth-yet-razor-sharp trickle of pure agave bit the back of my throat and spread like wildfire through my chest, warming me from the inside out like a liquid fireball. "Aaron loved this stuff," I said, handing the flask back to Lili. "I think he always had a bottle on hand."

"Where do you think I got this?" She took a deep pull from the flask. "You all have a well-stocked bar. You even have really cool to-go cups." She smiled, handing it back again.

"Yeah, those were an early wedding present from Linc." I took another swig. "I don't think Aaron ever had a chance to use them." I started to tear up.

"One more for courage," Lili said, handing the flask back to me. "The mourners are probably getting restless down there."

"Please don't remind me." I frowned, trying to pull myself together. Reluctantly, I got up, hung Aaron's jacket back in its spot, and raised the flask to the heavens. "Here's to you, babe," I said, taking another long pull. "Third one's the charm," I told Lili as I felt a welcome numbness overtake my senses.

I inhaled deeply, taking in as much of Aaron's essence as I could, and then opened the door and turned out the light, holding my breath for dear life.

Despite the fact that I could barely feel my feet, I managed to find my way back down the stairs and into the kitchen, where my mother and the church ladies were still hard at work. Upon seeing me, my mother shoved a plate into my hands and insisted I sit and eat something. "You look pale, darlin'," she told me in no uncertain terms. The deviled eggs, ham biscuits, and other assorted goodies gathered there made me want to puke, truth be told. But instead of making a fuss, I took the plate from her, smiled weakly, and headed out to the back porch. There was no way I could eat a bite, but I didn't need to explain that to my mother right now. She was just trying to help the best way she knew how.

The substantial screen door made a comforting thwack as it swung shut behind me. Pushing through the throng of well-wishers camped out on the porch—each of them repeating the same old, same old—I made my way across the room, out the other door, and into the backyard. It was a terraced affair, a stone wall parallel to the house sloping to the left down the hill toward the tall wooden fence that bordered the yard on all three sides. To the right, a rather uneven set of winding stone steps led down to a covered cement porch, which boasted a built-in stone fire-place with a grill, a wooden farm table with benches, and a slew of Adirondack chairs.

We'd been making plans to put in a pool at the edge of the lawn, a few feet from the covered porch. A long, slender ribbon of blue, stretching the length of the sturdy boxwoods—it would have been a place Aaron could swim laps with a vengeance. I'd entertained thoughts of learning how to swim, thinking it was something we could do together. I'd loved the thought of us slic-ing through the water side by side, swimming end to end and back again.

I pictured it now as I perched at the top of the stone stairs. Kicking off my shoes, I headed down the steps to cooler ground and sank into an Adirondack on the lower porch.

The honeysuckle swayed like a talisman on the early evening breeze, transporting me back to happier days—days I'd taken for granted…days I'd never get back. The porch sang and danced with conversations from the past. Visions of Aaron bubbled up through the cobwebs of time, overtaking me. All the evenings we'd spent entertaining friends and family, the laughter and deep abiding love that had filled those glorious hours resounded even now. I could hear Aaron telling one of his bad jokes, the rest of us groaning in mock disdain. I could almost taste the summer suppers, the corn and burgers we had cooked up on the grill, which we'd washed down with cold beer and happiness. Our life together had been new, and we'd felt invincible. And our love, which was both fortress and rocket ship, had seemed indestructible—a love that would last forever.

The voices of well-wishers escaped the windows above. Fragments of their conversations and laughter rode out to me on the plush evening air. I was so grateful to each and every one of them. But what would happen when they all went away? Went back to their lives and left me with mine? Suddenly, I didn't want to be alone another minute. Despite the exhaustion that gripped me like an overzealous newcomer at her first church social, I made a beeline for the kitchen and back to the land of the living.

There I found my parents, Linc, Lili, and Harper. I joined them as they emptied casseroles into Tupperware containers and packed them into the freezer, bundled up the trash, and started in handwashing the good crystal glasses and silver. This was a funeral after all. Maybe there hadn't been a body or visitation, but viewing or no viewing, we were ordered by law to bring out the good china, silver, linens, and crystal glasses when we were hosting a reception such as this. We weren't savages, after all!

As the last of the guests peeled off, I sank into my seat at the kitchen table. But sitting upright seemed like such a mammoth task. Making my excuses, I gave myself one last heave-ho, up the stairs, to my waiting bed and a long, deep sleep that welcomed me with open arms.

chapter four

It was the day before my wedding day... or what should have been my wedding day. I woke with the palpable sense that I needed to do something, get this show on the road, get "up and at 'em" and back to the business of living. I'd cried myself to sleep the night before, as had become my habit, and my head throbbed with the pain of a thousand tiny jackhammers. I'd heard it takes twenty-one days to form a new habit, and I wondered how long it would take to break this one. I was sick of feeling like crap!

I swung my legs over the side of the bed, the weight of grief still sitting squarely on my shoulders. But weight or no weight, I managed to pull myself out of bed and into the shower, where I lathered every part of my body a half dozen times in an effort to scrub away the misery that clung to me like a sheath. This effort proved fruitless. But even if I wasn't "at 'em," at least I was up.

Stepping out of the shower and into my oversized terry cloth robe, I padded back to the bedroom and made a beeline for the rolltop desk that sat in the middle of the large, sunny bay window. I'd loved that jigsaw of compartments, shelves, and hidden drawers since the days of my girlhood when it sat in my grandfather's study. The sturdy accordion of wood that hid those compartments was scrolled down and shut tight—the only thing standing between me and my "Wedding Bible," which was the be-all and end-all of collated, organized, color-coded bliss. Even though that tome had been my constant companion for close to a year, I hadn't had the heart to look at it since Aaron had met his maker. It had remained out of my sight, stationed underneath the rolltop.

I took a seat and a big breath and then opened the desk to find it sitting just where I'd left it. Pulling it toward me, I ran the flat of my palm across the face of the notebook where photos of Aaron and me—the happy us, the so-in-love-it-hurts-to-be-us photos—were pieced together like a crazy quilt. I began swishing my hand back and forth across the cover like I was rubbing a magic lamp, hoping a genie would appear and grant me three wishes. Really, I needed only one.

Sliding my thumb inside the binder, I slowly opened it to the first page. I willed myself to breathe. Just breathe. There was our wedding invitation: "Mr. and Mrs. Holmes request the honor of your presence for the marriage of their daughter, Julia Ann Holmes, to Mr. Aaron DeMinthe" read the beautiful calligraphy with the date, time, and place my dreams were supposed to have become reality. I began to leaf through the pages. As I did so, I found my mother's notes in the margins where she'd canceled the vendors. Each and every one had generously refunded our deposits once they'd heard my tragic story. But still, there were some loose ends to tie up.

First there were the gifts we'd received. I wasn't sure what the protocol was, but I knew I didn't want to keep a single one. Then there was the standing order for embossed thank-you notes and stationery that would have borne my married name. I'd planned to give the printers the green light once Aaron and I had said "I do." I wasn't superstitious about much, like having a first look with him before the ceremony, but I was superstitious about seeing my married name in print before it was official; now that, I thought, would bring us bad luck! But what had I known about luck, bad or otherwise? The only thing I knew was that none of the silly superstitions I'd kept or dismissed had prevented Aaron from falling off that mountain. I shuddered at the thought as the imaginary footage of his death flickered in my mind's eye, unlocking the floodgates I'd had a handle on a second ago.

Slamming the rolltop down, I scolded myself. "Why am I torturing myself like this?" I cried aloud, throwing my arms in the air. I should just go back to bed and stay there until the day after tomorrow! I thought. But that would never do, because, as my mama liked to say, God hates a coward. And I was anything but that!

Steeling myself, I pushed up the rolltop once again and took the Wedding Bible in both hands. I began to flip from one section of that big-ass binder to the next, like a woman possessed. Taking in every detail with the sweep of my puffy eyes, I cataloged the tasks my mother had taken care of: Cancel the caterer—check. Cancel the wedding cake and the silver pedestal it would have sat upon—check, check. Hair and makeup, the photographer, the videographer—check, check, check. The musicians, the guests— everyone knew my big day had ended before it had begun.

Like all the other vendors, Whitfield Chapel—my chosen ceremony site—had refunded my money in full, which was surprising because Whitfield never refunded anyone's deposit. Of course, they felt terrible about my tragic loss, but that hadn't been the only reason behind the unexpected refund. The truth was they knew they could fill my slot faster than a couple of born-again virgins dropping their drawers on their wedding night! I'm almost ashamed to admit it, but losing my big day at Whitfield to some other bride was equally as earth-shattering as Aaron's death. I know that sounds horrid, but that big, beautiful old church and I went way back. As a matter of fact, I'd dreamed of getting married there since I was five, the year I'd been the flower girl in my aunt Bitsy's wedding.

I'd been over the moon when Bitsy had asked me to herald her down the aisle, and not just because I was excited about being in my first wedding, but because the fact that Bitsy was getting married at all was a miracle!

Nobody, especially "poor" Aunt Bitsy, had ever thought her special day would come. By then Bitsy was thirty and just a hair's breadth away from being consigned to the worst of all fates: spinsterhood. The drama surrounding her marital status, or lack thereof, was my mother and grandmother's main topic of conversation. "How is it possible that such a beautiful, engaging, intelligent woman should have missed her chance for everlasting happiness, a houseful of new furniture, flatware, and the pitter-patter of little feet?" was the question on theirs and everyone else's lips but mine. I knew exactly why Bitsy was still a member of the lonely hearts club; it was her ridiculous nickname!

I never understood why anyone had chosen to call Elizabeth Jane Coulter "Bitsy" when she was no such thing! She'd sprouted up faster than summer corn and was nearly six feet tall, and this caused her to tower over most of her beaux. But I'd always thought if we called her Lizzie or Beth, rather than a nickname that drew attention to her towering stature, everyone would have been unfazed by it and she surely would have gotten married sooner. But what did I know? I was five.

From the moment she came home flashing that big old diamond ring, Bitsy's tragedy had turned into a cautionary tale.

"She was lucky to have slid into home plate right in the nick of time," my mother said.

"I was so afraid I'd never see this day," my grandmother confided, tears glistening in her eyes. And from that moment on, wedding fever gripped our household.

Bitsy, bless her heart, wanted a June wedding at Whitfield Chapel more than she wanted a chance to glimpse the pearly gates without having to die first. Seeing as how it was April, the chances of her getting her wish were slim to none. But as luck would have it, some June bride had decided to toss away her prime Saturday night slot, and Bitsy had caught it with both hands. It was a sign, the equivalent of Jesus turning water into wine, or finding the perfect pair of jeans! Whitfield was the chapel of every girl's dreams, and evidently all of Bitsy's were coming true.

My life took a dramatic turn the day we bought my dress. I had never beheld anything more beautiful; the delicious confection of taffeta and lace was perfection itself. And on Bitsy's big day, as I stood at the end of the aisle—my basket of petals hanging just so from my slightly trembling hand, a wreath of pale-pink baby roses atop my head entwined with white satin ribbons cascading down my back against a flurry of fluffy red curls—I looked back at Bitsy for one last encouraging smile. I was ready to go.

Stepping through the doors, I practically tiptoed to the aisle. There I stood for a spellbinding moment, suspended in time. I'd never seen so many people in one place, especially so many people looking right at me. Part of me wanted to turn tail and run! But the jigsaw of timeworn slate felt solid and sure underneath the soles of my white patent leather shoes, and as I took my first steps down the aisle, scattering my petals just so, my confidence began to take hold. By the time I'd walked halfway down, I began to feel like the magical nymph I resembled, blanketing the aisle with a trail of petals, like so many bread crumbs, leading Aunt Bitsy out of the woods of loneliness and into the light of true love. It was magic! It was heavenly and oh-so romantic.

Being Bitsy's opening act had given me a heady feeling. As I watched her walking down the aisle toward her true love, leaving not a dry eye in the house, I decided that one day I would be the main attraction, heading down that same aisle to the waiting arms of my very own groom, and we would live happily ever after. Yeah. That was the plan.

My rumbling stomach drew my attention to the hour; it was nearly noon, and I'd forgotten to eat breakfast again. Lucky for me, Linc would be here any minute, lunch in hand. That meal would carry me through until he returned at suppertime to share one of the casseroles that still filled the freezer.

From that first terrible night, Linc had rarely left my side. Without even knowing it, I had grown to depend on him. For all intents and purposes, Linc had moved in. It had just sort of happened. After Aaron's funeral he'd stayed in the guest room, and he'd been sleeping there ever since. The few times he had attempted to sleep at his own house, he'd invariably turned up at my front door in the middle of the night, his blond hair ruffled, his azure eyes churning with pain. But that was all right with me; I couldn't sleep either. Other than a few toiletries and a pair of sweats, he hadn't actually moved any of his belongings in, so I didn't think much of it. It just felt natural for him to be there.

Every morning he'd bring me coffee in bed before heading home to shower and ready himself for the day. I'd drift back to the land of nod until just before noon, when I would drag myself to the shower in anticipation of Linc arriving with lunch. Lili spent a lot of time at the house too, but her demanding job dictated much of her schedule. Likewise, Harper—who put Wonder Woman to shame as she fiercely wielded the double-edged sword of career and family—visited when she could. Of course, they were in constant contact via text and messenger. And my parents were always hovering close by, which was easy since they lived a few blocks away. But still it was mostly just Linc and me eating our way through a freezer full of funeral food.

Linc was always armed with snappy one-liners and an earthy smile, which bolstered my energy like the mother of all batteries and helped me cope as I tried to make sense of a world without Aaron in it. Having Linc around felt as natural as breathing. His easygoing company filled the empty spaces that Aaron had left in his wake. Linc's presence in the house was something I'd begun to take for granted. And I found that whenever he left to go to work or the grocery store, I counted the minutes until he returned, because when he was around it felt like a piece of Aaron was still there too.

My stomach redoubled its efforts to get my attention, and I hastily slid the Bible back in place and rolled the desk cover over it. Hoisting myself from the chair with not a little effort, I headed to my closet and whipped out the first sundress I could lay my hands on. Securing my curls on top of my head with my favorite tortoiseshell clip, I rinsed my face, brushed my teeth, and put on a touch of mascara and blush. Linc was bringing lunch; the least I could do was dress for the occasion.

The table was set by the time Linc walked through the kitchen door. I'd even had time to gather a handful of pink and white peonies from the side yard, which added an air of festivity to the room. They jostled for space in the cornflower-blue pitcher Aaron had bought for me on our third date—our outing to the Tennessee Craft Fair, a biannual event held in Centennial Park. Sturdy and squat, the pitcher was glazed with a blue so deep it could break your heart. But before I could even point to it and claim it as mine, Aaron had bought it and was handing it to me, a look of delight playing on his lips. The sight of those lips always made my knees buckle! And oh, my God, how I missed them.

I closed my eyes and began to breathe in the memory of him, wondering if I concentrated hard enough if I could will Aaron back into existence, even if just for a minute or two. And it wasn't long before I could feel him in the room, like he was standing next to me. Effortlessly, I felt myself being transported back to our date at the craft fair. I could hear Aaron's laughter rippling through the air as we shared our first inside joke. I gazed up at his face—sun-kissed and open—and as I reached to push back the unruly thicket of chestnut hair that was forever getting in his eyes, our lips met in a quick yet passionate kiss. We paused for one languid moment before continuing on our way. With the length of his arm wrapping around my waist, he guided me through the thick of the crowd, sure and true, like he knew every inch of his body and what it was capable of.

I opened my eyes and stared at the weathered farm table in front of me, which was illuminated by the cascade of peachy noontime light that streamed through the bank of windows behind it. That table had seen its share of lazy Saturday morning breakfasts and Tuesday night suppers for two. Our friends and family had regularly gathered here, sharing secrets and celebrating milestones. I let myself bask in the memory of the sights and sounds of every occasion. I just stood there, encased in a frozen chunk of timeless time, and it felt like Aaron was still with me, like I'd filled the blue vase with peonies just for him.

For a moment the world felt right again. It was as if Aaron had never been gone. I let myself be still . . . let myself just be. And oh, how I wished I could stop all the clocks and put away the sun and remain in that moment forever!

The sound of the back door opening shook me from my delusional haze. I turned to see Linc standing behind me, a black folio in one hand and a large bag from the Picnic Café in the other. There was a shadow hanging over his face, which made him look worn to the bone and frazzled, much like the way he'd looked the night he'd turned up at my bachelorette party. But as his eyes met mine the clouds lifted, his expression shifted, and he looked as he always did: like a golden retriever in a suit.

"I come bearing chicken salad and tea." He smiled as he set the bag on the counter. "And I took the rest of the day off." Crossing to the table, he set the folder down beside his plate and hung his jacket over the back of the chair.

"Is there pie?" I asked, hungrily unpacking the contents of the bag.

"Of course! Pecan and chess. I wasn't sure what you were hungry for."

"Both!" I laughed as I plated the contents of the containers and brought them to the table.

I actually felt like a human being for the first time in weeks—a human being with an appetite, apparently. I attacked my food with the gusto of a marathon runner, which was kind of surprising since I'd had little to no appetite for weeks. Maybe opening the big-ass planner and facing my loss head-on had made a dent in my grief. Or maybe reliving that perfect afternoon with Aaron had soothed my soul. Whatever the reason, it felt good to feel good.

"So why did you take the afternoon off? Getting a head start on the weekend?" I asked, coming up for air between forkfuls. It was then that I noticed Linc hadn't taken a bite. "What's up? I've never known you to turn down the best chicken salad in town," I said while I gesticulated with my fork before dipping it into a mound of coleslaw.

His hand moved toward the folder and rested there. "Just not hungry, I guess," he said through a lopsided smile. Now I was worried.

"OK, I give," I tried to joke it off, shoving a chunk of pecan pie unceremoniously into my mouth. "What's in the folder?"

He hesitated before flashing another uncomfortable smile. Standing to refill his glass of tea, which really didn't need refilling, he tossed his next remark over his shoulder like an unwanted tissue. "Just some papers for you to look at." He was trying to sound as casual as possible, which, as everyone knows, is a dead giveaway that someone is holding back bad news.

I dropped my fork, pushed back in my chair, and strode to the counter where Linc stood pretending to top off his barely touched glass. I, on the other hand, had drained my first glass. Shaking the inclination to pour something stronger in there, I refilled it to the top with tea and took a hearty gulp. "What kind of papers?"

The uncomfortable smile made a third appearance; now he looked like a golden retriever who'd been caught chewing up your favorite pair of shoes. "They can wait until you've eaten."

"I've eaten."

Linc turned to face me and, reaching out, ran his hand down my arm and gave it a squeeze. Crossing back to the table, he grabbed the folder. "Why don't we have a seat on the porch?"

He gestured for me to precede him, like the gentleman he was. This was going to be bad; I could sense it. Although what could be worse than losing Aaron? I wondered. Was I in danger of losing the house too, or did Aaron have a love child I wasn't aware of?

By the time we'd reached the wicker sofa, my stomach had turned in on itself, and I feared the lunch I'd inhaled was about to make an unwanted reappearance.

I sank into the overstuffed chintz cushions with an unladylike thud, grabbed a throw pillow, and clutched it to my chest. Settling beside me, Linc placed the folder on the low table in front of us, opened it, and withdrew a stack of documents an inch thick; that was just half of what was in there.

"So, as you know, I wasn't just Aaron's best friend...I was also his lawyer," Linc began, his voice all lawyerly and business-like. "And as such, I drew up his last will and testament. Did he ever talk to you about what is in it?"

"Sure," I stammered, looking at the stack of papers in Linc's hand. "He mentioned it. I mean, we never discussed the details really. It wasn't like we thought he was going to die any time soon. He was the picture of health . . ."

"Well, Aaron was meticulous about the details of his estate. Actually"—he swallowed, nodding at the large collection of papers he held in his lap—"he drew up a new version of his will a few weeks before we left for the AT. And to make a long story short, he left you very well taken care of."

I exhaled the breath I didn't realize I'd been holding, like somebody coming up from a deep-sea dive. "So I get to keep the house and there's no secret love child waiting in the wings?"

Linc smiled beneficently. "Just the opposite, Jules. Aaron left you a fortune."

I felt like somebody had knocked me upside the head with a two-by-four. "What? Aaron didn't have a fortune. We were comfortable...Aaron made a good living, but he wasn't rich."

"Actually he was." Linc nodded at me, thumbing through the freshly minted stack of papers. "When his parents died, he inherited a massive portfolio of investments, cash, and proper-ties worth millions of dollars." He indicated every few pages for emphasis. "Everything was initially held in a trust, and he just left it there. Let it ride, so to speak. He never wanted the money because he felt like it had cost him too dearly. But right after he proposed he decided it was time to embrace the money, espe-cially because after so many years the trust was worth ten times as much. He wanted to do it for you, and he changed the terms of the trust and put everything in both your names. Julia, you're his sole beneficiary."

I could feel the blood rushing to my head, and my ears buzzed like there was a swarm of bees in there trying to get out. I leaped to my feet and began to pace, the pillow still clutched to my chest. I felt like this news was the Titanic and I was the iceberg it was crashing into.

Linc was on his feet in seconds. Keeping pace with me, he tried to calm me. "I know this is a shock, Jules."

I stopped to look at him. "A shock? Is that what you call it? It's more like a fucking ambush!" I took up my pacing once more. "Aaron didn't want this money because it felt like blood money, right? So how the hell do you think it makes me feel?"

Linc stood stock-still in front of the low wicker table, Aaron's will sprawled across its surface, his arms crossed over his chest. "This was supposed to be a happy surprise, Julia!" His voice began to rise in pitch. "Aaron wanted this to be the wedding present to end all wedding presents!"

"Then why isn't Aaron the one giving me the wedding present to end all fucking wedding presents? Huh? Why isn't he here? Answer me that!" I threw the pillow to the floor and threw out my arms in exasperation.

Linc rushed toward me and forcefully grabbed me by the shoulders, shaking me a few times for emphasis, his eyes ablaze with confusion and anguish. "I can't answer you!" he screamed. "I don't have any answers! Don't you think I wish he was here giving you this news? Don't you think if I had it to do all over again, I'd stop him from climbing the last hundred yards to the top of that bloody mountain?"

I stared into his eyes as he held me fast, still hoping for an answer I knew he didn't have. I squeezed his arms in return, and drawing closer to him, looked up at him, shaking my head. "Of course you would have," I reassured him. "I know that."

I knew it only too well. The guilt and deep regret for the part

I felt I'd played in Aaron's death chased after me day and night like a bloodhound on the scent. "If only" had become my mantra, and the "should haves" that played on an endless loop in my head made it difficult to find any real respite.

RULE #31: *Don't, under any circumstances, spend even one night out on the town with that bastard Regret. Because he's gonna eat you for dinner, spit you out, and make you pay the check.*

"I should have forbidden him to go," I whispered in a ragged tone through the torrent of tears that had joined in the mix. I continued to search Linc's eyes, this time looking for the forgiveness I couldn't give myself.

"Oh, that would have gone over well!" Linc laughed through his tears, causing me to join him like a mischievous child.

He smiled down at me and reached to brush a fat, errant tear from my cheek with his thumb, the bottomless ocean of his eyes drawing me in. His palms came to rest again on my shoulder, but this time his touch was gentle. He pulled me toward him until we were so close I could feel his breath against my lips. We were a fraction of a second away from a kiss—a kiss I knew I wouldn't refuse.

"Jules?" Lili's voice came rushing from the kitchen, instantly breaking the spell. I heard the back door slam and her footsteps fast approaching. "Jules, where are you?" she called again.

Linc and I sprang apart like a couple of guilty teenagers as I pushed past him and headed for the screen door. "We're out here!"

A fresh batch of tears streamed across my flushed cheeks. Lili rushed toward me, arms flung wide. Grabbing me up in an enormously welcome embrace, she squeezed me just a little too tight. "I got Linc's 911," she said, alarm in her voice. "Are you OK?"

She finally released me and looked me up and down searching for visible signs of injury.

"I'm rich," I gurgled at her like a drowning cat.

"Say what?" Lili looked as confused as I felt.

"I'm rich," I repeated, a little more clearly, wiping at my face with the back of one hand while still holding on to her with the other.

"Well that's just terrible, Jules," she said in a mocking tone. "Now...how did this happen? And just how rich is rich?" She looked at Linc, who stood motionless behind us, and then back at me.

"Evidently, Aaron's parents left him a gazillion dollars, or whatever, but he kept the money in a trust because he felt guilty about spending it. And now he's dead and all of it goes to me. It was supposed to be my wedding present! Can you believe that?" I stared incredulously at Lili.

"Aaron was rich? Wow. Who knew?"

"I knew," Linc stated in an apologetic tone.

"That was meant to be a rhetorical question," Lili replied. "But that does make sense. You were the man's lawyer. Still . . ."

The sound of the back door flying open and slamming shut underscored the clickity-clack of Harper's three-inch heels. Like a helicopter mom on steroids, she demanded to know where we were. "We're out here!" Lili and I called in tandem.

"What's the emergency?" Harper pushed through the screen door looking like she might take it off the hinges and was fully prepared to do so should the need arise. "I got Linc's text."

"Julia's a gazillionaire," Lili explained in a slightly mocking tone.

"That's the emergency?" Harper looked confused for a moment before pulling her phone from the recesses of her designer bag. "If I hurry, I can still make the showing I pawned off on my assistant," she said, simultaneously sending a text and walking toward me. "I know that tomorrow was supposed to be your wedding day and you're probably freaking out. And I also know that this whole tragedy is affecting your self-esteem and your search for purpose in your life, sweetie. But I'm up to my ears in purpose, and I just wish that someone would leave me a fortune so I could afford a nanny for my kids." She hugged me firmly for a moment, let go, and looked me square in the eye. "I think you should go shopping." She squeezed my shoulders for reassurance.

"You know I hate shopping . . ." I weakly protested.

Promising to call me later, she turned on her heel and headed for the door. Her phone was going off before she even crossed the kitchen. She answered it on the second ring, assuring her baffled client that she was on her way and that her emergency had turned out not to be so emergent after all.

I stood stock-still, mouth agape, and waited for Linc and Lili to offer their reassurances about this bizarre situation or at least make rude comments about Harper's dismissive attitude. But they had nothing.

"Can you believe what she just said to me?" I pleaded with Linc and Lili when they didn't offer to back me up.

"Harper was just being Harper." Lili gave me another hug. "And honestly, Jules, I've got to say that I'm with her on this one. This isn't the worst news in the world! If I could, I'd stay here and explain the dozens of reasons I know this to be true. But I can't. In case you've forgotten, I have an actual date with a real, live man tonight, and I need to go home and shave my legs." She kissed me on the cheek, gave my arm a squeeze, and she was gone.

The air felt thick and syrupy in the silence that followed in her wake, and I suddenly felt so uncomfortable in my skin that I had to fight the urge to tear it from my bones.

I looked to Linc, hoping he would make everything all right. But apparently, he had nothing to say either as he busied himself tidying the papers that had been scattered across the table. Staring at the back of him, I flashed back to our almost-kiss, the thought of which made my head spin—and not in a good way. So I turned and followed the trail Harper and Lili had blazed, Linc's voice trailing after me.

chapter five

I ran out the door, my heart beating like a caged bird that was demanding release. I strode past house after stately old house that lined block after shady block of my neighborhood, trying to see beyond the lake of tears that flooded my eyes. The heat of the late spring afternoon hung around me like an unwelcome cloak, which only added to my distress. My breathing had become so labored I thought I might pass out. Great! Now I couldn't see or breathe! But the last thing I wanted to do was turn and head for home; despite the relief I would have found in the perfectly chilled air, I feared Linc's reception would be even chillier. I could tell from the stream of anxious texts that were dinging my phone that Linc had gone from worried to angry to who knows what, so finally, I turned the damn thing off.

The overwhelming heat and sheer exhaustion of my incredulity finally slowed my pace. And as I ambled along, I held my hand up in a flat-palmed wave to residents and passersby, as is the custom in these parts. From their vantage point I probably looked like an ordinary woman taking a walk in the punishing afternoon heat. But inside I felt like an alien studying the behavior of the random earthlings who were walking their dogs, weeding their front flower beds, or sitting on their porches nursing cool glasses of tea and praying for just a hint of relief from the bellowing humidity. I wondered what it must be like to be them, going about their normal, day-to-day routines with no knowledge of who Aaron had been or that he'd left the land of the living. I felt like a ghost of my former self going through the motions of living, and I wondered if I'd feel like an apparition forever.

When I couldn't stand the heat a moment longer, I reluctantly returned to the house, my skin bathed in a thin veneer of sweat, my hair ablaze in a tangle of damp curls. But as disgustingly wet and sticky as I felt, at least my walk had soothed the savage beast that had overtaken me earlier. I hoped Linc would be waiting inside so we could pick up where we'd left off. I felt like I needed to clear the air.

He stood on the back porch, almost in the same spot I'd left him, surveying the emerald-green backdrop of lawn and trees. Despite the fact that he appeared not to have moved an inch, he was now wearing jeans and a T-shirt as opposed to the suit he'd sported earlier. Unfortunately the wardrobe change extended only as far as his face; nothing had changed there. He walked toward me, doing his best impression of a man who's nonplussed, but I could see that I'd worried him. The thought made my heart sink a little. I opened my mouth to apologize, but before I could say a word, he let 'er rip.

"Where've you been, Jules?" he shouted at me like I was a teenager who'd missed her curfew.

"I was just walking around . . ." I shrugged my shoulders.

"Didn't you get my texts?" he continued to scold.

"All ninety-five of them?" I joked.

"Funny! You're a funny lady!" He twisted his mouth into his best impression of a smirk, but a deep rivulet of anger dug in across his forehead and overran his eyes. He wasn't fooling anyone with those eyes.

For once in my life, I didn't know what to say. We just stood there for a moment staring at each other. All I wanted was for Linc to reach out for me and fold me in his arms. I wanted to wrap myself in the cocoon of his aliveness and revel in his heartbeat, his steady breath, and the faint scent of vanilla and sea salt that rose from him in comforting waves. I took a step toward him and reached out my hand, but he took a step back, shaking his head. That snapped me to attention.

"I'm sorry if I worried you, Linc. I just needed to clear my head."

"I get that, but you didn't have to be so dramatic about it!" he shouted.

Evidently, he wasn't ready to let go of how pissed he was.

"But you know something?" he continued. "Your disappearing act got me to thinking. I've been hanging around here, trying to come to terms with Aaron's death by spending time with you, when really what I needed to do was to get out of here for a few days."

I was stunned! "Are you saying I've driven you away?"

He began to pace in an exasperated manner. "No! I just need to get out of this city. Maybe head to the Smokies and do some hiking. I see Aaron everywhere I look, and it's taking a toll on my sanity."

I wanted to scream, "Don't you think I feel the same way? Don't leave me, Linc! I need you so badly!" But instead, I opted to put a brave face on it. "So when are you leaving? You must have to go home and pack." I hoped my voice sounded calmer than I felt.

"Already did. After I figured out that you were going to be AWOL for a while, I headed home and threw my gear together. I was just waiting here for you so I could say goodbye."

My heart jumped into my throat and lodged there, thick and heavy, and it was all I could do to croak out my acquiescence to his unsettling plans. "If that's what you've gotta do, then all I can say is safe travels."

I walked to Linc and grabbed him up in a quick hug, trying to ignore the rush of confusing feelings that swirled through my veins like a Molotov cocktail that threatened to blow a giant hole in my already tripped-out mind.

"Take care of yourself, Jules. I'll call you when I get back." He kissed me on the forehead and exited stage left.

I hardly knew what to do with myself. I had come to count on Linc, and I'd thought he had come to count on me as well. Our grief had woven itself around us like a raggedy blanket, pieced together by the shared tears and endless Aaron stories that kept us from the bitter cold of misery and the cavernous ache of missing him. But in the process, I had begun to develop feelings for my dead fiancé's best friend, a man who had probably saved my life after failing to do the same for Aaron. As the memory of our almost-kiss came roaring back into my mind's eye, I realized that this crush, or whatever it was, had to come to a grinding halt. Linc deserved better than to be dragged into an untenable situation with an emotionally spent woman who didn't have sense enough to pour piss out of a boot with the directions written on the heel.

I needed to slow things down and get us back on an even keel, where we belonged. This would require shifting the relationship back to one Aaron would have approved of, which did not include my taking a trip to rebound-town with the man who had been his best friend in the world. How to accomplish this, I had no idea. All I wanted to do was run after him and drag him back into my kitchen, bury myself in arms, and stay there until the storm that had engulfed my once-perfect life had passed. And all I could think to do was head upstairs, fall into my bed, and pull the covers over my head, despite the fact that the sun had not yet fully set.

By some miracle, I slept through the night, the dreamless sleep of the dead. I woke to gray skies and a gloomy disposition, the rain falling in sheets, and the wind rattling the ancient windowpanes, which sounded like they might give way at any moment.

I can certainly afford to fix them now, no matter what the cost, I thought. And we'd had the money for those windows all along, hadn't we? We'd been rich, and Aaron had kept that fact from me. The more I thought about it, the angrier I got. What was I supposed to do now?

"Really, I can do anything I want to do," I muttered to myself as I jumped out of bed with a fury. I could travel, start a business, buy a dozen houses in as many cities, fly to Paris for lunch; the world was my fucking oyster. But that gave me no comfort. I'd been given thirty pieces of silver in exchange for a life with the man I loved, and I felt like I'd been cheated.

I descended the stairs to the kitchen, all the while muttering to myself and slamming things around. I'd been trying to figure out what I wanted to do with my life for as long as I could remember. And, as Harper had so kindly pointed out, being handed a giant pile of money was really pushing my buttons. The question I'd struggled with for years—"What do I want to be when I grow up?"—had been the itch I couldn't scratch. And now it looked like Aaron had up and scratched it for me. It made me wonder if he'd ever had faith in me or if he'd just seen me as an adorable loser who couldn't take care of herself.

Most of my life I'd been a jack-of-all-trades and a master of none. I'd graduated from Vanderbilt University with a bachelor of fine arts, which meant I dabbled in everything and was suited for nothing. I'd become an enthusiastic professional dabbler, as I tried my hand at everything from interior design to real estate, with a detour to the world of hotel management somewhere in the middle. That was a mistake from the word *go*! I realized that I liked to stay in fancy hotels and order room service, not serve those who came to stay.

I'd then thrown myself into the world of airport management, followed by a stint as development director for a prominent charity, but neither of those careers rang my bell either.

Then I'd met Aaron, and everything changed. He'd applauded my joie de vivre and encouraged me to follow my bliss. So I continued to follow it, and this time it led me from restaurant management (but again, I wanted to be served, not serve others) to the wonderful world of retail. Here I discovered that the only time I wanted to say that word was when it was followed by the word therapy and the patient was me.

A few months before our wedding, Aaron suggested I stop trying to figure things out and just throw myself into the wedding with abandon; I could think about all of that career stuff later. He made more than enough for the both of us. I saw no reason to say no, so I let go of trying to find myself and devoted my energies to planning our wedding, down to the last sequin.

Within a few days, I realized that I was completely content. And I wasn't just happy for the obvious reason—the fact that I was planning the wedding of my dreams—but I reveled in creating the spreadsheets, staying on budget, and styling every aspect of the day. I thrived as I made the final choices for the china and linens and drew up timelines and shot lists for the photographer. I was good at every aspect of this job! Maybe I'll try to find a job in the wedding industry when this is all over, I thought. I had employed the services of a day-of-wedding planner; maybe I could do that. Or maybe Aaron and I could just get remarried every year and I could keep redesigning our wedding over and over again.

But that was then, and this was now. There was no more wedding to plan, no Aaron to love, no life to get on with. I was a wealthy wiancée with a fortune to spend and nowhere to go. What was I going to do now?

I filled my favorite coffee mug to the brim and plopped down at the kitchen table, staring out at the dreary day, which matched my mood to a tee. And then it hit me—maybe Harper was right. Maybe it was time to go shopping.

chapter six

To say that I shopped 'til I dropped would be the understatement of the century; I shopped until I was in a coma. It all began innocently enough. I simply googled "sundresses," and before I knew it I had purchased a dozen. Of course, I needed shoes to go with the dresses and the right bras to wear with them as well. Then I thought, you can't buy a new bra without buying the matching panties, so I added a dozen to the cart.

Naturally, a girl can't be expected to live in sundresses alone, so I bounced around the internet like a woman determined to do some damage and bought every manner of skirt, slack, jean, short, capris, tank top, jacket, and shirt that struck my fancy. Then I scooped up a countless number of sweaters, coats, boots, leather gloves, warm scarves, and hats; why not get a jump on winter?

I came up for air $51,287 later. I'd spent more money in two hours than I'd ever earned in any year to date. Honestly, that made me a little queasy. Maybe Harper wasn't right after all. So far, blowing a hole in my inheritance had brought me nothing but a feeling akin to the onset of food poisoning. Where was the joie in that?

As I stood up from my chair, I caught a glimpse of myself in the large mirror hanging over the desk and gasped. I looked like a refugee who'd been on the road for weeks, caked in a layer of dried sweat and dust. Had I forgotten to shower before falling into bed last night? Evidently so. I gagged a little as I got a whiff of myself. I'd also forgotten to eat supper and breakfast. Maybe I'm simply too hungry and dirty to enjoy my shopping spree, I reasoned as I ran up the stairs.

An hour later, sparkling clean and fed, I renewed my campaign to diminish Aaron's fortune by spending $28,922.29 on every electronic device I could lay my cyber paws on—and in forty-seven minutes, no less! I should have felt pumped up after spending so much money in so little time, but I didn't; all I felt was sick and empty. I know it sounds unladylike of me, but I've always found shopping to be more of a burden than a thrill. Plus, I'd gotten used to living lean over the years; my penchant for career hopping didn't exactly make my bank account scream "financially secure!" So all in all, I could understand why this shopping excursion might be an exercise in futility.

OK, I thought, if buying things for myself isn't the cure for what ails me, maybe giving the money away is the way to go. So for the rest of that afternoon, I threw myself into the task of making the planet a better place. But by the time I'd donated another large chunk of my ill-gotten gains to Greenpeace, UNICEF, the Red Cross, Gilda's Club, St. Jude's, the National Wildlife Federation, Amnesty International, and several dozen more charities, I still felt no better than I had that morning. And as the gloomy day gave way to an even gloomier night, I finally decided to give up my quest and settle in on the sofa with the last of the frozen funeral casseroles, a bottle of tequila, and the TV remote.

I'm sure I made a pretty picture, sitting cross-legged in my pj's, eating directly from the casserole dish, and swigging from the tequila bottle like the devil's spawn while channel surfing maniacally. But I felt no shame. Shame was eclipsed by a cloud of self-pity that was so enormous it blocked out any positive thoughts that might have had the temerity to try and get a word in edgewise.

How could Linc have deserted me in my hour of need? I cried as I tried to find just one decent romantic comedy on the premium channels. Harper and Lili had finally texted to see how I was doing, but I hadn't answered, not even with an emoji. I was mad at them, and I had every right to be! Where was the unconditional love? They knew I had hopped the train to crazy town! And they also knew that they were supposed to either drag me off the train or get on board and ride the rails with me. Those were the rules!

Lili texted again asking if she should come over, and once again I ghosted her. Nothing was going to put a damper on this festival of resentment. I didn't need her! I was just fine! I was the guest of honor at the pity party to end all pity parties. All that was missing was the confetti and the lonely cry of a solitary noisemaker.

Of course, my mother—God love her—called me every hour on the hour, and if I didn't pick up she'd call again and again until I did. Despite the fact that the house was silent as a tomb, I found her attempts to "come over and keep my baby company" contemptible. What did she think I was, a child who didn't know how to be alone? Of course, she knew that Linc had deserted me (Mr. Responsible had sent a group text), and the worry in her voice combined with the fact that she found Aaron's legacy "truly magnanimous and loving" only further pushed my self-worth buttons.

"I just want to be alone," I whined like the child I was pretending not to be.

"Have you eaten anything, Julia? You're not over there starving yourself, are you?"

"No, Mother!" I snapped. "I am not over here starving myself. If you must know, I've just eaten an entire casserole right from the dish."

I heard her audibly gasp. "Well that doesn't sound good at all! It's not like you to eat right out of a covered dish. I hope you're not standing over the sink while you do it!"

"I'm a rebel, Mama. What can I say?"

"Are you sure you don't want me to come over there? Your daddy is all wrapped up in one of his woodworking projects, and I have nothing but time on my hands."

"I'll be fine. I'm just going to go to bed early," I lied like the good Southern-girl-making-the-best-of-a-bad-situation she had raised me to be. I was never going to be fine again. But if I told her that, she'd be over in a flash, making a big fuss over me—and that was the last thing I needed.

RULE #13: *No matter how sorry you feel for yourself, don't give in to a visit from your mother who thinks she can fix everything with hot food, determination, and a pleasant attitude.*

"Really, Mama," I assured her with the last shred of patience I had left, "I am *fine.*"

Just to prove my point, I hung up the phone, gobbled down

four double-fudge brownies while leaning against the counter with nary a plate or napkin in sight, and chased them with a hearty chug of tequila. Several actually . . .

RULE #14: *Never mix chocolate and Tequila. It will instantly make you barf.*

Lucky for me, I made it to the bathroom in the nick of time. Once I'd come up for air, I headed back to the sofa for another fruitless round of channel surfing. Of course, there was nothing on. "Why the hell do I subscribe to four hundred twenty-three channels if there's nothing to watch but *Friends* reruns, reality shows, and infomercials?" I screamed at the well-coiffed woman who was trying to sell me jewelry. And then the world went dark.

Several hours later, the voice of an angel was coaxing me into consciousness. Opening my eyes was challenging; my eyelids felt like they were made of rusty metal flaps that had been welded shut. It took every ounce of strength I had to pry them open even the tiniest bit. But the dulcet tones of that voice continued to beckon. "Open your eyes! You need to see this fifteen-piece handcrafted baking set! It goes from oven to table to freezer, and it can be yours for just four easy payments of $29.99!"

Her voice was so enticing, so reassuring. "You're not alone," she promised. "Four hundred forty-three other people just like you are awake and alone in the middle of the night, and they've already purchased this limited-time offer. You won't see this price again for months!" She sounded alarmed, like she herself might miss out on this collection of bakeware with its handy set of lids that made storing leftovers a breeze if she didn't act right away.

I pushed my stiff, aching body into a sitting position and tried to get my bearings. It was still dark outside. What time was it? How long had I been out?

"None of that matters," the TV woman crooned. "All that matters is that there are only three hundred fifty-nine sets left and they're going fast!"

Somehow this made perfect sense to me. I scrambled to my feet and lunged for my credit card, which was sitting by the computer where I'd left it. Picking up my phone, I dialed the number on the screen. A knowledgeable operator picked up instantly.

"Have you ever shopped with us before?" she inquired.

"No," I told her uncertainly. "This is my first time."

"Well welcome to HSN!" she proudly trumpeted. "What can I help you with?"

I ordered the bakeware, making sure it came with a money-back guarantee if I wasn't completely satisfied. I was new at this, and I wanted to cover all my bases.

"Would you like to speak with our on-air host?" she asked once my order was complete.

This sounded like a bad idea, especially because I was still wasted from the half a bottle of tequila I'd downed, so I politely declined.

But I didn't decline to keep watching. Fifteen minutes later I was on the phone again, this time ordering a slinky top with matching jacket. It was a "bonus buy situation" the new hostess informed me, and I could get two for the price of one. I ordered six sets in as many colors.

This went on for hours. When I got bored with HSN I flipped over to QVC, which had a whole new set of affordable crap I'd never realized I needed. I felt like I'd come home. The perfect storm where my grief and loneliness ran up against a live human with a comforting voice was impossible to resist. Seeing as the house was eerily quiet and everyone I loved had deserted me, it was suddenly all I needed. These strangers on TV became my soul salvation—hallelujah! I had found my shopping heaven.

It was almost dawn by the time I gave in to exhaustion. I didn't have the energy to drag myself back up to bed, so I decided I'd just stay put. "Yesterday was supposed to be my wedding day," I chirped unhappily to the peppy hostess who was selling an assortment of magic hairbrushes. "I should be in Hawaii right now."

The rain was still falling in sheets, and I took this as a sign that the heavens were just as sad as I was that I wasn't sunning myself on the beach with a mai tai in my hand.

As I curled up in a fetal position and pulled the blanket up around me, the voice of a jaunty woman selling Wolfgang Puck's complete set of cookware lulled me into unconsciousness, and I dreamed about funeral food.

chapter seven

It's amazing how fast your house can fill up with boxes when you spring for overnight shipping or, in some cases, same-day delivery. This hadn't actually occurred to me until the stuff began to arrive by the truckload. But I figured all of these details would sort themselves out, so I ignored the mounting pile of parcels and just kept shopping.

I shopped, grazed, and drank my way through the remainder of the weekend, shunning family and friends and catching catnaps on the couch as dirty dishes piled up around me. By midday Monday, I had already received a couple dozen shipments from FedEx, UPS, and the USPS. Feeling too stunned to open them, I let them take up residence in the foyer as I took my place on the couch. I'd gotten really good at this shopping thing, and I didn't want to stop.

By Tuesday afternoon, there were so many packages stacked by the door that I could no longer open it. It took me a good twenty minutes to get them moved into Aaron's study, where they'd be out of sight. In the back of my mind, I knew I was trying to shove more than just those boxes out of the picture, but at that moment I didn't see the problem.

By Wednesday, the stacks of boxes once confined to the study began to spill out into the living room, stopping just short of the stairs. I reasoned that I wasn't using that part of the house anyway. This rationale gave me license to keep on shopping. It was the only thing that filled the gaping hole in my soul, and I had no intention of slowing down.

My mother had dropped by unannounced a couple of times, as I'd been largely ignoring her calls and she wanted to make sure I was still alive. Luckily, she always entered through the back door and never ventured into the rest of the house; she would have absolutely lost her shit had she seen the collection of dirty dishes, food containers, and boxes that were beginning to overtake my house.

Linc was still off Lord knows where doing his mountain man thing, and I had managed to put off Lili and Harper by telling them that I'd finally given in to exhaustion and just wanted to hibernate. I'd given into madness, was more like it, but they didn't need to know that—and, evidently, neither did I. I'd dived headfirst into the rollicking river of denial. But I felt calm for the first time since Aaron had died, and I clung to that feeling like a life preserver.

The one bright spot in my week-of-shopping-dangerously was the unexpected friendship I struck up with Hazel, the UPS driver. Hers had been the first delivery—or should I say deliveries—that Monday morning. After she'd made multiple trips from her truck to my door, she commented blithely, "That's a lot of boxes."

As I signed for my gaggle of goods, I attempted to explain myself and wound up inviting her in for a cold glass of tea; it was hot as hell out there, and she did look parched after all! As she ambled through the door I noticed that she resembled a stork in UPS clothing, her knobby knees riding shotgun between her regulation brown shorts and socks. A crown of short dishwater-blonde hair topped off her tall, gangly frame. The sinewy muscles in her arms looked as if they were constructed of miniature steel cables, which were made for a life of heavy lifting.

As I poured Hazel's tea, I spilled my story. She was a very good listener—which, at that point, I needed more than I realized. She rarely gave advice, and when she did it was generic. "It's important to get that eight hours of sleep in. Keeps the mind sharp!" she imparted with a wink, pointing to her head. She was a breath of fresh air and a welcome departure from my nearest and dearest who'd given me so much advice I was drowning in it.

This unassuming stranger-turned-confidant never monopolized the conversation (that was my job!). Looking back, I realize that I never asked her anything about herself. I didn't even know her last name. But that didn't keep me from claiming her as my new BFF. I guess she was like an extended version of one of those friendships you strike up in the line to the ladies' room or on a plane; they feel like real connections, but they only serve the moment. Still, I didn't see any of that, and I came to look forward to Hazel's morning deliveries and our one-sided chats.

I'd pulled another all-nighter, and I was a total mess. My hair looked like a squirrel's nest. My pajamas, which I'd been living in for the better part of a week, were covered with food stains—the latest having been the result of a pizza accident, which had left a bright red stain just over my heart. I'd wiped it off as best I could using the stray napkins that were strewn about the couch and coffee table. As if this wasn't enough, I smelled like a chicken coop, and my face was covered with unsightly blemishes that were the side effect of not having washed for days.

Somewhere around three o'clock that morning I had decided that I really was going to build that pool and learn to swim, which led me to google "pools." Things went downhill from there. By dawn I had ordered every conceivable chaise, chair, umbrella with and without tables, and a dozen varieties of pool floats. I had no idea where I was going to store this new inventory. Just as it came to me that I should build a cute pool house to go with the pool, I heard the unmistakable sound of my front door hitting cardboard followed by Linc calling my name.

I jumped to my feet and spun around just as he strode into the living room like a man on a mission. "Julia! There you are!" He looked aghast as he took in my unkempt countenance. "What the hell is going on here? What's with all the boxes? Are you moving or something?"

"No . . ." I answered as if I wasn't sure whether this was true or false. I could tell by the way he was staring at me that he was shocked by my slovenly appearance, and I don't think the Eau de Garbage Pail that was coming off me in waves made the picture any more palatable.

I raked my fingers through my snarled hair, as if this would do anything to tame the Bride of Frankenstein look I had going at the moment, and then crossed my arms in an effort to hide the enormous pizza stain on my shirt. But there was no point; it was so large and obvious you could have seen it from space.

"What are you doing here?" I said accusatorily.

"I just got back, and I thought I'd surprise you."

"Well it looks like you were successful," I tried to joke off my appearance. "As you can see, I've been very busy with a project and I wasn't expecting company." I turned and began collecting as many dishes and junk food wrappers as my hands could hold and headed toward the kitchen. "Would you like some coffee?" I called over my shoulder, as if it were just another day.

"No, I would not like some coffee!" he shouted, following after me. "What is going on, Julia? I hate to say this, but you look like you just fell off the back of a truck."

Dumping the trash and dishes into the sink, I tried to brush off this remark. "Like I said, you caught me by surprise. I haven't had a chance to shower."

He let this slide. "Okay . . ." he said in the tone of voice you'd use to coax a jumper off the railing of a bridge. "But you still haven't answered my question. What's up with all the boxes?"

"I took Harper's advice. I've been doing a little shopping."

"A little shopping? Jules, there are so many boxes in here I could barely fit through the front door let alone the garage!"

I didn't know what to say. I was hardly prepared for this onslaught of questions. So I did what any guilty defendant would do—I became indignant.

"You have no right to march in here like the king of the hill and start asking me all these questions! I'm a grown-ass woman, and I can do whatever I damn well please!" I glowered at him. "Besides, you're the one who ran out on me!"

I could see that my comments had hit the mark, as Linc looked hurt and angry all at the same time. "I'm leaving now, but I'll be back," he declared as he stomped out of the kitchen. "You haven't heard the last of this!"

Uh oh, I thought. Here comes trouble.

chapter eight

Linc rode out of my house on his high horse and returned a few hours later with a posse in tow. Lili and Harper were hot on his heels, followed in quick succession by my parents. I could hear the sound of my front door hitting boxes as each of them tried to squeeze through the doorway. This was soon followed by my mother's voice: "Julia?"

"In here," I called out from the kitchen, where I sat chatting amiably with Hazel over a big glass of tea, clean as a whistle and sporting one of the new sundresses I'd purchased.

Crowding through the door like an unruly pack of dogs, my nearest and dearest came to a halt at the edge of the room and just stood there with their mouths agape. And then they began peppering me with questions.

"Julia Ann Holmes!" My mother looked as if I had just hauled off and smacked her. "What is the meaning of this? What are all those boxes? And who, may I ask, is this woman?" My father, as usual, just shook his head in acquiescence and gave me a long, disapproving look.

"What the hell, Jules?" Lili took a step toward me. "Linc told us you'd become a shut-in and a hoarder, but I thought he was exaggerating! Is this why you haven't been returning my calls?" She indicated the boxes, which had even begun filling up the kitchen.

"You all deserted me in my hour of need, if you remember correctly," I retorted. "And Harper's the one who told me I should go shopping," I raised my voice.

"Hey! Don't blame this on me!" Harper stood shoulder to shoulder with Lili. "I told you to do a little shopping, not stage a coup on Amazon!"

"You don't even like shopping!" Lili's outrage toppled over Harper's.

"I've come to enjoy it," I stated proudly, even though this couldn't have been further from the truth. It hadn't brought me any real joy. But I wasn't about to admit that to them!

I turned to Linc, who stood off to my right, silently boring a hole on the side of my head with his gaze. Mirroring my father, who stood to the left of the gaggle, they could have been bookends—quiet, judgmental bookends. This infuriated me. "Don't you have something to say?" I addressed Linc alone. I knew Daddy was a lost cause.

"I really don't know what to say, Julia."

My mother regained control of the floor by pointing—rather rudely I might add—at Hazel, who sat frozen in her chair, her lips stretched in a thin, tight line. "You still haven't told us who this is!"

"Forgive me! Where are my manners?" I smiled at my mother. "Mama, this is Hazel. Hazel, this is my mama and everyone else."

I gestured to the assembled mob. That ought to do it, I thought. I thought wrong.

"Hazel, I am sure you're a very nice person and all, but would you please excuse us?" My mother smiled through clenched teeth.

"Anything you want to say to me you can say in front of Hazel." I gripped poor Hazel's shoulder ever tighter, jutting my chin out in solidarity.

"Look at the time!" Hazel said, glancing at her watch and forcing herself up, out of her chair and my demented grip. "It was nice to meet you all," she threw over her shoulder as she scurried from the room.

And then there were five. Five people who had come to corner me in my own home and pepper me with questions I had no answers to: "What were you thinking?" "Why didn't you call us?" "What the hell is in all these boxes?" Their voices wove together in a tapestry of sound that made my brain ache!

"Just stop!" I wailed. "What is wrong with you people? First you desert me, and then you come in here and try to manage me. What are you going to do next? Have me committed?" I waved my arms in the air wildly. "I think you all should leave my house!" I stomped my foot like a defiant two-year-old.

I was met by utter silence; everyone just stared at me, and no one made a move.

"All right then!" I grabbed my purse from the table. "If you won't leave, then I will!" And like a woman on a mission, I turned on my heel and headed out the door.

This was the second time in less than two weeks that I'd run away from home. To be honest, I was mad as hell that I'd allowed myself to be chased off. What gave my family and friends the right to chastise me about my shopping habits? If I wanted to spend Aaron's fortune on hundreds of impulse buys that were now stacked like the Great Wall of China throughout my house, so be it! What business was it of theirs?

I drove around in circles, with no destination in mind and a definite sense that there was no rush to turn back for home. So when I pulled up in front of Whitfield Chapel, I was surprised to see where I'd landed. Yet it made sense in a sad kind of way; it was like I was returning to the scene of a crime. Although, from my perspective, I was the victim here—the victim of fate.

Parking beneath one of the stately oaks that lined the front walkway, I took in the formidable Gothic structure that sat before me, looking for all the world as if it had magically risen from the earth. The limestone walls ran up to meet the ornate cornices that evenly flanked the slate roof. The arms of fluffy rosebushes in full bloom reached around every corner, open and welcoming as a June bride—the bride I might have been. The sun winked down from the stained glass windows that soared above the oversized front doors, which fit into the carved stone archways like a prayer. Then, from the towering, stately bell tower, the bells began to toll the hour. For a moment, I believed they were ringing just for me. I turned the engine off, leaned my head against the headrest, and tried not to throw up. I was a train wreck in progress, and I'd given no thought to anything further than the moment in which I was crashing and burning. Life was hell on wheels, and I was along for the ride.

"So this is what depression feels like," I would mumble at the TV whenever those commercials for antidepressants came on. I never realized that emotions could actually weigh that much! Or that they could pull you under so fast and hold you down for so long that even the thought of dragging yourself to your bed and pulling the covers over your head was a feat.

There was your predictable losing the will to live, loss of appetite, and loss of time as the days ran into each other like an endless string of bumper cars. Then there was the loss of my identity and the life I'd envisioned for myself. But I'd also lost contact with Whitfield's wedding director, Sally, with whom I'd grown quite close. Maybe I'd subconsciously come here to see her and find some closure.

Or maybe my willfulness has taken the helm and driven me here so I can face my fears, I reasoned as my heart began to slow its pace. My mother had often scolded me for being a willful, stubborn girl. But maybe this character defect had finally served a purpose: it had driven me to Whitfield to face the spot where my dreams had begun and ended.

I forced myself up and out of my car and walked toward the chapel I'd loved for so long. I passed through its massive front doors and headed toward Beaumont Hall, the adjacent building, which housed the wedding office and dressing rooms. And there, in the cool of air-conditioned bliss, I was finally able to steady myself. Before I knew it, my hand was poised to knock on the frosted glass door that stood between the wedding director and me.

Needless to say, Sally was surprised to see me. She jumped to her feet immediately, and I made my way from the doorway to her outstretched arms. After a short yet sweet flurry of condolences, she asked me to have a seat and then returned to her place opposite me behind her large, imposing desk. But no sooner had she asked me how I was holding up than the phone began ringing madly, and I had to put my answer on hold. Apologizing, she took the call, indicating that it was an important one but that she'd like me to wait a moment so we could say a proper goodbye.

"Yes," she stated to the person on the other end of the line as I sat back and folded my nervous hands in my lap. "That should read 'Now taking applications for the position of weekend wedding assistant. Applicant must be knowledgeable about weddings and be willing to work weekends and holidays.'"

She smiled at me as the person on the other end of the line repeated the content once more. "Yes," she replied, motioning with her index finger that she'd be only another minute. "That all sounds right. Let me see it before you post it. Thanks, Doris."

And with that, she turned the conversation back to me momentarily and then, glancing at her watch, explained that she had an appointment and stood to see me out.

"Wait a minute." I motioned for her to stop. "I'm sorry to be rude, but I couldn't help overhearing your conversation. Are you looking for someone to work here?"

"Yes, I am." She seemed surprised by my question. "Do you know someone who might want the job?" she asked.

"Yes," I answered, before I could even think to stop myself. "I do."

chapter nine

W hat the hell compelled me to say "I do" to a job, instead of the man I was supposed to marry, in the chapel of my dreams? I had no idea. I didn't know if it was kismet or confusion that led me to Whitfield that morning; maybe it was a combo platter. All I knew was I could barely see what was right in front of me, let alone the big picture, so I just went with the moment.

Driving away from the chapel, I felt a mixture of ebullience and dread coursing through me. It was clear—I'd officially gone all the way 'round the bend! I was confused and elated, dumbfounded and giddy, and I scolded myself and justified my actions until I'd run out of words. As my phone chirped for the tenth time in as many minutes, I knew it was time to head home and face the music. My mother was sure that I'd driven off a cliff, at least that was the content of her latest text. And in a way, I guess I had.

My mother cornered me the minute I walked through the front door. "Where have you been?"

I pushed past her and dropped my keys on the hall table, the only spot not covered with parcels. She followed me into the living room where the rest of the gang stood with cocktails and worried expressions. "I went to Whitfield Chapel," I replied in as steady a tone as my trembling throat would allow.

"What?" my mother looked confused. "Why?"

Why? What did she mean why? How could I begin to explain my reasons for charging out of the house, facing Whitfield Chapel by myself, and taking a job getting other brides down the aisle?

"So...funny story," I began in as normal a voice as I could muster. "After I ran out of here this morning, I ended up at Whitfield. So I decided to drop in to see Sally, the wedding director." I looked from Lili to Harper to Linc to my parents to make sure they were with me. "Apparently, she's been looking for someone to work there on the weekends. You know, someone to oversee things. She asked me if I knew anyone who might want the job, and do you know what I said?"

"I can't imagine," Lili said and smirked, thinking I was about to hit her with a great punch line.

"I said, 'I do.' I do! Isn't that funny?" I tried to sound upbeat about this bizarre turn of events.

"Well...that was one way to go . . ." Harper said unenthusiastically before taking a sip of her wine.

"What is that supposed to mean?" I winced in anticipation of her explanation.

"It means...it sounds a little crazy to me, Jules."

"Crazy?" I stuttered. "So is that 'lock her up in the attic' crazy or just, you know, 'zany and impetuous, you can't keep that girl down' kind of crazy?" I began, my voice suffused with an eerie kind of calm. "Or maybe you meant that I am buried so deeply under the weight of this unimaginable grief that I'm just not rational right now?"

Everyone just stared at me. Then Linc broke the silence.

"Jules," he began like he was a doctor taking the measure of a psych patient, "I think what Harper is trying to say is that she's...we're surprised that you ran off half-cocked and took some crazy job."

"Well, I'm sorry you all feel that way!" I snapped, waving my arms. "Maybe my decision was a bit unorthodox, but I was just following my gut. Haven't you ever done that?"

"Sure!" Linc's voice began to rise in tandem with mine. "Sometimes I take an alternate route to the office if I think I might hit traffic. And I've been known to pick a rogue stock a time or two. But this? I don't think I've ever made as rash a decision as the one you made today! I mean really, Jules, what were you thinking?"

I had no idea how to respond to that. The truth is, I hadn't been thinking, not in the rational sense anyway. (Isn't irrationality the very basis of going with your gut?)

My mother fell into the nearest chair with a thud. She could barely contain her tears. She'd been concerned when I'd been unable to drag myself from the house, but this about-face of mine seemed even more distressing to her than the blinding curtain of depression that had fallen over me these past few weeks. "This isn't in your best interest! It just doesn't make any sense, Julia." She got up, shaking her head, and walked toward me.

My father, meanwhile, just paced and drank intermittently from a tumbler of bourbon the size of Atlanta, chiming in with the requisite mm-hmms and "Your mother has a point!" comments that were his stock-in-trade. Though outspoken and opinionated about politics and the rising price of real estate, when it came to emotional problems, my father preferred to defer to his wife.

Lili, on the other hand, was not shy. "You have done some crazy things in your day, Julia, but this takes the cake!" she shouted. "What in the Sam Hill were you thinkin'? You're still in mourning, for God's sake. Aren't you worried that getting other people down the aisle at Whitfield—where you were supposed to get married—is gonna be painful for you?"

"I think she's still in shock," my mother surmised, the highlights of her caramel-colored bob shaking with every syllable. Everyone just nodded their heads in agreement. "Maybe we should call Dr. Reynolds and have him write you a nice prescription," she added. "You know...something to calm your nerves."

"That's a great idea," Harper chimed in, pulling out her phone. "I think I have his number on speed dial!"

At that, Linc and my father finally joined the fray, exclaiming how none of this was really my fault since I was too steeped in grief and confusion to know my own mind. "You could just call the nice lady at Whitfield and tell her you changed your mind," my father finally spoke his piece.

I felt like a two-year-old who'd had an unfortunate accident after weeks of successful potty training. They were treating me as if I couldn't think for myself or talk, let alone make a simple career move. I still didn't understand why they couldn't support me the way I needed to be supported, and that made me spitting mad.

"I am grieving, damn it! And it's messy and confusing and lonely as hell!" I yelled. "I said, 'I do' to a job! How is it possible that no one but me sees the irony here?"

Once again, there was no response from the peanut gallery.

"Can't you all see that I need something to fill the hours that are stretched out in front of me? If anything, my shopping madness is proof of that!" I continued to shout. "This pain is going to bury me if I give it any more ground. I need to drive through it and never look back. And, as crazy as it may seem to everyone, taking this job makes me feel like I'm in the driver's seat, like I have some control over my life!"

Finally, my mother broke in. "Sweetheart," she began gently, "why don't you come sit down with us and have something to eat?" She motioned toward the kitchen, waiting for me to lead the way.

Linc joined forces with my mother, as any upstanding sheriff would do. "Really, Jules, let's just all sit for a few minutes and talk."

But I knew what that was code for; what he really meant was "sit down and let us talk you out of this." That was the damn lawyer in him talking.

And that's when I realized he'd been taking care of me in order to avoid his own grief—and I'd been letting him do it!

If he was an alcoholic or a drug addict, I would be his enabler right now, I thought. Enabling him has not only been wrong, but it's also helped me avoid the inevitable: learning to live alone.

I knew what I had to do. As much as I hated to do it, for both our sakes, it was time to push Linc out of the nest for good.

"Look," I said, the pitch of my voice beginning to rise. "I *want* to be alone." I hoped that my excellent impression of Greta Garbo would ease the tension and make light of the moment despite the fact that I meant every word.

I looked from my mother to my daddy, from Harper to Lili to Linc, and slowly shook my head. "I think it's time everyone went back to their respective corners."

After a moment of uncomfortable silence all around, Linc jumped in with his usual aplomb. "Maybe she's right," he addressed the posse. "You all are a stone's throw away," he said, indicating my parents. "And Lili and Harper are on speed dial."

Obviously, he intended to stay. I think that he hoped the two of us would then have a chance to clear the air and start over. After all, we hadn't even begun to address the fight we'd had before he left. But going there just seemed like an insurmountable task. There was way too much baggage and backstory to even know where to start.

"I mean everybody, Linc." I looked at him pointedly. "You're probably exhausted from your trip, and you'd get a better night's sleep if you were in your own bed."

I practically choked on every syllable, and I could tell I had hurt his feelings. I suspected that he thought I was still angry about our fight. It was easier to let him believe that than it was to start explaining feelings I didn't understand myself.

I was wrung out. Hugging each of them in turn, I headed toward the stairs and away from the people I loved most in the world. "I'll talk to you all in the morning," I tossed over my shoulder.

"Jules . . ." I could hear Lili's voice behind me as I hit the stairs. "Julia!" she repeated, her voice becoming more insistent as she followed, hot on my heels. Only she would have the nerve.

I spun on the landing, taking her in, as every fiber of her being reached out to me in psychic understanding. Even though she was going to give me permission to run as hard and as far into the dark night of my soul as I needed to go, she wanted me to know that she'd be there to pull me from the brink if ever I ran too far afield.

"I just have to do this thing," I told her, referring to my crazy new career choice. "If I don't see some kind of forward motion soon, I'm afraid I'll keep falling backward and I won't survive."

She didn't say a word; but then, she didn't have to. She just reached out and gave me the biggest bear hug she could muster, which is a feat, considering her diminutive size. And in that, she gave me the jolt of energy I needed to propel myself the rest of the way up the stairs. As I fell into the welcoming embrace of my familiar sheets and fluffy duvet, I thanked God this day had come to a close.

chapter ten

I was floating in a large wooden rowboat, a veil of silvery fog draped around me in every direction. The fog was so dense, it looked like I could grab handfuls of it. But when I reached out to do so, it slipped through my fingers like the weightless air it truly was.

The sounds around me were distorted. Although I could hear the clanging of a buoy nearby, it very well could have been one hundred yards away. The prow of the boat met water, raising tiny waves, which spilled into one another like an endless row of Bolshoi ballerinas. The fog lapped at the surface of the water like a feathery tongue.

Except for the occasional whine of creaking wood against water, all I could hear was the sound of my breathing, which, heavy with anticipation, lifted and fell in tandem with the oars. They slapped the surface of the water as someone pulled them rhythmically to and fro. I couldn't see the oarsman. Although I knew I should feel panicked by this fact, I felt calmer than I had in weeks, so I leaned forward to get a better look. And as I did, the fog lifted to reveal Aaron grinning at me like a Cheshire cat. My heart lurched outside its well-anchored spot as I gasped in surprise. He was just feet from me and seemingly very much alive.

His teeth shone breathtakingly white in the silvery air, and that shock of chestnut hair falling over the arch of his left brow took me back to the first time that I saw him. As his eyes caught mine in a mischievous gaze, I felt like not a single second had passed since I'd looked into them last.

I leaped to my feet, nearly capsizing us, and then promptly sat back down. Holding on to the sides of the tiny boat, I tried to steady it as best I could. "Oh my God! Aaron! Where have you been?" I shouted.

"I've been with you, Jules. I've been with you the whole time," he stated matter-of-factly. I wanted to haul off and throttle him.

"No you haven't!" I shouted. "You missed our wedding! Our beautiful, perfect wedding, Aaron!"

"I know, Jules," he stated calmly (again!). How the hell could he be so frigging calm?

"I miss you so much, Aaron. When are you coming home?" I sounded like a little girl, but that was how I felt—like a lost, lonely, and confused child. And I knew that, more than anyone, Aaron could understand that.

"I miss you too," he said, smiling blissfully. "But the veil between the worlds is so thin...I can reach out and touch you."

"Is it really? Is that true?" I wanted to believe him so badly! I began to stand again in my excitement and grasped the seat of the boat as we once again started to rock unsteadily.

"Of course. We're floating around in it now."

Somehow, this made perfect sense. I turned to look around. There was water. And there was a boat. And they felt totally real. I mean, I was afloat and dry, right? So it made sense that I could touch Aaron, because he would be tangible too—flesh and blood, warm, alive. I decided to test this theory and reached out to him. He set down the oars and took my hands in his.

"So can I visit you like this any time I want to?" I asked him, holding his hands as tightly as I could, sounding childlike still. But no answer was forthcoming. Aaron's hands—his flesh-and-blood hands—slipped through my fingers like the fog had done just moments before, and he was gone.

I was alone, floating in the rowboat in a cloud of fog. I began to call his name over and over, but my voice stilled in the thick, cold air, as if it had no power to penetrate the liquid wall that billowed and twirled all around me.

"Aaron!" I called his name again. "Aaron!" It was then that I woke, tangled in the sweat-drenched sheets of our bed, without him beside me. And I realized it had all been a dream.

Despite the sun streaming in through the bank of windows on the east side of the room, I felt a blackness welling up inside that threatened to choke the life right out of me. I sat up in bed and looked around, still feeling disoriented. The house was deathly quiet, although the echoes of Aaron's name still rang in my ears and I could still feel the weight of his name on my tongue.

I turned to look at the clock. Despite the fact that it read 6:45, I reached for the phone and dialed Linc. But before the call could go through, I hung up and threw the blasted thing on my rumpled bed. No! I told myself. Calling him would be wrong. But shouldn't I at least apologize? my rational, people-pleaser voice chimed in.

No. I knew better. I would look desperate if I called him and told him to hurry over and give me a hug because I'd had a bad dream. Of course, I wanted to share the dream with him, and he would want to hear all about it. But the fact that I wanted to call him so badly made me back off even further. What was I doing? Whatever it was, it wasn't right!

I propelled myself out of bed and headed for the shower, thinking that the water and steam would clear my head. Instead, they only brought me back to the dream I had just screamed awake from. I sank to the floor of the shower and began to weep, the ache in my chest churning like rapids in a river, the sound of water rushing in my ears.

The morning dragged on, the minutes stumbling one into the other as I busied myself with menial tasks and a lengthy visit to Facebook. There were still new postings on Aaron's feed every day, and it was comforting to know I wasn't alone in missing him. His friends continued to post old photos of him doing any manner of things—from hanging off the face of a sheer rock wall with a thin rope and a few grappling hooks between him and certain injury, to him knocking back tequila shots, crowned with a ridiculously large sombrero and surrounded by his college buddies.

Closing the computer, I wandered out to the back porch with my coffee and tried to shake off the ghosts of the life I had lost. Despite the fact that everything had changed, everything still remained the same. Aaron's clothes still hung in his closet. The hamper was still jammed full of the socks and sweats he'd promised to launder upon his return.

The drawer of his bedside table still housed a variety of personal items: a box of Breath Right strips, a pen with a cap that bore his teeth marks, and the broken watch he kept meaning to bring to the jewelers. And sitting on top was the spy novel he was reading, with the bent and faded queen of hearts—his go-to bookmark (a reminder of me, he'd always said)—sticking out from between the pages.

The second sink in the master bath patiently awaited his return, his razor and toothbrush at the ready, a few errant beard hairs forgotten in the rush of his departure still littering the drain. I had swept most of the hairs into a small, tidy pile and then into a sandwich bag one afternoon. And unbeknownst to anyone, I slept with it underneath my pillow, as if it were a tooth I had lost, hoping in the morning it would have been mysteriously claimed by the death fairy and Aaron would be lying there next to me once again.

Around every corner, on every surface, there was evidence that he was expected back at any moment. There was so much left undone. I'd been marooned here for weeks, and Aaron had been too. He was everywhere around me, everywhere I looked. But he wasn't where I needed him to be—standing tall, flesh and blood, beside me.

Every few minutes, I glanced at the phone, willing it to ring, willing Linc to call and wondering if I should, indeed, be the one to make the first move. After all, I did owe him an apology, and we really needed to talk. I needed to know if I was the only one who felt like we were treading on possibly dangerous turf.

The phone finally rang at eleven thirty, and I pounced on it, only to find it was my mother checking up on me. I assured her I was still in the land of the living, that I had eaten breakfast (coffee and a handful of Multi Grain Cheerios is a healthy meal, right?), and that, no, I hadn't lost my ever-loving mind like Aunt Martha (who was nearly one hundred years old and had every right to be one or two chips shy of a cookie from time to time). And yes, I was still determined to keep the wedding assistant job.

She tried to sound like she wasn't worried half to death, but if I knew anything about my mother it was that she was going to worry whether I wanted her to or not.

No sooner had I hung up the phone than it was Lili's turn to call. After assuring her that I was really OK, I decided to ask her advice about whether or not I should call Linc.

"You were pretty rough on the guy," she scolded ever so slightly. "I mean, all he wants to do is take care of you like Aaron would have. What's wrong with that?"

"Nothing," I admitted halfheartedly. But there was a lot wrong with it, at least in my mind. "I guess I should call him," I conceded. Maybe it was natural for Linc and me to rely on each other right now. We had both loved Aaron, and we needed that shared feeling to keep him alive in our hearts. Maybe I was just imagining that I was developing feelings for Linc. "Thanks for being my sounding board, Lil," I sighed.

"It's what I live for," she retorted.

Signing off, I steeled myself to make the call that I'd been avoiding all morning. But just then, I heard the back door open and close. And as I turned around, there was Linc, wearing his button-down best and an apologetic grin. And wouldn't you know it? He'd brought lunch.

chapter eleven

n anticipation of the job starting Friday, I began dismantling the Great Wall of Cardboard that had taken up residence in my house. This entire exercise in acquisition had been so unlike me! I've never been a material girl, I thought as I affixed return labels on box after box of the crap I'd purchased during my shop-till-you-drop-over-the-top bingeathon.

As the bulk of my purchases were returned to sender and the pile of parcels began to dwindle, I started to feel like I was finally getting things under control.

And then Friday morning dawned. A panic attack named "What the fuck have I done?" woke me from a sound sleep. Crazy was back in town.

I had no business saying yes to this job! It must have been the grief and sleep deprivation talking! I screamed, hurling myself from bed. What have I done? What was I thinking? I'm in no shape to start a new job. Hell, I'm not even in shape enough to do the laundry! I'll just call Sally and tell her I made a mistake, I decided as I lunged for the phone.

"Back away from the phone!" the voice of reason crowed like some overconfident TV detective as I slowed to a crawl. "That's right. Easy…easy . . ."

I managed to get myself dressed and arrange my hair into some semblance of order. Get a grip! I told my reflection in the mirror as I brushed my teeth a little too vigorously. You can do this! You can *do this*! I wanted to believe my image more than I wanted to believe Pop-Tarts actually contain real fruit. And just to prove I was right, I stumbled down to the kitchen and grabbed a couple from a box in the pantry as I headed out the door.

I walked through the mighty oak doors of Whitfield Chapel and into Sally's open arms as she greeted me with a warm and welcoming hug. Leading me into the sanctuary, she began her tutorial, laying out the parameters of the four-hour time blocks each bride was allotted and how I would be tasked with making sure she and her party arrived and exited on time. "That's very important when you have two back-to-back weddings like we do tomorrow," she explained. "We have only an hour after the first wedding to clean the place and get ready for the second one."

The weekend was divided into four four-hour time slots: one on Friday evening, two on Saturday, and one on Sunday. And the time slot was all you had for decoration, photography, ceremony, and cleanup, which seemed like a lot to get done in so short a time. But these rules had been in place since time immemorial and were key to keeping the place running like the little wedding factory it was.

Once we reached her office, Sally handed me a notebook—which weighed as much as a human head—containing every bit of information I'd need to do my job. Every rule and regulation as well as the location of every light switch and lock was explained in great detail, as were the rehearsal and wedding schedules. Because the Sunday weddings rehearsed after the second Saturday wedding, I came to understand that I'd often be working fourteen-hour days. But I had no problem with long days; it meant that I would have less time left to my own devices, and that was certainly a plus.

Pulling the folder for the first wedding, Sally pointed to the vendor sheet, which had been signed by the photographer, florist, and musicians who'd been contracted by the bride. "This is the first thing to look for," Sally explained, pointing to a line on the form where the wedding planner had signed. "Half the time there is no planner, and those will be the hard days! But we're lucky this weekend. All the weddings have one." She smiled as she led the way back to the chapel.

I would soon come to realize how right she was. Having a wedding planner on board—a real, bona fide wedding planner here, not Aunt Cora or some nice lady from church—could mean the difference between a well-run affair and a chaotic one. Sure, the brides have been to lots of weddings, as they will happily tell you, but that doesn't mean they know how to run one. That would be like saying, "I could be a tightrope walker because I like to go to the circus."

RULE #34: *Never underestimate the importance of hiring a wedding planner; it can make or break your day.*

No sooner had we walked into the chapel than the front doors parted, and in came the clattering, cajoling, and raucous sound of the bridal party making their entrance. There were at least fifty of them, including ten bridesmaids, ten groomsmen, two flower girls, a ring bearer, grandparents, parents, and assorted family members who, although they wouldn't be in the wedding itself, had come to watch the spectacle and hitch a ride to the rehearsal dinner.

Sally got everyone settled and made her obligatory announcements about Whitfield's rules. Then, after handing the reins to the wedding planner du jour, Sally and I took a seat in a side pew, which was not, she explained, something I would regularly do. My job was simply to facilitate the venue and make sure nobody set the place on fire; I'd never be responsible for actually running a rehearsal, but she wanted me to see how the rehearsal was supposed to flow. And suddenly it made total sense why a professional wedding planner was preferable to Aunt Cora; someone had to run the whole thing, and that someone would not be me!

Wow! I thought. This is going to be easier than I imagined.

But oh, how naïve I was.

That first weekend was a blur of brides and grooms, promises made, tears, laughter, and bubbles exits. I kept my head down and soldiered through each of the weddings-of-someone-else's-lifetime. At the end of that first unmercifully long day, I drove straight home, ate a few bites of the supper my mother had left me in my fridge, and dropped promptly into bed, where I slept the sleep of the dead (so to speak).

Harper and Lili kept me on a short leash when it came to communicating. I knew they were worried I'd fall apart on the job and were relieved to hear I hadn't, but that didn't lessen their fears. Of course, my mother continued to call every hour.

Linc, on the other hand, was mostly silent. We'd never really talked about the almost-kiss or the fight. Despite the fact that he'd brought lunch the day after the intervention, he'd mostly been absent; after all, wasn't that what I'd wanted? But when he did text, he was upbeat and supportive, sending the thumbs-up emoji or a smiley-winking face. I was glad he wasn't mad at me for pushing him out the way I had.

For the most part, I was able to let go of my own personal drama at work. The pain and unrelenting grief that had marked every waking moment for weeks was ferried to a small, airtight compartment, where it remained under emotional lock and key as I focused on the brides. I basked in the radiance of their wedding-day glow and shivered with excitement when they walked down the aisle. And I found myself welling up with tears each and every time, which was odd when you got down to it, as I didn't really know these girls.

RULE #17: *Don't even try to fight the tears when you're catching a glimpse of pure joy.*

As each bride glided down the aisle, my head would fill with imaginings of what my own wedding day would have looked like had Aaron not gone off and died, and I'd feel myself start to sink into the abyss of his loss. But each time I caught myself sinking below the radar, I'd swat this image from my mind and snap my attention back to the moment at hand—a moment that had nothing to do with me.

But mostly, I found that I was bathed in a sense of relief because, for the first time in weeks and weeks, I was not the center of attention. Nobody was fussing over me, asking me how I was holding up, or second-guessing my needs. I was a stranger to those around me; nobody knew my sad story, and that came as a huge relief. And to top it all off, the job that everyone had said I was crazy to accept was something I was actually good at. For the first time since Aaron's death, I saw a tiny speck of light at the end of the long, dark tunnel of grief in which I'd been abandoned.

I trained for the rest of Friday, Saturday, and Sunday, shadowing Sally and the four wedding planners who pulled off one perfect ending after another. By the time Sunday afternoon rolled around, I was wasted, but happily so.

"You've done a great job!" Sally said. And with that, she handed me a fistful of keys and smiled her all-knowing smile. "Welcome to Whitfield," she said. "I think you're ready to run things on your own."

And as I climbed into my car and pointed it toward my house, I breathed a giant sigh of relief. I had done all right, and that was just all right with me.

I wound my way home as if in a trance. My face hurt from a weekend of nonstop smiling, and I was so tired I had to sing along with the radio at full blast just to keep myself awake.

To my utter joy and surprise, Linc and Lili were waiting at home with Thai food. As we gobbled it down, I recounted my weekend, epiphanies and all. They agreed that taking this job hadn't been so harebrained after all. I basked in the glow of vindication, despite the fact that deep down I'd had as many reservations as they'd had.

I felt a bone-deep weariness settle over me. Perhaps it was the long hours I'd put in or the hypnotic rhythm of the late afternoon rain that had begun out of nowhere. Whatever the reason, I could barely hold my head up.

After volunteering for cleanup duty, Linc walked Lili to the door while I collapsed on the living room couch and proceeded to pass out.

I was in the rowboat again. The fog was still impossibly thick and was suspended around me in a fortress of silvery clouds. Aaron sat before me, clear as day, his smiling face a familiar beacon shining through the mist. Lulled into contentment by the rhythmic swishing of oars against water, I was not surprised when a patch of blue sky appeared above us. It was as if some portal had opened up, sending big, fat rays of sunshine to bathe us in a translucent light so measured and perfect I felt a sense of joy the likes of which I'd never imagined.

As the curtain of fog melted away, I came to realize that we were in the middle of a large lake surrounded on all sides by hills so green they took my breath away. Trees blanketed the landscape, creating a thousand dimensions of shape and color. I marveled at the beauty of it all. Is this heaven? I wondered. And although I had only thought the words, Aaron nodded as if I'd spoken them aloud and then continued to row across the face of the cornflower-blue lake, which was exactly the color of the vase he'd given me.

I drank it all in like a woman who'd been deprived of water for her entire life—the lake, the landscape, the way Aaron glowed from every fiber of his being as if he were lit from within by his own personal sun. And for the first time since he had died, I was able to forgive him for leaving me and turning my world upside down. This gave me a sense of peace I hadn't even known I was longing for. Aaron beamed at me for all he was worth, like he understood this too.

Steering us into a narrow inlet framed by a shelf of translucent sand, Aaron rowed us to the shore. It looked like a million diamonds had been crushed into a fine powder and sprinkled there. The surface danced and glistened in the sunlight. Aaron jumped ashore and, offering me his hand, helped me make my way onto the soft, inviting sand.

A cool patch of emerald-green grass winked at us from several yards away. As we lay back on the soft, welcoming carpet, I was enveloped by the scent of an early spring morning. Aaron's arms encircled me, and I leaned in to rest my head against his chest.

We still spoke not a word. But words weren't necessary; our love was everything, above and below and within us. We were one. We were complete. We were infinite.

I began to drift off, like I was having a dream within a dream. And then the ground gave way, like one of those sinkholes you hear about on the evening news. I was falling and tumbling away from Aaron and back into the dark, gray curtain of fog.

"Aaron!" I cried. "Aaron! Aaron!" I called and called, repeating his name over and over, like an echo in the void, expecting him to reach out and pull me back into his embrace, away from the cold and vapid expanse of the foggy tunnel through which I was falling. But instead, I slammed awake with an audible thud, or so it seemed to me, and found myself twisted up in the thin afghan Linc had evidently draped across me. Drenched in a layer of cold sweat and unable to catch my breath, I sat up and tried to figure out just where I was.

Traces of the dream clung to me like a fine spider web, cloaking me in suspended disbelief. I tried to shake free of the dream that had seemed eerily real. In the fading evening light, I could see the foggy drizzle that hung just outside the bank of windows framing the back wall. And this made me think I was still alive in that other world, alone and scared.

The echoes of Aaron's name still hung in the air as Linc appeared out of nowhere, wrapping his arms around me for all he was worth. He began rocking me back and forth like a child who'd just awakened from a nightmare, crooning the only phrase that might bring me back to the land of the living. "It was just a dream, Jules. Just a bad dream."

But I wasn't so sure about that. My heart pounded in my chest with a ferocious speed that made it hard to catch my breath. I was still not back in my body, trapped in a netherworld of panic and fear. I began shivering, as if I had suddenly been plummeted into a pool of ice water. Linc just squeezed me tighter, like he would never let me go. He kept rocking me and repeating, "You're OK now, it was just a bad dream" into the nape of my neck.

I pulled back a few inches and looked up at him, his fingers pushing back the damp tendrils of hair that clung to my face. And then Linc leaned in, fingers tilting my chin up to meet his lips as he bent them to mine. And I let myself become lost in that perfect, succulent moment, his breath coming fast, his kiss urgently meeting my own.

I doubt that the kiss lasted for longer than a few seconds, but it felt like we might have been there for hours. Time was suspended, as was all sense of reason, of right and wrong. And for that brief moment, I felt as if I had come home and everything felt so right. And then it didn't.

"Oh my God!" Linc gasped as he pulled away and stood up, half stumbling as he backed away from the couch. "I am so sorry, Jules! I don't know what came over me!"

I knew exactly what had come over him! We'd been sitting atop a slow-burning flame for weeks, and my emotional meltdown had finally turned up the heat to a fever pitch neither of us could deny. This was exactly what I'd been afraid of; this was why I had suggested he move out! But although I should have been mortified and ashamed, I was not. I wanted to kiss him again!

Instead, I scolded myself back to the land of reason. That was not—I repeat—not a good plan! This could end only one way: badly! Sure, my feelings for Linc had been growing like a wild, untamed weed. But he was in no position to act on them, and neither was I. I certainly didn't want to lose him as a friend! We had to nip this thing in the bud, and fast.

"Linc"—I stood and began pacing in circles—"it was my fault! I had this crazy dream that made me all hysterical, and you came riding to my rescue...again . . ." I stammered.

Of course, he would hear none of it and continued to lay the blame squarely on his own big, broad shoulders. "Aaron was my best friend, and this is how I behave?" Linc would probably have slapped his own face if he could have achieved the right angle. "I should probably go." He turned and started walking toward the kitchen.

What could I say? He was mortified. And I was so hot for him! Yep. He should probably go.

Without saying a word, I lowered my gaze and followed him to the back door, where he gathered his coat and umbrella. I couldn't help but notice our dinner dishes drying on the rack and surmised that Linc had finished cleanup duty long before and had been waiting for Sleeping Beauty to awaken from her long and tortured sleep so he could kiss her back into the land of the living. Well, I thought, he'd certainly done his part!

As this realization dawned on me, I found myself feeling even worse than I had a moment ago. Just as he was about to open the door, he turned to meet my eyes and asked if I was OK. Of course, he would care more about my feelings than his own; what was his deal with being so damn wonderful?

"I'm fine," I lied. "I'll give you a call in the morning." And as he made his exit, I had to turn away lest he see the fresh host of tears that were poised to explode the moment he closed the door. But tears were no match for this conundrum. I realized just what I had to do; it was time to call in the cavalry.

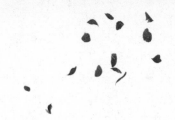

chapter twelve

Thirty minutes later, my mother came charging to my rescue with a suitcase in one hand and a cooler full of food in the other. She knew just what I needed: to eat some of her home cooking served with a heaping helping of her can-do attitude. I was a hot mess—a mere puddle of the person I'd been just hours before.

I hadn't been able to stop thinking about the kiss. That kiss was the icing on the friggin' cake! Whatever had possessed me to kiss Linc like that? And what still possessed me to want to do it again? I'd always been a rational person, a reliable person others could count on not to have a big, fat, messy breakdown. A messy breakthrough? Sure. I'd heralded my share of epiphanies into the world. But this was just the opposite of that. This was an anti-epiphany. Not even an Eagle Scout with a compass could lead me out of this quagmire. I didn't know who I was anymore.

Without Aaron I was a mere shadow of my former self. And with Linc I was a certifiable, kiss-wielding lunatic! "Pathetic!" I screamed to nobody in particular. "Pathetic," I repeated, slumping back on the couch.

Sitting wrapped in a balled-up, sweaty afghan while staring into space is not the optimal state for your mother to find you in when she comes walking through your door. But that's exactly what happened. Dropping everything she carried with a crash, she came dashing toward me like a house afire, shrieking my name.

"My God, Mama! You scared the life out of me!" I shrieked back, jumping to my feet.

But within seconds, she'd caught me up in a bear hug and I was right where I needed to be—in my mama's arms. Then I lost it. Who wouldn't?

"My poor, poor girl," she whispered. "You must be wrung out." After a closer inspection she went on. "Doesn't look like you've been getting much sleep," she scolded. "Or eaten much of anything." Pushing my damp mop-of-a-hairdo away from my face, she stroked my cheeks with her thumbs, as if she was trying to erase every tear I'd cried these past weeks but was helpless to do so.

Really, I think it would have been easier for my mother had I had some visible sign of injury to which she could attend—some scrapes and bruises, a fever, broken bones—something she knew how to fix. If anyone was content only when she was at the helm of the ship, it was my mother. She was a veritable force of nature. If Velma Sue Holmes was not in her wheelhouse, she would work like hell to get back there.

"Now!" She jumped up as if someone had lit a small firecracker under her. "Let's get you fed and put to bed!" This was her solution for the moment. And to tell you the truth, it sounded pretty darn good to me. Despite the fact that the twilight was still hanging on like a dinner guest who's overstayed his welcome, I was ready to call it a day. It had been a long one.

One hot shower, three yeast rolls, and two bowls of vegetable soup later, I was crawling into my bed and being tucked in like a little girl. I felt as vulnerable as a child who was running head-on into life.

I envied my mother. Married for nearly thirty-five years, she and my daddy were still happy and seemingly in love. "How do you do it, Mama?" I asked her as she settled beside me.

"Do what, sweetheart?" she said, resting her hand on my arm.

"You and Daddy have been married forever. How have you made it work all these years?"

She looked wistful for a second, and then she looked me straight in the eye. "Half the time I want to kill him. Now, that may sound like an insensitive thing to say, especially after you've just lost Aaron, but it's the truth!"

For a moment I was dumbfounded; I'd never detected even a hint of marital discord between my parents. Never. But then, for some reason, I began to laugh—perhaps a bit too hysterically, but I couldn't stop myself. Mama joined in.

"Don't get me wrong, sweetheart," she said between guffaws. "I love the man with all my heart. But ever since he retired, he is underfoot all the time. It's getting on my last nerve! I'm used to having my space. You know what I mean?"

Indeed I did; I was wired just like her. But these days space was precisely what I had too much of, and it was making me loony tunes. "I've been having these dreams," I told her.

"What kind of dreams?" She crinkled her brow and took my hands in hers.

So I took her on a tour of my nocturnal journeys—the rowboat, Aaron glowing like some goddamn jack-o'-lantern, the way time was suspended, how alive he seemed. "And then I come crashing back to earth! It's awful!"

"My poor baby! No wonder you can't sleep!" she cooed. "Maybe this new job of yours is too much."

"Honestly. The job is the only thing keeping me sane!" I told her. Then I began to recount my weekend, which was a tonic of sorts. As I ran over the litany of stories filled with brides and epiphanies, I felt lighter than I had a few moments before. However, there was still one thing weighing me down: Linc and that unbelievable kiss. But there was no way I was going to share that tidbit with my mother!

Aaron had been everything to me—my closest confidant, the man who could make me laugh out loud in the middle of a fight. He'd been my champion and most honest critic, and he made me want to be the best woman I could be. He had been my soul mate, my destiny…and now he was gone. What a cosmic joke!

And there was Linc. He had stepped into Aaron's empty shoes and filled them so perfectly I'd hardly noticed he'd done it. He'd taken care of me these past weeks as if I were job one, and he'd managed to fill in the cracks where the pain had been festering. In turn, I'd done the same for him. Night after night, we'd stayed awake late recounting our craziest and saddest and sweetest memories of Aaron until we'd exhausted ourselves. And then we'd wake up the next morning and do it all over again.

Slowly, Linc had begun to fill in the void Aaron had left, in every way but romantically. Now, it's not that Lincoln Douglas isn't one hell of a good-looking man—I mean, the man is a rock star in that regard—but I'd always thought of him as an older brother. I'd never thought of him in a lust-crazed way. Now I couldn't stop thinking about him in a lust-crazed way—his lips, his hands, the scent of him that hung in the room even after he'd left it. He clung to my senses like a well-worn memory, and yet every thought of him was like an explosion of confetti that settled over me in disarray.

The good Southern girl in me wondered what people would say if they only knew. And the grieving wiancée in me was shocked that I could feel this way at all, especially so soon after the love of my life had bitten the dust! I'd been brought up better than that!

I looked through the bloodshot slits I was using for eyes and pleaded, "Mama, will you sleep in here tonight?"

Again, she was up like a shot. Back in her wheelhouse and ready to steer me all the way from crazy town to dreamland, she said, "I'll brush my teeth, put on my nightie, and be back before you know it!"

And with that, I slid down into my bed, repeating Scarlett O'Hara's mantra over and over: "I'll think about that tomorrow. I'll think about that tomorrow." Because honestly? It was the only thing I could think of to do.

chapter thirteen

W hat doesn't kill us makes us stronger; at least that's
what my mother kept telling me for the few days
she continued to keep me company. Somehow, I'd
survived the shock and terror of Aaron's death and was still here
to tell the tale. But waiting for Linc to get in touch with me and
tell me that we were still OK was something I was sure would be
the end of me.

In the spirit of healing me, Mama kept me busy. And it felt
good to be consumed with banal chores like dusting, polishing,
and deep cleaning every square foot of my house, which was
sorely in need of a good going-over. In my desperate state of
mourning, I had barely lifted a finger to tend to any chores, other
than those that were absolutely necessary—like making sure I
had clean underwear and doing the occasional, cursory bout of
vacuuming. But citing her mama's adage that "idle hands are the

devil's workshop," I gave the cleaning jag my all. After a couple of days, we had the place spic-and-span and sparkling.

I worked so hard that when I finally dropped into bed each night, I fell into a deep, dreamless sleep and therefore had not been traveling to the strange and beautiful otherworld in which Aaron now resided. Also, I was way too busy to wonder about Linc until I dropped into bed. But it was then that I allowed myself to be lulled to sleep with visions of our fateful kiss...the kiss that had compelled him to flee the premises and never look back! Except for a couple of innocuous texts—"Hope U R OK" and "B N touch soon"—there was radio silence.

I called and left a couple of upbeat messages telling him that I missed his face, when really it was his lips that were mostly on my mind. I figured he would call or come by when he was ready. Until then, I had no choice but to leave him alone. I had no idea what he was thinking. And as for myself, I was thinking way too much.

My mother departed midweek saying she had to get back to Daddy. I guess the fact that my house and I were in a better state than she'd found us made her feel like it was safe to leave me on my own. "I'm right around the corner if you need me," she cooed as she prepared to exit the premises.

"Thanks for everything, Mama." I hugged her, tears pooling in my eyes.

"None of that now," she said. And then she was gone.

The deafening silence that followed her departure rattled me for a moment, but I busied myself with little projects and turned up the volume on my playlist until it outpaced the cacophonous voices in my head, which were tap-dancing across my frontal lobe. And then it hit me. I knew just what to do to make things right with Linc. I'd simply call and ask him to come by. And when he showed up, I would come clean; I would tell him everything!

Sure our timing was off, I would confirm. Well, OK. Our timing was in bad taste and totally wrong, I would admit. But shouldn't we be true to ourselves? Shouldn't we give this crazy romance a chance?

A few seconds later, I snapped back to reality. Maybe saying that last part was too much; maybe I should work up to the part where I confessed that I didn't give a crap about what the rest of the world thought about us! And after I'd delivered that lovely and oh-so-logical speech, what could he say? What would he say?

I'd come to realize that just because someone's life is snuffed out, it doesn't necessarily snuff out the relationship you had. That relationship still lives on, despite the fact that the other person does not. Linc was still Aaron's best friend, despite the fact that Aaron was dead. And I was still his fiancée. This realization forced me to take a big step back in my mind.

Maybe I should take a chill pill and a breath! I heard a little voice say. *Or maybe… maybe I should just start out with a softer version of things and work my way around to the rest*, the devil on my right shoulder whispered in my ear. *Maybe you should just take that chill pill and breathe*, the angel on my left repeated.

I could just tell him that I'd missed him and there was no reason for him to stay away. Things happen. We're both adults, I would laugh. That way I could test the waters.

I was pacing back and forth in my kitchen when I heard a familiar knock at the back door that stopped me in my tracks. It had to be Linc. He must have read my mind! But wait, why the hell was he knocking? He had a key, and besides, the back door was almost always unlocked. This was not a good sign. I headed toward the door, boasting a smile that was about as natural as a death mask, ready to face the music. But before I'd taken two steps, the door swung open and Linc stepped over the threshold. Whew! I thought. He had found the polite knocking a little bizarre as well.

I took his dropping by unannounced as a positive sign and reached out to him, pulling him to me in a fierce hug. He returned the gesture, although his hug was more tentative than fierce. "You're a sight for sore eyes." I stepped back, smiling as he shrugged out of his jacket and crossed to drape it over a chair.

"You are too, kiddo." He half-smiled. Then he took a seat, staring at me in an expectant way.

That was weird. First of all, he always ambled about when he first walked in. And what was with the "kiddo"? He never called me that. "Want something to drink?" I offered, continuing the perky party all by myself.

"Maybe just some tea." He half-smiled again. "I've gotta head back to the office, I'm afraid."

"That's too bad. I was hoping you could stay for dinner," I said, busying myself with the tea, the glasses, the ice.

I set our drinks in place and took my usual seat. The seating arrangements were the only thing usual about this. Linc was quiet. I'd never known him to be so quiet. He was the kind of guy who bounded through most doors, excited to see what lay on the other side. But today his usual golden retriever imitation was sorely lacking. He seemed downhearted, more so than I had seen him in a while.

Time hung heavy between us as Linc stirred his tea, seemingly mesmerized by the swirling and clanking of the ice cubes that do-si-doed from one side of his glass to the other. I wanted to break the spell, to say something clever like, "That tea isn't gonna drink itself" or tried and true like, "Cat got your tongue?" Or maybe I should say something sporty like, "It's so quiet in here, all we're missing is a putting green." Or perhaps the moment called for something honest and caring like, "Are you OK? I've been so worried about you!"

But since none of these pithy sound bites sounded rational or particularly cute, I chose to opt out of being the first one to speak and stirred my tea too, staring at the carousel of ice cubes that spun in perfect circles in my own glass.

Finally, he looked up. I could feel his gaze trained on me. Slowly, I drew my eyes up to meet his, trying to stay calm, but shaking like a leaf. "Julia, I . . ." he stammered the words, which ran headlong into my "Listen, Linc . . ."

That broke the tension for a moment as we both laughed nervously. "You go," he said politely.

"No, you . . ." I volleyed in return.

He looked so breathtakingly handsome, the late afternoon sun framing him from behind, ribbons of light bouncing off his golden mane like a halo. I knew he was forbidden fruit, and that made me want him all the more. The evil twin of my better self wanted to launch myself across the table and kiss the lips right off his face. But instead, I just sat there, a lifetime member of the school of good manners still in good standing.

"I don't even know how to start," he began. "But I need to apologize for my behavior on Sunday. I don't know what came over me, Julia."

"There's nothing to apologize for, Linc." I looked him in the eyes and smiled. "It was just one of those things. You know things that happen out of the blue like that . . . they just happen." I kept smiling and nodding my head like a first-class idiot.

He sighed and reached for my hand, as if he needed an anchor before he could continue. He gave it a squeeze, sending a bolt of lightning up my arm. It took all my strength just to nod my head quietly and wait for him continue. "I don't know how I would have survived Aaron's death without you, Jules. You saved my life."

"Are you kidding? My parents would have had to commit me if it hadn't been for you. You know that, don't you?" I looked into his eyes, and he returned my gaze with a smile that pierced my heart with its tenderness. Could this mean I had reason to hope?

"I know we've gotten really close these last couple of months. And it's felt really great to have you in my life." He continued to look me in the eye. Once again, it was all I could do not to jump his bones. But I wanted him to make the first move, and I squeezed his hand to let him know we were on the same wavelength and all he needed to do was make his feelings known.

This kind of behavior was so new to me. I had never been the bad girl before, but now I understood what the fuss was all about. It was exhilarating, breaking all the rules and not giving a damn. It was as if the blinders I'd been wearing since birth had been stripped away. I saw things in the margins I'd never seen before. Black sheep bounded through lush green meadows without a care for the nattering naysayers and gossip-mill queens whose dictates had always ruled the world. And I felt like I was flying above the fray, to a place where the air was fresh and new and clean.

"But . . ." He let go of my hand.

But? I screamed silently. There's a but?

"Julia, I was not expecting that kiss." He pushed back from the table and stood, walking to the other side of the kitchen. He turned, leaned against the counter, and just stared at me for a moment. I stared back. "It totally threw me for a loop!"

"Me too!" I answered a bit defensively, still in my seat despite the fact that I wanted to leap up and throw myself at him.

"Aaron was my best friend! He was like a brother to me. And what do I do at the first opportunity? I betray him. I betray his trust!" He was kind of screaming now as he paced back and forth over the entire length of the room.

I stood and walked over to face him. I didn't know whether to slap him or kiss him, but I felt like the universe had bitch-slapped me back to reality. This whole thing had been one big cosmic joke—and the joke was certainly on me.

"I don't know what to say," he kept talking. Why was he still talking? "If I could take it back, I would! Believe me, I would!"

That was it. That was all I needed to hear. The shame of allowing this fantasy not only to take shape but to take over my psyche, my equilibrium, and my heart was almost more than I could bear. I felt as if my insides were being ripped out through my eyeballs. I had to shut him up! One more word, and I would lose it.

"Look," I said, a little more firmly than I had intended. "Let's just put this whole unfortunate incident behind us. We are equally at fault. And considering the circumstances, we can't be held responsible for our insane behavior."

He had stopped pacing by this point, and now he just stood there staring at me like I had hit him with an entire truckload of truth pellets. I could tell he was stung, if not truly wounded, and I realized I had gone a little too far.

"Thank you for coming by and talking this out," I said, trying to bring a modicum of normalcy back into the room. I reached to hug him and he returned the gesture, but I knew that both of us felt uneasy. It would take a while to get back to being the good friends we'd always been. "It really meant a lot," I said, releasing him as quickly as I'd embraced him.

"I'd better get going," he said, crossing to grab his suit jacket and then throwing it over his arm.

"Let's have dinner soon," I offered, walking him to the door as if he were a casual acquaintance and not the man for whom I'd been prepared to throw over my entire life. And as I closed the door behind him, I almost wondered aloud how something that had felt so absolutely right just moments before could possibly have become so absolutely wrong.

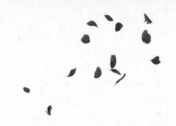

chapter fourteen

Never before in my life had I been so glad to see a weekend arrive. Sure, when I'd had a nine-to-five job you would have found me leaping with abandon from conference calls to cocktails on a Friday afternoon. But now the weekend held an entirely new connotation for me, because it was work, not play, that I was looking forward to. I needed a distraction from my life.

But while I was happily anticipating my escape from the cloud of emotions that had overcast my week, I was also rather nervous. I'd be flying solo at Whitfield for the very first time, and I felt less than prepared to take the wheel. Sally had assured me I was ready and that there was only so much training she could give me. "The rest comes with experience, honey," she had replied when I'd voiced my concern.

I arrived at Whitfield shortly before two o'clock that Thursday to open the chapel for the Friday wedding's rehearsal. Opening the door to my new office, I was hit by the smell of well-worn oak paneling and potpourri. Suddenly, I felt at ease, the way you do coming home after a long trip. The room was large and airy and filled with light. And behind the oversized wooden desk, a row of casement windows covered the entire rear wall of the room, which afforded a view of the parklike expanse of Whitfield's grounds. "Maybe this won't be so scary after all," I murmured.

Taking a seat behind the desk, I began to riffle through the neat stack of canary-yellow folders for the weekend's weddings. Flipping open the one that belonged to the Friday evening bride, I glanced at the vendor list and breathed a sigh of relief; there was a wedding planner assigned to my first wedding. And not just any planner—it was Grace Kennedy of Graceful Weddings. She was one of the best.

I'd met Grace when she'd shepherded Harper through her big day, which would give me a bit of a leg up during my first solo flight at the chapel. As I prepared to look through the remaining folders, I sent up a prayer that they would yield equally good results. They did. "Thank the good Lord above!" I cried out to my empty office, feeling grateful for this small miracle.

RULE #26: *Always remember to count your blessings when they present themselves; they're as rare as rocking horse shit.*

What had been the hushed confines of Whitfield soon became an echo chamber of raised, exuberant voices as the wedding party, family, and friends came crowding through the front doors. I smiled and nodded as they passed by, but to be honest I was a bit intimidated by the bride and her attendants. They were all tall, gorgeous, and had the ability to make walking in three-inch heels look effortless. The bride was a stunner! Luminous folds of wavy auburn hair fell effortlessly over her perfectly tanned, bare shoulders, setting off the creamy-white linen of her form-fitting cocktail dress, which looked expensive and luxurious. If she looked this breathtaking in her rehearsal dress, I could only imagine how glorious she would look in her gown!

Grace called everyone to attention and introduced me, whereupon I took a couple of minutes to run down the dos and don'ts of Whitfield: no smoking or firearms allowed on the property, in and out times, parking restrictions, and the like. Then I exited stage right and headed for the quiet of my office. That couldn't have been easier, I smiled to myself.

RULE #27: *Never count your brides before they hatch.*

Friday dawned with a mixture of blustery winds and the heat of a thousand saunas, typical August weather. There was a 20 percent chance of rain, which meant scattered showers at best, but that was also typical for this time of year. I hoped, for the bride's sake, that the rain would blow past us.

After running the rehearsals for the two Saturday weddings, I set up for the evening wedding. By four thirty, all systems were a go. I was a half hour ahead of schedule.

Grace arrived fifteen minutes later, which was great because it meant I'd have a few minutes with her to get my ducks in a row. I certainly didn't want to appear as clueless as I felt when the bride and her entourage came charging through the doors at five o'clock.

The wedding office was located ten feet from the entrance to Beaumont Hall, which housed the dressing rooms, restrooms, and a large, open sitting room that ran the length of the building and featured row after row of casement windows that looked out over the same grounds I could see from my office. The polished oak floors stretched forty feet in either direction and were topped with Oriental rugs and groupings of overstuffed couches and chairs. Fireplaces banked each end of the room, and a baby grand piano sat askew in one corner, giving the place the air of an old-fashioned drawing room where comfort was king.

At precisely 5:00, the bride and her entourage made their entrance. From my desk I could hear the excited tap, tap, tap of their shoes, keeping time with their high-pitched voices, as the women bounced through the door in an excited gaggle. I rose to greet them as they scurried past my door. Their makeup was flawless, as was their hair, which was piled loosely at the sides of their heads in the feathery updos that were all the rage. But despite the coifs and makeup, the magic halted there, because every one of them wore short shorts and tiny tees, which made them look like young girls playing dress-up from the neck up. Of course, it made perfect sense for them to get dressed here; they needed to look crisp and clean, not sodden and wrinkled from the heat of this steamy day! But still, it was an odd sight.

Traveling the few yards to the breezeway that connected Beaumont Hall to the chapel, I was struck by the overwhelming number of flower arrangements and wrought iron candelabras that were being assembled on the stage.

A riot of white hydrangeas, cabbage roses in various shades of pink and coral, and other assorted blooms were piled in a glorious, tall arrangement, which sat atop an enormous sterling silver trumpet vase at the center of the altar table. This would tower above the heads of everyone in the wedding party as they stood on the dais, framing the couple and the minister, who would be front and center. Two identical yet smaller arrangements, also perched on trumpet vases, flanked the centerpiece. Dozens of oversized pillar candles were woven in and out between the arrangements along the length of the ten-foot-long altar table, while four enormous black wrought iron candelabras graced either side of the stage in pairs. Hydrangeas and roses, tied with white grosgrain ribbon, marked every other pew from one end of the chapel to the other. And in the foyer, an even smaller replica of the altar centerpiece sat just behind the couple's guest book and the neat stack of programs printed on thick linen paper, with the bride's and groom's names embossed in raised print. It was clear that no expense had been spared!

The whole thing was majestic, a bridal dream come true. And this made my heart feel like it was going to burst out of my chest—but not in a good way, I suddenly realized. I was having a panic attack.

This had only happened in the confines of my own home before, not in the middle of someone else's frigging wedding! It felt like the walls were closing in on me, and I'd suddenly forgotten how to breathe. Luckily, no one but the florist and his band of helpers were in the chapel, so I was able to scurry back to my office without anyone noticing. Closing the door behind me, I threw myself into the nearest chair and put my head between my knees in order to stave off the waves of dizziness that were rippling through me.

Once again, I began to question my decision to take this job. What had I been thinking? I was such a fool! But really, what could I do about it? I couldn't very well bail on the bride!

After a few moments of this mindless back and forth, I got to my feet. Fixing my face as best I could, I applied a new coat of lipstick to the mouth that wanted nothing more than to scream bloody murder, opened the office door wide, and went to sit behind my desk. No sooner had I done so than I heard the click-clack-click-clack of nine pairs of high heels echoing from the far end of the building. The bride and her entourage were on the move.

One after another, the bridesmaids paraded toward the chapel, all dressed in identical strapless coral chiffon and silk gowns and pearl necklaces and studs. Their matching three-inch open-toed shoes peeked out from beneath the flowing hems of the floor-length creations that made each and every one of them look like Miss America on steroids.

And then—last but certainly not least—here came the bride, followed by her maid of honor (or MOH, as we say in the biz), who valiantly held the five-foot cathedral train of the bride's ivory silk gown aloft. This was no easy task; the train of that gown, studded with pearls, looked like it weighed as much as she did. But she managed to keep pace with the bride, who looked positively regal in her pearl-encrusted, strapless, dropped-waist creation, the skirt of which went on for days. Spun of cream-colored silk, it caught the breeze, dancing around her as if it had a mind of its own. She was a magnificent sight to behold, head held high. She was queen for a day—her special, magical day.

Oohs and aahs emanated from every corner of the sitting room where friends and family were gathered. "You can look, but you cannot touch!" Grace informed the crowd of onlookers as she followed behind, assisting with the train. After all, they were on a strict schedule, trying to get as many photos as possible of the bride, her attendants, and her family before she was hidden away in her dressing room and the groom had a chance to do the same.

After the girls had filed out of the building, I breathed an audible sigh of relief; I had at least an hour before anyone would need anything from me, which would give me sufficient time to recover from my panic attack.

But no sooner had I congratulated myself than into my office strode one of the most handsome older men I had ever laid eyes on. He was every bit as sexy as George Clooney, and he had Carey Grant beat by a mile; even Hugh Grant would have had to work to outrun this guy in the total-package department. I figured him for the father of the bride (that's FOB, if anyone even cares to know this), and I stood to greet him, asking how I could be of service.

"I am so sorry to bother you," the syllables spilled out of his mouth on a waterfall of Southern melodiousness. "I'm afraid our ring bearer's boutonniere has come unpinned." He gently propelled a much-shorter version of himself forward and displayed him in front of me.

He waited for me to leap to my feet, which, of course, I did, assuring this ruggedly chiseled man—who smelled like old money and perfectly ripe pears—that I would get it done!

"Thank you so much," he drawled.

"My pleasure," I said, repinning the boutonniere like an old pro. I smiled up at all six foot four of him. "That ought to do it," I said, patting the ring bearer on the shoulder.

"Wonderful!" Mr. Handsome Pants smiled back at me as he turned to go. "Thank you so much."

And as I told him he was very welcome, I noticed that I no longer felt the sea of bile writhing in my gut and the walls were staying put exactly as they should. Maybe staying busy is the key to my emotional success, I thought, making my way back out into the hall to see if anyone else needed assistance.

Time flew by after that as people continued to click-clack up and down the hall. The flurry of activity persisted like a beehive at full throttle. At ten minutes to showtime, Grace and one of her two assistants had the wedding party lined up in Beaumont Hall and ready to make their way to the chapel. I watched them file by my door: the grandmothers and their escorts, the mothers and theirs, the bridal party, and finally, the bride, this time with Grace personally bringing up the rear. And as they made their way through the doors and down the sidewalk to the rear entrance of the chapel, I couldn't help but notice how blissfully silent the building had become. It was palpable, like the enormous silence that settles in just after a thunderstorm has passed.

But then this quietude was sharply broken as I heard the door to Beaumont Hall being thrown back and a scurrying of heels accompanied by the sweet, plaintive tones of a Southern belle. "She's gonna kill me! She's gonna kill me!" the voice sang out between slightly hysterical sobs as one of the women from the wedding party ran past my open office door.

Following on her heels as fast as my sensible shoes could carry me, I called after her, telling her that I'd unlock the bride's dressing room (which we kept locked when the ceremony was taking place). "What happened?" I asked as I fumbled with the still-unfamiliar keys.

"I lost the ring!" she cried, pushing into the room.

"The bride's ring?" I probably sounded even more panicked than she felt.

"No! The groom's," she sobbed, tearing through every bag, box, and purse she could get her hands on. "I had it on my thumb, and it must have slipped off! Oh my God! Oh my God! She's going to kill me!"

"I'm sure she's not going to kill you," I tried to reassure her as I pulled the sofa cushions and pillows aside, hoping to unearth the lost ring.

"You don't know my sister!" she cried, still frantically searching the room.

Just then, thank God, Grace appeared in the doorway. Calm and collected as always (that's why she makes the big bucks!), she assured the young woman—who, it turned out, was not only the bride's sister but also the MOH—that everything would be fine. Someone could just lend the couple a ring for the ceremony, she explained, and then we'd have time to search in earnest for the real thing once they'd tied the knot.

As Grace hurried the harried MOH back to the chapel, you could hear the bride from the sidewalk that ran parallel to the building; she was screaming that loud. And despite the fact that a string quartet and pipe organ were playing the preceremony music at full volume, I was certain the entire congregation could hear her screaming about her sister's idiotic negligence and the fact that her perfect wedding had been ruined! It was quite theatrical, I must say, and a bit over the top. But in a matter of minutes, Grace had taken control of the situation and arranged for the best man to loan his wedding band to the groom. The bride reined in her hysteria, and they were off and running as if nothing had ever happened.

But something had happened. The bride had gone full monty bridezilla on everyone's ass just moments before walking down the aisle. This would be her wedding memory, the one that she would carry with her forever.

Of course, once they had made it down the aisle, everyone carried on as if nothing had happened. Vows were spoken, tears were shed, the groom kissed his bride, and they were pronounced husband and wife. But as the new couple recessed down the aisle, you could feel the air between them rippling with tension.

As soon as they were clear of the chapel, the groom began to scold his new wife for her abhorrent behavior. The entire wedding party had come back into Beaumont Hall at this point. The logical next step was for them to reenter the chapel to pose for about four thousand more photographs before heading off to their over-the-top reception at one of the premier country clubs in town. But the unrest had not abated. In reaction to the whole mess, the bride's father paused at my door, apologizing for his daughter's behavior.

"We did not raise her to be like this!" he exclaimed in my general direction.

"If you didn't, then who did?" I wanted to say with my outside voice. But the well-bred woman who wanted to keep her job and still thought this guy was hands down the foxiest man in Christendom kept her mouth shut.

Not getting the reinforcement he obviously sought, Debonair Dad turned and marched on down the hall, voicing his brand of standby parenting to anyone who would listen. It was time for a formal apology, he announced, steering the wedding party back to the chapel.

From the far end of Beaumont, I heard the pitter-patter of heel-clad feet, which carried the bride's mother along at quite a good clip. And above the clickety-clack rode her melodic and gleeful voice. "I have got to see this! Oh my! I have just got to see this!" she exclaimed as she trotted by my office door.

I definitely did not want to see this. I'd had enough drama for one day. And besides, I knew Grace would give me the lowdown.

At her father's insistence, the bride had apologized to everyone—everyone but her sister, that is! This she would just not do. I was astounded and rather horrified that this bridezilla was still holding such a grudge, especially on what was supposed to be the happiest day of her life! This behavior did not bode well for the newlyweds, whose marriage, I surmised, was headed for a long walk off a short pier.

The drama really never subsided after that. As the next hour dragged itself slowly to a close, the miracle worker of a photographer managed to cajole big smiles and romantic poses out of the newly married couple and their posse. Finally, they climbed into their stretch limo and headed to the reception—where, I later learned, the bride and groom continued to rage on for quite a while. After she had cried off all her makeup and had it re-applied, the couple was finally announced into their reception, over an hour late.

By the time they'd left the chapel, I was utterly exhausted by the whole ordeal, so I couldn't imagine how they must have felt. But I didn't care. All I wanted at that moment was to go home and crawl into my waiting bed.

chapter fifteen

S even o'clock came way too early the next morning. As I dragged myself out of the cool oasis of my nine-hundred-thread-count sheets to head into a hot shower, I wanted nothing more than to crawl back under them and stay there. Visions of the previous night's wedding danced in my head with the tenacity of a polka band on meth. Good Lord! What if all the weddings were that insane? Was this the reason the job had been up in the first place?

Loneliness coated the pit of my stomach, leaving me with a hollow feeling that could not be drowned no matter how much coffee I inhaled. But this persistent ache was nothing new. Work was the only remedy for this malady of mine. So grabbing a Pop-Tart in one hand and my travel mug in the other, I headed to the job.

I let myself in a side door. Struggling a bit under its weight, I found that the heft and solidity of it gave me a sense of reassurance. This place had stood the test of time; maybe I could as well. Walking from one end of the building to the other and then on to Beaumont Hall, I was bathed in the beams of delicate light that danced along the stone walls and floors. The cool quiet of this magical place transported me to a moment of calm, a place where I could feel still.

I unlocked doors and flipped on lights, fluffed couch pillows in the hall and rearranged a few chairs so that everything was ready for the two weddings that were scheduled for that day. But I still had thirty minutes to kill before any of the vendors or the wedding party arrived, so I sat at my desk, trying to amuse myself by scrolling though the hundreds of items contained in the Groupon email I'd been ignoring for days. I had never seen such an array of goods; everything from a twelve-pack of camisoles to all-inclusive beach vacations whizzed by. What harm could it do to buy a few things? I asked the universe as I continued to cyberstalk merchandise I didn't need. Even the set of wrenches with interchangeable heads called my name, despite the fact that I was mechanically challenged. But before I could make any kind of crazy impulse buy, I heard a cacophony of voices entering Beaumont Hall. The wedding party had arrived; all inane purchases as well as all bets were off.

Greeting the bride and her wedding planner, I was happy to see that the civilized and small group that had rehearsed the day before hadn't grown in size or attitude, which made me breathe a sigh of relief. Perhaps yesterday's wedding had been an anomaly after all!

For the next four hours, all I did was a whole lot of nothing. I pointed guests in the direction of the restrooms and the chapel, helped the florist find a water source, and locked and unlocked dressing rooms during and after the ceremony, which was brief and stress free. It became obvious that I was merely going to be the keeper of the keys for this wedding, which was fine by me.

The morning flew by, giving way to a glorious afternoon with temperatures hovering in the eighties. The second wedding party was due to arrive at any moment, and I felt renewed and ready to meet any and all challenges that might come my way. But forty-five minutes into their four-hour block of time, they hadn't arrived, which made me a bit anxious. I called Sally, who explained that the evening wedding was going to be quite a small affair, so it wasn't surprising that no one had arrived yet. Just then the door to Beaumont swung open, and she and I signed off.

In walked the bride, her mother, and the wedding planner; no giggling bridesmaids teetering on three-inch heels, and nary an adorable flower girl was in sight. As soon as they'd made their way to the bride's dressing rooms, in came the groom and his parents, who said polite hellos and then retreated to his dressing rooms. I made my way to the chapel, where white hydrangeas and roses were being assembled into a large arrangement on the altar table. There were no pew markers and, other than a few pillar candles on the altar table, no other adornments, which was unusual for Whitfield brides. In addition, there was no guest book and no programs. Stranger still, I thought.

When the wedding planner asked if I could help open the doors for the bride's entrance, I was thrilled. I would get to be a part of "magic time": those last few seconds before the big walk, when father and daughter would exchange a few heartfelt words or just share a little hug and kiss.

This made me wonder what my father would have said to me if I'd made it down that aisle just a few months before. He probably would have said something irreverent; he can never pass up the opportunity to crack a joke. Perhaps I'd have said something heartfelt like, "I love you so much Dad!" To which he'd have replied with a nod and a wink, "You're not keeping the credit card." We both would have laughed out loud as those big, wooden doors opened wide, and the congregation would have risen and turned to watch as I took the first steps toward a new life, my arm entwined in his.

I noticed the chapel was eerily quiet. Peeking through the space between the doors, I understood why; save for the bride's mother and groom's parents, there was not a single guest seated inside. How odd. Why on earth would anyone book such a huge venue for such an intimate wedding? It didn't make any sense. I knew there had to be a story behind this mysterious wedding, and I intended to hear it! But that moment would have to wait.

As the organ began to play Cannon in D, we opened the doors. The luminous bride and her father glided through them. I welled up with tears almost instinctively. It was so beautiful and a little bit sad, seeing this gorgeous girl walking down the aisle with barely anyone to witness her processional. And yet, it was not without magic and majesty. She still had that unspeakable glow.

Once we had closed the doors, I turned to the planner and asked in a whisper, "Why aren't there any guests? What is the story here?"

In hushed tones, she spilled the beans; and oh, what a pile of beans they were. Evidently, this bride had booked Whitfield and the planner eighteen months before. An only child from a wealthy Belle Meade family, she had been engaged to someone else. Originally, the wedding was supposed to have been an absolute extravaganza. Two hundred fifty guests had been invited. The reception was to be held at her parents' resplendent home, the backyard of which would have been tented, complete with a wooden floor, tables, chairs, and centerpieces—the works. But she had fallen in love with someone else just three months before the wedding and had called the first engagement off, trading in the new groom for the old.

In the old and moneyed circles from which she came, the whole affair had been a scandalous one. She couldn't very well have pulled off her big society wedding in the wake of it all. So, despite the fact that she had planned an over-the-top affair, love had triumphed over all; the bride had given up the fancy trappings of her big day to marry the man she loved. It was so brave and so romantic!

As I slid into a pew at the back of the chapel to watch this young couple exchange vows and rings—so sure of the love they had for each other, so happy to be taking this big step in their lives—I felt myself begin to lose it. And just as they said I do, I slipped out the side door and headed for the safety of my office, where I knew no one would hear me as I fell to my knees and wept.

By the time I made it home, I was totally spent. It was almost nine thirty, and although the sun had long since set, the air hung heavy with heat and moisture and the electric, grassy scent that fills the air just before a big rain is about to fall. Complete with rolling thunder and lightning it came, knocking out the power, and with it the blissfully cool air that usually fills the inside of my home.

Grabbing the first glass I could find, I filled it with white wine and went out to the screened-in porch, where I could sit protected from the storm while still feeling as if I were in the midst of its raging elements. I swigged and cried, cried and swigged. And when the first glass was empty, I went for a refill and began the ritual again; although, to be honest, the tears really never abated.

The past twenty-four hours, I'd been on the roller coaster ride of my life. Like a pair of crazy, mismatched bookends, the Friday and Saturday evening weddings had been as different as night and day. Each had shaken me to my core in different ways, but both had left me missing Aaron more than I had in weeks. How was it possible that he was gone? That he was never coming back? How was it possible that the craziest bride of them all had gotten to walk down the aisle to her happily-ever-after and I had not? Where was my groom? My beloved? My happily-ever-after? And what was to become of me?

The second glass of wine led to a third. As the maudlin thoughts piled one on top of the other, like cheerleaders in a pyramid, I fought to keep them from tumbling into a heap, realizing I'd have a hard time reassembling any rational train of thought after that. I needed someone to talk to. After reaching for my phone, I instinctively dialed the first number that came to mind: Linc's.

I knew it was wrong and that seeing him when I was in such a fragile state might be a mistake. But I made the call anyway because, at that point, he was the only one I wanted. Besides, Lili was out of town for an entire week, and Harper was probably asleep. I didn't dare dial my mom when I was three sheets to the wind. She would have been there for me, of course, but I had no patience for her brand of stoicism at the moment. Besides, I needed a strong pair of arms around me more than I needed a motherly touch.

The call went right to voice mail. The sound of Linc's deep, comforting drawl brought fresh tears to my eyes. He had gone hiking, his familiar voice stated, so he would be unreachable until Monday. And then I remembered; Lili had told me that he had set out to hike the Appalachian Trail all over again, as a testament to Aaron and with hopes for a different ending.

Stopping just short of finishing off the bottle, which now sat on the table by my side, I put a cork in it and dragged myself up the stairs. Just then the power returned with a resounding whir, bringing my darkened, empty house back to life. And I only wished it could have done the same for Aaron or, for that matter, for me.

chapter sixteen

The phone was ringing, a far-off tone. It trilled three times, and then he answered.

"Hello?" Aaron's voice sounded groggy.

I had obviously woken him. "I'm so sorry! Did I wake you?"

"That's OK," he reassured me in a gravely tone. "It's good to hear your voice. How are you?"

How was I? How was I? That was a loaded question. "I miss you," I whispered.

"I'm right here, Jules. Closer than you think." I thought I could hear him smiling as he said this and suspected he knew something I didn't.

"I have a new job, Aaron. I think it's a good fit for me. And I'm trying to get on with my life, but it's just so hard. I miss you," I repeated. But no reply was forthcoming; all I could hear was dead air. "Aaron?" I began raising my voice. "Aaron, are you there?" Nothing.

And then I felt like I was struggling to rise to the surface of a deep body of water. "This is just a dream," a voice said inside my head as I fought to regain consciousness—rising, rising, up, up, up.

I woke with a start, my heart racing. As crazy as it sounds, I knew in no uncertain terms that I had just spoken to Aaron on some cosmic telephone line. It had been so real; he'd been so close, just as he had said. It felt eerie and strangely comforting all at once. Impossible, yet it had happened. Wow! I threw back the covers, kicking free of them, and stared at the ceiling. The rain outside continued to fall in torrents. The cocoon of sound, as steady as a heartbeat, made me feel less alone, as if someone's arms were encircling me, keeping me safe.

The bedside clock told me it was only 3:00 a.m. But despite it being the middle of the night, I knew I didn't have a prayer of going back to sleep anytime soon. So up I got, wandering downstairs in search of a midnight snack and some late-night TV. Maybe I'll get lucky and find a rerun of *Ghost*, I thought facetiously.

This wasn't the first time I'd woken up in the middle of the night. Since Aaron's death, it had become a bad habit—one whose rhythm my body had decided to dance to, on a nightly basis, come hell or high water. One of the reasons I'd taken to midnight shopping sprees was to quell those dark hours, the hours in which I ached for Aaron in a distinctively painful way. The air weighed more at night. And the ghosts of my failed life, those masked marauders of my best-laid plans, took up every inch of real estate in my brain, leaving me indefensibly sad.

People tell you all sorts of things about the grieving process— how you'll get over him in time and how the first year is the hardest. But no one tells you about the nights and those empty hours before dawn when sleep won't come and solace eludes you.

Certainly the passage of time had helped lessen the burden of grief. And I knew that as it marched on, like a foot soldier who knew the tried-and-true path to and from the battlefield, things would start to improve. But they would never be the same.

Sunday's wedding came and went without much fanfare, which was fine by me. I had no patience that night for watching a glistening creature in a poufy white dress glide down the aisle that I should have glided down. Now, I know this sounds like sour grapes—most likely because that's exactly what it was. But I was happy to have those grapes, as they gave me something to chew on.

RULE #11: *Bitterness never tastes as sweet as you hope it will. But knowing that won't keep you from taking a big bite and swallowing it whole.*

Linc finally returned my call later that evening. It was so good to hear his voice. I felt like I could breathe for the first time in days. He told me all about his plans for hiking the AT a second time.

"I'm hiking only parts of it this time, but I'm hoping it will bring me a bit of redemption," he quietly explained, as if hiking miles and miles of rough and unpredictable terrain might erase the tragic ending he had witnessed at the finish of his first pass.

I listened and interjected supportive phrases like "uh-huh" and "I know what you mean" whenever they were clearly called for. I actually felt jealous of Linc for having found a way to deal with his grief, a tangible tribute to Aaron's death and the life he had lived so fully. I felt like I was still knee-deep in the tar pit of my own grief and unable to unearth myself from the weight of my sorrow.

Linc rambled on about hiking buddies he had assembled, many of whom had known Aaron, who wanted to embrace the challenge. They included a couple of lawyers from Linc's office as well as some guys from Aaron's firm and a graduate student from the Vanderbilt Law School who was interning at Linc's firm. They'd all been training together for the past few weeks. Linc sounded as if this whole endeavor was helping him.

"So it is kind of a support group in hiking boots," I joked, and he laughed his agreement.

Hearing that rumbling, melodic laugh of his made my heart race, faster than it should! But it was just so good to hear him laugh. And I guess it was infectious, because I joined right in, teasing him as I had always done—that is, before the fateful kissing incident.

We hung up after confirming that we'd both be attending Harper and Jeff's annual Labor Day bash. I actually hadn't given much thought to their party until that moment, despite the fact that their original Evite and subsequent reminders had been sitting in my inbox for weeks begging for a reply. The party always signified the end of summer and the run-up to the holiday season. And since it was a long weekend, it was always held on Sunday, because all of us knew we had a national reprieve the following day and could throw caution to the wind. It had been a staple of Aaron's and my social calendar ever since we'd started dating. The thought of being there without him was not without its challenges. But the thought of not being in attendance made me even unhappier, so I promised Linc I'd be there.

Immediately after hanging up, I began to feel restless and jittery. I knew the only thing that would quell my nerves was tackling a big project. So many choices, so little time, I mused to myself as I mentally paced from room to room, cataloging the reorganizing required in each and every nook and cranny, closet and drawer. I rattled around in the kitchen for a while, but that did nothing to stave the incessant thrumming in my solar plexus.

Like the feeling you get when a word is right on the tip of your tongue, I felt a strong pull toward the guest room—despite the fact that it was the last place I wanted to go. It was there that I'd find Aaron's closet. Getting rid of his stuff was the thing I was dreading above all else.

But I wasn't avoiding my dead fiancé's closet because I couldn't face seeing his things, knowing he'd never wear them again; on the contrary, it was because I loved seeing his things. I actually savored the moments spent with his jackets, shirts, and khakis. They were the only tangible things that remained of him on God's green earth. Packing his stuff up and giving it away meant that he'd be gone for real, and I wasn't ready to face that fact. Not even close.

A few days after Aaron died, his dry cleaning had been delivered, like it always was on Tuesday afternoons. And there it stayed for several days, hanging on the front door like a man-shaped wreath, until someone finally brought it in and saved it from the late spring rain and mighty wind that threatened to take those freshly pressed suits of his to kingdom come. But what did I care? Maybe it would be a good thing if they were carried off. Maybe they'd find their way to him in the great beyond and he'd be smartly dressed when he arrived at the pearly gates.

There is a belief in many Eastern religions that the souls of the deceased hang around for thirteen days to get their emotional affairs in order and settle scores with those they've left behind. And as much as I considered myself to be a good Christian girl, when I heard this theory of the afterlife I knew in my heart of hearts it was true. I constantly felt Aaron's presence around me like a weight in the air, like a soothing, quiet voice whispering at the nape of my neck. And every day during those first thirteen days after his death, I had spent hours shut away in his closet commiserating with him.

I'd close the door, turn out the light, sit down on the carpeted floor, and just breathe him in. The scent of him was a balm for me. Even though he wasn't there in the flesh, the earthy, salty-sweet scent of him still inhabited the place.

I'd talk to him as I held one of his favorite shirts or unwashed socks up to my face. I'd beg him to return. And all I wanted to do in these moments was seal myself away in this little space filled with his garments and shoes and sporting equipment, like I was a Pharaoh's widow who'd been entombed while she was still alive, in order to keep her sphinxy husband company. Eventually, my mother or someone else in the house would come searching for me, open the door, and coax me back to the real world, such as it was. But it was just another dreary step in the rhythm of life that required me to put one foot in front of the other and trudge ahead, so I savored those closeted moments.

After a few weeks of these daily pilgrimages, Aaron's scent began to dissipate. I feared I'd been too greedy. I'd spent too much time sucking in the last vestiges of him and not enough time keeping the place hermetically sealed. So I'd begun visiting the closet more sparingly, seeking refuge there only when I really needed a fix.

In addition to Aaron's things, the closet held another garment I had a hard time looking at: my wedding gown. More of a pavilion than a dress, it took over most of any space in which I tried to confine it. In an effort to keep Aaron from seeing it before the wedding, that dress had been stashed at my parents' house. After Aaron had died, my mother had hung it in the guest room. But when Linc began camping out at my house, the dress obviously had to find other accommodations. So naturally I stuck it in the only place it would really be out of the way: Aaron's closet. And there the dress remained.

But during one of my pilgrimages to "The Aaron Memorial Room," as I'd come to call it, I'd had kind of a confrontation with the dress. I actually went into a bit of a jealous rage because this behemoth was getting to spend 24/7 with Aaron's clothes, and I felt like it was getting a better deal than I was. Irrational? Yes. Loony and over-the-top behavior? Most definitely. But it didn't seem like that at the time.

After berating my once-beloved wedding gown for taking full-court advantage of Aaron's things, I promptly moved said dress back to my closet, hoping that would put an end to the silliness. But, unfortunately, it got worse. My dress mocked me from the closet. The dress I had worshipped and fawned over, an item of clothing that cost more than the GDP of a small country, would never be mine to wear! It would remain an empty shell of lace, satin, and silk forever, a hanging reminder of what I had lost. Even if I fell in love with some random stranger and decided to tie the knot, I would never wear that dress! The thing was cursed, destined to be alone, it's only company the cast-off clothes of a dead man whose scent was slowly but surely disappearing.

So here I was, climbing the stairs as I had done on so many nights before. Here I was, heading for Aaron's closet...but this time it was different. This time I was on a mission: to pack Aaron's stuff away. But once I opened the door and stepped inside, all I could think about was shutting off the light, slipping to the floor, and sitting alone in the dark with Aaron's things. "There will be no packing tonight," I said to the ghosts of Aaron's life. And there I sat for a very long time.

chapter seventeen

The last weeks of August dragged on interminably as one-hundred-degree days baked the city, and afternoon rains did little to cool things down. The pavement sizzled, sending steam rising like smoke from a recently doused campfire. Attempting to do more than run from air-conditioned house to air-conditioned car after eight in the morning made you feel like you might just spontaneously combust. I often wondered how anyone had survived heat like this back in the day when women wore corsets, button-up boots, and multiple layers of petticoats. Just the thought of it made me grateful that I was born in the age of the flip-flop. At least I was grateful for something.

By the time Labor Day weekend rolled around, I had super-vised another dozen weddings, which mostly ran smoothly. I say mostly because, of the dozen blushing brides I'd helped down the aisle, ten of them had had the good sense to hire wedding planners—the other two had not.

The first DIY bride's day had gotten off to a rocky start. After underestimating the time it would take to do hair and makeup for herself, eight bridesmaids, and two anxious mothers, she'd arrived at Whitfield twenty minutes late. Her photographer didn't have a second shooter (a must at a big wedding), so he was running around like a crazy person, which threw her schedule even further afield. And as if that wasn't enough, this poor girl had not paid the organist's deposit, so said organist hadn't shown up. This was a disaster in the making! But I knew what I had to do; it was time to take charge.

Taking the MOB aside, I broke the bad news: there was no preceremony music being played and, oops, there wasn't going to be ceremony music either because there was no organist. "But," I told her in a reassuring voice before she could freak out, "I've called another organist, and he's on his way. He even knows her music."

She looked at me like I had just parted the Red Sea.

RULE #44: *Always have a solution before you present a problem. This will make you look like a genius. It will also help you to continue looking like the good guy when you hit the MOB with the next piece of bad news: someone needs to tell the bride about the delay, and this someone is not going to be you.*

I knew the bride had been given the news when I heard her wailing at a deafening pitch from the far end of the hall. "Noooo!" she howled so loudly I was afraid the walls would come down!

RULE #45: *When disaster strikes at a wedding, always keep the bride in the dark until the last possible moment. Why ruin her entire day?*

I rode to the rescue once again, stressing to her the fact that this kink in her big day would eventually be her funny wedding story. And within moments, she had reapplied her makeup, the music had begun, and everyone in the wedding party was lined up and ready to go down the aisle. Luckily, the bride had chosen classic pieces for the ceremony (which had been listed on her program, thankfully), so she was able to walk down the aisle to the music she had planned on as if nothing had ever been awry.

My second DIY bride did pretty well for herself, I must admit—that is until she and her newly minted husband were stranded at Whitfield. The family and wedding party had left the chapel after formal photos had been taken. After the new Mr. and Mrs. had posed for a handful of portraits, the photographer (once again, minus a second shooter) had scurried off to the reception to set up for the couple's grand entrance. But much to her chagrin, the bride realized, a little too late, that she'd neglected to arrange transportation. Before you could say "Be sure to reapply your makeup before you make your grand entrance," I was tucking the distressed bride and her groom, who was trying to console her, into a taxi. Off they sped to an unknown future.

After I'd sent the stressed-out couple on their way, I began my methodical process of shutting Whitfield down for the day. And as I turned off the last light and locked the last door, I thought, I was knee-deep in the trenches all weekend, and I lived to tell the tale! Maybe I'm going to be good at this job after all.

Labor Day weekend is a big one for the wedding industry because there's always that guaranteed Monday off, so Sunday weddings are actually a realistic option, even for out-of-towners. My first Labor Day weekend at Whitfield, all four timeslots were booked. Lucky for me, all four brides had professional planners on board.

By Sunday at four o'clock, the last wedding had wrapped up and I was on my way to Harper's. There was a hint of fall in the air, so I drove with the windows down. And as I began to make the ascent to the top of Love Circle—where Harper and Jeff lived—a stream of memories rode in on the cool afternoon breeze. Aaron and I had driven this way countless times, taking each foot of the windy, unevenly paved journey for granted, as if we would be traversing it forever.

One of my favorite streets in Nashville, Love Circle was aptly named. The un-paralleled view of Nashville combined with its secluded nature had once made it the spot for lovers to "park." And as I stepped out of my car and took in the amazing view, I was glad I had come even if it meant facing this new milestone of life without Aaron.

Walking through the wooden gate and up the stone walk, I was bombarded by well-wishers who were camped on the front porch and obviously on their second round of cocktails. These were my dear friends, some of whom I'd known my entire life. I felt like I was coming home after a long absence, which wasn't far from the truth. Harper was on me in an instant. Ever the consummate hostess, she led me to the bar despite the fact that I'd been to her house a thousand times.

"I'm so glad you could make it, Jules!" She hugged me and poured me a glass of my favorite chardonnay. "Jeff is around here somewhere," she added as she turned to greet another newcomer.

Wandering through to the kitchen, I began to feel more relaxed than I had in months—actually since before Aaron had died. The sun was loping in the late afternoon sky, melting slowly into the Nashville skyline. I followed it onto the back deck, running into Lili in the process.

"I thought you'd never get here!" she squealed, throwing her arms around me and hugging me for all she was worth. "Ready for our slumber party, girlfriend?" she quizzed as I accompanied her back to the bar for refills.

Was I ever! I'd been looking forward to having Lili over for weeks now, and I smiled broadly at the prospect of the hell we were gonna raise. "The pantry is stocked with all kinds of goodies neither of us should be eating, and the liquor cabinet is, of course, fully loaded," I told her.

"Sounds like we're all set!" She raised her glass to mine in a toast, and we hugged again as if to seal the deal.

"Have you seen Linc?" I asked.

"Not yet," she said, scanning the room. "Let's go scout him out!"

We took off in a flash, like a couple of wild teenagers on a scavenger hunt, looking behind couches and chairs, under tables, and behind doors for Linc. It was such a silly thing to do, which really cracked us up; we were laughing so hard I thought we'd fall over. And for a few minutes, it felt like the old days, as if I had never been in mourning for my fiancé and I was just another carefree, party-going woman charging through a house, on a mission.

Doubling back to the kitchen, I cornered a little too fast and ran smack-dab into Linc. We gave each other a giant bear hug, as if there had never been any weirdness between us, and I let myself melt into his arms for a minute.

Snap out of it, Julia! I silently scolded myself, wresting free of his embrace.

Linc stood back to take me in, as if he were assessing a prize he'd just won at a carnival. "You look great, Jules!"

"So do you!" I exclaimed, taking him in as well. "I guess all that hiking you've been doing agrees with you."

"Yeah," Lili chimed in. "How cool that you're tackling the AT again!"

"It's even harder the second time." He winced in mock horror. "But I have a posse to keep me going. Did Julia tell you there are a bunch of us doing the trail this time? Kind of a tribute to Aaron," he informed Lili.

No sooner had those words escaped his lips than the duo of gratitude and regret began doing their obligatory two-step in my chest, and I felt the tears begin to rise. Will life ever feel fucking normal again? I wondered, choking back the tears into the recesses of my throat. Chasing the hot salt that hung there with the remainder of the wine in my glass, I fixed my eyes on the floor and tried to still the inner rumba that was, evidently, the duo's second number. Lili and Linc were chattering away like a couple of long-lost cousins, and I was grateful they hadn't noticed that the earth was falling out from under me. I was so tired of being the sad girl.

It was then that I sensed, more than saw, a young woman approaching Linc from the side, vying for his attention. He turned and smiled at her, reaching out his arm to draw her into our circle; there it stayed, wrapped around her waist as if it belonged there. "Julia Holmes, Lili Sinclair, this is Emmalyn Carter Grimes. Emmalyn, meet two of my dearest friends in the world."

Friends? I thought. What does he mean by that?

"It is such a pleasure to meet you," Emmalyn Carter Grimes gushed, flashing her sparkling white teeth in my direction. "And please, call me Em. I have heard so much about you...and Aaron, of course. I am so sorry for your loss."

My loss? To what loss was she referring—Aaron or Linc? I couldn't believe that this was the question flashing though my mind, but there you have it. Life is a trip.

Without missing a beat, Linc continued the explanation of why this annoyingly charming creature also had her arm wrapped around him like it had every right to be there. "Emmalyn is part of my posse." He grinned, turning to her and exchanging a ridiculous high five. They found this quite amusing. I did not. "She's the grad student I told you about, from Vanderbilt."

Ah…now it all made sense. Linc's renewed vigor for life was not just a result of all the hiking he'd been doing; he'd been climbing atop much more than the lofty peaks of the AT! I felt the blood drain from my face and hoped it didn't show. But I had nothing to worry about. The adorable couple had eyes only for each other. As they leaned in for a brief yet electric kiss, I was sure I was going to throw up.

"It seems I'm in need of a refill." I smiled, holding my empty glass up for everyone to see, as if I needed a reason other than abject nausea to escape this unholy scene. "So nice to meet you…Em," I said, emphasizing the "m" for good measure.

"Think I'll join her." Lili grabbed my arm, and we retreated across the kitchen and back toward the bar.

As we helped ourselves from the pitcher of margaritas—it was definitely going to be a tequila night—Lili looked me square in the eye. "What was that?" she asked.

"What was what?" I tried to act all innocent.

"What is going on with you and Linc?" she demanded in a stage whisper.

"It's a long story." I sighed, taking a big gulp of my drink.

"Well then," she said with a smile, "it's a good thing we have all night, 'cause I have a feeling it's gonna be a long one."

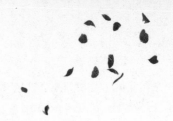

chapter eighteen

ili was right about one thing: it was gonna be a long night. I couldn't very well leave Harper's party after having just arrived, so despite the fact that I wanted to flee I stuck around. I tried to act natural, mix and mingle like a normal person, which would have been great if I knew what that looked like.

I kept turning my attention back to Linc and Emmalyn like some rubberneck who can't take their eyes off a horrific accident. They flirted and flattered, kissed and cajoled as they shared some private joke that was, evidently, quite hilarious. They had private jokes already! How long had this been going on, and why was I the last one to know?

Oh my God! I thought, turning my back on the young lovers and heading out to the front porch, my drink sloshing onto my shoes as I trekked with great determination. I'm jealous! I'm jealous of Linc and this pixie in pumps he's obviously fallen for! That is crazy! What the hell is wrong with me? Aaron's body is barely cold, and here I am chasing after the last man to see him alive! I chastised myself as I knocked back the thimbleful of margarita that had survived my sprint across the house.

But who could blame me for being jealous? I slumped into the porch swing. Emmalyn Carter Grimes was a gorgeous girl and obviously perfect for Linc in every way. This made me hate her even more. She could have been his doppelgänger, if you were to discount the six to eight inches in height that separated them. Otherwise she was a mini-him. Blonde, like Linc, her thick honey-colored hair was cut in a stylishly chunky bob, and her eyes were the same lapis blue.

And she was so right for him! She was going to be a lawyer, she had a casual elegance that mirrored his, and they sparred point for point with exceptional wit. She was a smart cookie, a baby doll with a brain, and a charming Southern girl to boot. She was the whole package. And there is no messing with that.

We Southern girls have it hands down when it comes to getting our way and getting what we want. Like a well-cut diamond, a Southern woman of quality can be recognized by the four Cs: charm, confidence, coyness, and control. These we know how to employ with panache.

When a good Southern girl sees a man she wants, she goes out and gets him—because, sister, she knows how. She can attract and corner him, wrangle and hog-tie him. And while she's holding the reins of the invisible halter she's slipped around his neck, she's enjoying the ride of her life while making sure he's enjoying it too. All of this happens with barely the wave of a little manicured finger, because we Southern girls were born and bred to be in charge while letting our menfolk think they're the ones calling the shots. And if you have the know-how and play your cards right, you can make the man of your dreams do your bidding from now until eternity. I know this may sound like a harsh assessment of my kind, but it's just the facts.

So there she was, all lithe and lean, wearing a flowery sundress that hugged her in all the right places, working her Southern girl mojo on Linc—who was not complaining one bit, I might add. I have to admit it got my goat; OK, it got the whole herd! But once again, I had to remind myself that I had no right to feel this way. I was practically a widow, for God's sake! And the unholy trinity of me being in love with my dead fiancé and his best friend at the same time was a scenario I found hard to explain.

And then all of a sudden it hit me! I actually did have a reason to feel the way I did, and I needed to get out of there, fast.

I spilled the beans the minute we got to my house, thanks to Uber and Lili, who was sober enough to use her phone to call for a car. I told her everything from beginning to end without apology on my part or judgment on hers. She sat rapt, her mouth agape, her eyes never leaving my face.

Like every bad love story ever written, mine was original but also derivative. And as we settled into the cocoon of my over-stuffed couch for an evening of drinking and deep conversation, I explained what I'd been thinking and feeling about Linc, about Aaron, and about the fact that I'd become an amoral floozy in wiancée's clothing.

"I could feel something brewing between you months ago," Lili confided. "Especially when you all had that big fight about your new job. But why did you keep it to yourself?"

"Was it that obvious to you?" I was dumbfounded. "'Cause it wasn't obvious to me for quite a while. I mean, I kept thinking Linc and I were getting close, but I was such an emotional heap of goo, nothing felt like it made sense."

Lili stood up and headed toward the kitchen. I followed her, busying myself with the blender and a new batch of margaritas while she pulled assorted bags and boxes of junk food from the pantry and poured the contents into bowls.

"And the kiss! How come I never heard a word about that kiss?" she demanded.

I filled two large glasses with icy lime-green cocktails, and we plopped down at the kitchen table. "I was afraid you would think I was the biggest slut on the planet!"

"I already thought that!" She laughed.

Swatting her arm playfully with the back of my hand, I took a sip of my creation. As it slid down my throat with an icy jolt, I took a second to remember that kiss. "I still get chills just thinking about it . . ." I admitted.

"Are you sure it's not just that drink?" Lili laughed again. "So what happens now?"

"Before today, I would have said I need to get on with my life like any reasonable person would do," I said. "But I kind of had an epiphany at the party, and I think it might change things."

"Go on . . ." She reached for a handful of chips.

"Do you remember the night Aaron and I met?" I asked before popping a handful of cashews into my mouth.

"Sure I do. We were about to leave that boring fundraiser, when you saw him standing across the room."

"Right!" I took a drink and paused. "But do you remember who was with him?"

"Linc, of course. So what?"

"Well, there were two of them and two of us, and I thought how great it would be if we could pair off . . ."

"Which is when Aaron crossed the room with that enormous grin of his and headed straight for you."

"Yeah." I remembered the moment—Aaron so strikingly

handsome in a dark-blue blazer and gray slacks, his shoes polished to perfection, every hair in place. He had claimed me with that first touch when he shook my hand and introduced himself. "But that thing I realized this afternoon? It was Linc I noticed first, and it was him I wanted to meet. But then Aaron made his move, and who could say no to that? Until tonight, I'd forgotten all about my initial attraction to Linc! But I got so jealous when I saw him with Emmalyn, and everything clicked into place."

Lili stared at me, her mouth, once again, agape. "Wow, Jules." She sat back.

"Naturally, I'd hoped you and Linc would hit it off that night, the way Aaron and I had."

"Which didn't happen, for obvious reasons. The dude felt like my brother from the word *go*." She took a long sip of her drink and shook her head in disbelief. "So what are you going to do now? Are you gonna tell him?"

I popped out of my chair and went to grab a bottle of water from the fridge. "I can't do that!" I said before draining the entire thing. This emotional boomeranging was so dehydrating. "That kiss was a mistake, and Linc and I both know it. Besides, he's moved on. Maybe I need to do the same."

"Are you sure you're ready to do that?" Lili asked me, a look of concern crossing her face. "Aaron's been dead for only a few months."

"Well, I don't mean move on, move on," I said, sitting back down. "It's not like I'm looking for someone to replace him. I don't think anybody could ever do that. But I feel all pent up, like I need to at least get out and have some fun."

"Well, if it's fun you're looking for, I have just the ticket!" Lili smiled her most mischievous smile. When she looked like that, I knew she had hatched a plan. And I knew I would like it just fine.

chapter nineteen

Frist Fridays were a weekly staple of Nashville's summer social calendar. Since I'd missed every single one that year, Lili and Harper thought that attending the final "Friday" of the season would be a great way for me to get my groove back.

Sponsored by the Frist Art Museum—Nashville's answer to the Met in New York—this event combined food, drink, and live music and was set outside on their giant back lawn. The place was packed by the time we got there. The Long Players, a band made up of Nashville's best studio musicians, was kicking off the night with their rendition of the entire *Sticky Fingers* album. These guys sounded exactly like the Rolling Stones as they sang and played every song, note for note.

"This is really fun!" I toasted my girlfriends happily after we'd successfully attracted the bartender's attention and had our drinks in hand. Taking in the crowd and a swig of ice-cold beer, I began to move to the hypnotic rhythm of the music. "I'm glad I let you all talk me into this," I shouted, trying to be heard above the fray.

"Let's dance!" Harper shouted back as the three of us waded into the crowd to the strains of "Brown Sugar," singing along at the top of our lungs.

One dance led to another, followed by more beers and more dancing. The sun began to dip behind the clock tower of the historic Union Station Hotel, which provided the backdrop for the stage where the band was rocking harder and louder by the minute. Psychedelic wisps of neon pink, Creamsicle orange, and deep purple wove across the azure-blue sky as the silvery twilight cast the magnificent old building in silhouette. In need of a fresh beer and a breather, I signaled to the girls that I was heading to the bar. They quickly followed suit.

It was nearly impossible to get the bartender's attention, as the band had taken a break and everyone in attendance wanted their thirst quenched at the same moment. I was about to give up, when a rather tall man to my left, having flagged the bartender, asked me what I wanted and ordered up an additional three cold beers.

Lili and Harper, who were still by my side, were obviously impressed.

"Well, well . . ." Lili smiled deviously.

"Look who's popular!" Harper added.

"What do I do now?" I asked my friends just as the tall, dark stranger turned to offer us the drinks he'd purchased on our behalf.

"You could start by smiling at him," Lili suggested, accepting the proffered beer with a smile and a thank you of her own. Harper nudged me in agreement.

"Thank you!" I tipped my beer in his direction, taking his measure.

The guy was a heart-stopper who owned each and every inch of his six-foot-two frame. Judging by the wide expanse of his well-muscled shoulders, I was certain he was hiding a perfect six-pack under the fashionably cut black T-shirt that hung on him just so. His well-worn jeans and cowboy boots rounded out his casual brand of elegance.

"My pleasure." He toasted me back. His captivating smile lit up the even planes of his chiseled face. "I'm Garrett, by the way."

I'm dumbstruck, I thought.

As usual, Lili had her wits about her and leaped in where I had obviously fallen short. "I'm Lili, and this is Harper and Julia," she said while gesturing to each of us in turn.

He extended his hand, long fingers wrapping first around Lili's, then Harper's, and finally mine as we were introduced. "Nice to meet you all," he said, staring mostly at me.

I had no idea what to say or do. Should I thank him again for the drink? Make small talk? Flirt and laugh like some college girl? None or all of the above? I was glad the dim lighting hid the blush that had spread from my neck to my forehead. "Thanks again," I blurted out as I released his oversized grip.

"You looked thirsty," he replied evenly through his crooked grin. "Wanna dance?" he asked as the band started their second set.

The great thing about dancing to a really loud band is that it prevents you from having to carry on a conversation, which is super helpful when the cat's got your tongue. And from the moment I'd said yes and followed Garrett to the dance floor, mine had been tied up in knots. It had been years since I'd danced with anyone other than Aaron, and I could think of nothing else. But the moment Garrett turned to face me and took my hand in his, all that pesky thinking stopped because Garrett had all the right moves. And once we'd found our place in the middle of the undulating crowd, I lost myself in the rhythm of the music. All I wanted was to dance until I was breathless.

RULE #33: *When rational thought flies out the window like a parakeet that's escaped its cage, let it go. It might be the only adventure the little sucker gets.*

Taking a break from the action, we returned to the bar. Naturally, Garrett began the conversation I'd been able to avoid on the dance floor. "So what do you do, Julia?" he asked after a long pull on his cold beer.

"I'm between lives at the moment," I confessed.

"I see," he said, stepping closer, leaning in, and lowering his voice. "That sounds rather mysterious."

I had no idea what to say. That I was an almost-widow? That my fiancé had kicked the bucket doing something on his bucket list? That I had taken a job as a wedding planner at the place we were to be married? That it had been years since I'd done this and therefore had absolutely no idea what to do next? "Let's just say that my life has changed majorly in the last few months and I'm still getting my bearings. I really don't feel like going into it," I summed things up.

"OK. Fair enough," he said, swallowing me whole with those limpid pools he was using for eyes. "Why don't I buy you another beer and we'll talk about the weather or something?" He motioned to the bartender to bring another round. "So, do you believe in climate change?" he asked as if in all seriousness.

I laughed. "That's how you talk about the weather?"

He began to laugh as well—a warm, low, and earthy sound that, annoyingly, reminded me of Linc. All of a sudden, the image of Linc and Emmalyn together crowded out every other thought in my head, and I began to feel a little bit angry. I had to shake this green-eyed monster loose, and I knew of only one way to do it; I had to distract myself. And what better way was there than to distract myself with the handsome stranger who smelled like a warm summer night at the beach.

But just as I decided to throw caution to the wind and ask Garrett some personal information—like his last name and what he did for a living—Lili and Harper came barreling toward us, wringing wet and dying of thirst.

"Hello, ladies!" Garrett greeted my girlfriends with a couple of cold ones he'd procured in advance.

"I guess chivalry isn't dead," Lili said before taking a long drink of her beer.

"I hope you all aren't driving." Garrett looked serious for a moment.

"Oh no," I assured him. "Harper's husband is our chauffeur for the night."

"Speaking of which," Harper said, glancing at her phone, which had pinged into action, "I think the witching hour is upon us. Our chariot awaits!"

"I guess that's my cue." I looked apologetically at Garrett. "I have to work tomorrow anyway. Early day."

"On a Saturday?" He grinned. "That does sound mysterious. Now I really am intrigued."

"Thanks for the drinks." I offered my hand.

And as he took my hand in his, he pulled me to him, leaned in, and planted a kiss on my cheek. "The pleasure was all mine," he purred.

I fought the urge to lean in and kiss him ever so gently on the mouth, just a light brush of my lips against his. It would have been so sweet, I told myself as I walked toward Jeff's waiting car. But I shook that thought loose as quickly as it had entered my head, because in my heart of hearts, I knew it was probably just the beer talking.

chapter twenty

It was early, and the sun was hanging low in an impossibly clear blue sky. The air was so crisp I felt like I could reach out and snap it into little pieces, yet I didn't feel chilled, despite the fact that I wore only shorts and a T-shirt. But I also wore hiking boots, which was so unlike me; as a matter of fact, I had never worn a pair of hiking boots in my life. Nonetheless, there they were, standing stoutly upon my feet. And here I was at the top of a grassy hill, which allowed me to take in the incredible scenery that wrapped around me in every direction.

Voices rode like sirens on the wind. From my vantage point, I could see a line of people making their way up the side of the hill and over its crest. And as they wound their way up the steep path to my left, I realized that Aaron was leading the pack and that he was headed right for me. "Jules!" he shouted happily, breaking into a run. "I was hoping you'd come!" He caught me up in a giant hug, releasing me as he took a step back, in order to inspect me. "I never thought I'd see this day." He laughed. "Julia Holmes in hiking boots!"

I hardly knew what to say. I never thought I'd see this day either. I hated hiking! "I don't have any gear," I began making excuses.

Aaron pointed to a bundle that lay at my feet. "There's your pack, silly!"

Funny, it hadn't been there a moment ago . . .

"So, who are all these people?" I asked, taking in the dozens of assorted hikers who bent to fill their canteens from a crystal-clear stream, settling in for a rest under startlingly green trees. Except for one young boy, standing with a man who appeared to be his father, there were no children in the crowd. But it was obvious that father and son were quite close, and I watched them as they joked and laughed together like they were having the time of their lives.

"Everyone here died on the AT," Aaron said matter-of-factly, as if he was remarking on the weather. "So we decided to hike it again, together. Kind of an exercise in moving on, I guess."

Startled by Aaron's remarks, I looked at the father and son again. OK, so maybe the dynamic duo wasn't exactly having the time of their lives. What had happened to them? I wondered. Had they died instantly like Aaron? Had there been pain?

I reached out and wrapped my arms as tightly as I could around Aaron, feeling him solid and real beneath the expanse of my arms—alive, breathing, all mine. Everything felt right. My world was whole.

"You know, Linc is rehiking the trail again too," I said, thinking I was delivering a giant news flash.

"I know. He told me. I'm glad he's doing it. I think it will be cathartic."

I felt my heart start to pound and pulled back to look him in the eye. "He told you? When did he tell you?"

"You're not the only one who visits me, babe." He took a step back to put on his pack. "So, are you gonna join us today? Looks like it's going to be a beautiful one." He smiled that all-knowing smile he'd recently acquired and looked out toward the hills that stretched above and beyond us.

I couldn't believe how nonchalant Aaron was being about his death and the deaths of his hiking companions. And why was he talking about how he died; he'd never done that before! Would he keep hiking the AT from now until the end of time? And would all of these people be with him? There were so many questions I wanted to ask, so much I needed to know.

But before I could ask a single one, Aaron had begun to walk toward his compatriots. Turning back to face me, I noticed how his eyes sparkled in the translucent light that hovered around him like a cloud. He lifted his arm, and with an open-palmed wave, he faded from view, as did everyone else who'd been standing around me a moment before.

I spun in circles looking in every direction, shielding my eyes with my hand as the sun rose higher and higher. How could they have disappeared just like that? Did they just get a really good head start? None of this made sense!

I began to run as fast as I could over the next hill, where the vista was even more incredible than the last. But when I reached the top, there was still not a soul in sight.

Sinking to the ground, winded and exasperated, I felt the once-solid earth beneath me begin to give way. I clutched at the tall grass for dear life, but it was no use. Suddenly I was free-falling, weightless. Thudding back into my body, I awoke alone in my bed, the covers thrown off in a heap, the room dappled by the lemony sun, which had begun to peer above the horizon.

As with every dream I'd had about Aaron, this one felt uncannily real, leaving the remnants of him scattered in my mind's eye for several moments. I had held him; he had been warm and solid. I could still feel his touch on my skin. And I had been wearing hiking boots, for God's sake! Talk about a nightmare!

Sliding into the pair of jeans I'd dropped by the bed just a few hours before, my mind drifted to Garrett, and I felt a little shiver of something akin to joy trailing up my spine. I remembered the way his lips had brushed against my cheek, warm and inviting, and how he'd made me feel alive again in a way I hadn't expected to feel. But it was too soon for someone new. Besides, I knew nothing about the man. Hell, I didn't even know his last name! Truth be told, he was more than likely just a fly-by-night flirtation, which was a good thing; I had enough to handle with this new job of mine.

Speaking of which, I had two weddings to prepare for, I realized, shifting into full gear despite the fact that my head felt like it was stuffed with wet cotton. Luckily, I had no decisions to make that morning other than what I was going to wear and how many cups of coffee I'd need to drink in order to get my head screwed on straight.

Naturally, when you have even the teensiest of hangovers, every little thing—like impossibly slow drivers who hog the road ahead of you or the fact that you spilled most of your coffee when you were trying to get out of the car—eats away at the fabric of your being until you just wanna slap someone. That was exactly how I felt that exceedingly hot, damp morning as I opened the doors and stepped into the blissfully cool sanctuary of Whitfield Chapel.

I still wore traces of Aaron, like a lingering scent that should have lost its verve hours ago yet still permeated every pore. "Is it time to move on?" I asked his flimsy apparition still hanging on by the threads of my dream. "Was that what you were trying to tell me last night?" I wondered in a whisper, closing my eyes. "Give me a sign if that's what you meant. Give me a sign . . ."

The insistent sound of the side door rattling off its hinges made me jump. What the hell? Someone was trying to get in, and the unexpected intrusion was filling me with rage! Not only was this idiot thirty minutes early, but he or she had just interrupted a very important one-way conversation!

I suspected the offending party was a vendor trying to bend the rules by showing up before their allotted time, hoping to get in. Usually I was generous with the florists who arrived early, afraid their arrangements would wilt in the heat, or the videographers who wanted to get set up so they could capture the bride's arrival. On those occasions, I allowed them early entrance. But not today, I wanted to scream out loud! Today I was in no mood!

Knowing that the person on the other side of the door could neither see me nor hear me gave me a secret thrill; I was safe in my lair for a few moments longer. I went on with the business of setting up. But when I heard the door rattling at the other side of the building followed by someone pulling at the double doors in front, I began to fume anew. This clown was working on my last nerve!

I then heard the door to the left of the altar rattling away before the offending party headed for the door I'd come in, which I'd had the good sense to lock behind me. Marching across the chapel, spewing venom under my breath, the outline of a man trying to peer through the thick, frosted windowpanes appeared. I nearly lost my cookies.

Flipping back the lock with purpose, I thrust the door open, hitting the would-be intruder squarely in the head, sending him staggering backward. "Sorry," I apologized halfheartedly. "But you're thirty minutes early! The chapel doesn't open until ten thirty."

Trying to right himself, he vigorously rubbed at a spot on his temple, blocking his face with his hand. "I'm the one who should be sorry," he said in a voice that sounded familiar. "This is my first time here, and I had no idea there were such strict rules." As he lowered his hand, I realized with a start that this familiar voice belonged to none other than my mystery dance partner from the night before, the ever-handsome Garrett. My irritation gave way to a steady trembling, and I could feel the color rising in my cheeks.

"Well look who almost knocked the wind out of me!" He grinned at me while continuing to rub his head. "Second time in under twenty-four hours," he said flirtatiously. "That must be some kind of record."

Stepping through the door, I moved a few steps closer, trying to assess his injuries. Then I began stammering like a schoolgirl. "I am so sorry! Are you OK? Why are you here?"

Pointing to a large black case that rested by the door, he cocked his head. "I'm shooting the Smith/Wilder wedding. Actually, I'm the second shooter on this job, so I wanted to get here early and familiarize myself with the place."

"Ah," I said, embarrassed by my inane babbling. "I didn't know you were a photographer." I stared at him for a moment longer than necessary, like I was the one who'd just been smacked on the head.

"I guess that makes us even. I didn't know you worked here." He continued to smile indulgently, waiting for me to make a move. "So, is it OK if I come in?"

"Sure!" I said, trying to recover my dignity. I took a step back and motioned him inside. Thus far, this man had seen me drunk and stunned—not the kind of first impression one hopes to make. "Actually, I think you'll want to set up in Beaumont Hall. Follow me, and I'll show you where to put your stuff."

"I'd follow you anywhere!" He laughed, lifting the hefty case as if it weighed nothing.

Showing him to the large drawing room at the center of Beaumont Hall, I suggested he take a look around and then excused myself in order to finish setting up the chapel.

Just inside the door, I fell against the cool brick wall and tried to center myself. Although my heart was still thumping with the beat of a hundred carrier pigeons, my head, thankfully, had ceased its thrumming. Well, I thought, that's one way to get rid of a hangover!

Get it together, Julia! I reprimanded myself as I straightened my skirt, ran my fingers through my thick, unruly curls, and then continued about my business.

No sooner had I unlocked the rest of the doors than several vendors piled into the sanctuary hauling flowers, candelabras, and video equipment. After greeting them, I headed back to Beaumont Hall, all the while counseling myself to keep my cool. But rounding the corner, anything resembling cool fell away because there was Garrett with his arms wrapped around a petite brunette, giving her an enthusiastic hug.

I stepped back, wondering what I had stumbled onto, and then turned and headed for my office, hoping Garrett hadn't seen me.

"Julia," I heard him say as he approached from behind.

Too late; he'd seen me! I turned back to face him.

"This is my boss, Georgia Knox." He pointed to the adorable creature who'd walked up to join him.

"Hi, Georgia," I said, flashing my most charming Southern-girl smile, hoping to hide the fact that the wind had just been knocked out of me. "I'm Whitfield's weekend wedding assistant, Julia Holmes. Nice to meet you."

She reached for my outstretched hand, shaking it firmly. "I heard there was a new girl in town. Welcome to the wonderful world of weddings," she joked.

I liked her instantly, a fact I absolutely hated. But donning my professional hat, I asked if there was anything I could do for her before I went to check on a few things—mainly the state of my untethered brain. She assured me that she had shot at Whitfield dozens of times and knew the lay of the land, which made me wonder if that was the only thing she knew the lay of. As I turned to go, I smiled once more at Garrett. He smiled back with equal parts amusement and lust. Once again, I fought to still my racing heart. This was going to be a long day.

Whitfield was choked to capacity with 250 guests in attendance and ten bridesmaids and groomsmen standing up for the happy young couple. The father of the bride was a wealthy developer who'd wanted his daughter to have the best of everything on her big day, and have everything she did. I was sure her gown had cost at least $10,000, and the array of flowers adorning the chapel and the wedding party probably had come with a matching price tag.

There was really no need for me to be in the chapel during the ceremony, as the wedding planner du jour had two assistants. But I just had to see Garrett in action. Slipping into the foyer, I tried to make myself useful by showing latecomers to the side door and repinning a couple of uncooperative boutonnieres.

Garrett moved around the sanctuary with the skill of a dancer, sliding up and down the aisle with ease, getting shots of the ceremony from every possible angle with a lunge here and a side step there. He was poetry in motion. Every now and then he would catch me staring and shoot me a sly smile or wink, which made me pulse with excitement. But mostly, he was caught up in his work, as was Georgia. Every few moments, they would cross paths and nod to one another, and then one of them would ascend to the choir loft while the other crossed to the side aisle for a different angle. I could see that they worked well together. What else do they do well together? I wondered while trying to tamp down the visions of them dancing in my head.

The minister had pronounced the happy couple, and I slipped out of the chapel before I could see them seal it with a kiss. After busying myself with unlocking the dressing rooms and collecting the stray water bottles that peppered Beaumont Hall, I retreated to my office as Georgia and Garrett corralled the extended family and wedding party to take the after-ceremony pictures that would eat up the hour they had left. Not wanting to get in the way, I busied myself in my office. Before you could say "cheese!" a hundred times, it was 2:25 and everyone was getting ready to head to the reception.

"It was great seeing you again."

I looked up to see Garrett leaning against the door frame as if he hadn't a care in the world. You'd never know that he'd spent the past four hours working like a madman (talk about being cool!). We locked eyes as he sauntered over to my desk.

"Looks like you had your work cut out for you today," I said, not knowing what else to say. I still wasn't all that sure that he and his "boss" weren't some kind of item, and I didn't want to be mistaken for some kind of fool.

Placing both palms on my desk, he leaned in. He smelled like dried orange peel and cloves, and I let his scent waft over me as we locked eyes. "Georgia is quite the taskmaster." He laughed and righted himself. "I'd forgotten how much work these weddings are. I shoot them so infrequently."

This seemed like just the opening I needed, a way to be nosy without giving myself away. "Oh, so you don't work with her on a regular basis?" I asked as casually as possible.

He grinned at me as if he were wise to the real question I was asking. "Actually, we used to work together a lot, but it's been months since I've seen her," he responded as if this should explain everything.

It did explain the present, certainly, but not their past. But what had or had not been between them was really none of my business. I hardly knew this man. And besides, I wasn't in the market for a big romance.

"Well, I should be heading to the reception," he said. I stood and extended my hand across the desk, glad to have the buffer of solid wood between us. But instead of shaking it, he just held my hand for a few seconds and gave it a little squeeze before letting go. "Call me," he said with a wink and a smile, sliding a business card from his pocket and setting it down on the desk. And then he was gone, leaving me restless and unable to breathe.

Reaching for his card, I ran my index finger over the raised letters and shivered. "Garrett McLeod Photography," I read aloud, enjoying the sound of his name in the room.

chapter twenty-one

What's a girl to do when she's got a crush on a guy she has no business having a crush on? Call her girlfriends, of course! I was conferencing with Lili and Harper before I left Whitfield's parking lot.

"You will never guess who I literally bumped into at work today," I began, as if I was in the habit of swinging wooden doors into handsome men every day of the week.

"I give up," Harper replied before even bothering to hazard a guess.

"Remember the guy I was dancing with last night?"

"Who could forget?" Lili swooned.

"Well, it turns out he's a photographer, and he turned up at Whitfield to shoot this afternoon's wedding!" I said, pictures of him reeling in my mind.

Filling the girls in on the details, especially the one where he gave me his card and asked me to call, I reminded myself of a teenage girl. "Should I call him?" I asked, hoping they'd egg me on.

"I'd give it at least a day or two," Lili advised.

Harper had other ideas. "Wait a week," she said. "He'll be chomping at the bit by then!"

"He'll be chomping all right," Lili countered. "But by then he may have chomped right through the idea of dating you and moved on to someone else who doesn't play hard to get. Is that really what you want?"

Way to throw a curveball, Lil, I thought. "I don't know what I want!" I complained. "I mean, Garrett is totally gorgeous and funny and charming...but I'm not ready to date, date. I might meet him for an innocent cup of coffee, you know, just to tell him I'm not interested . . ."

"Jules, there's already been a date of sorts with alcohol involved, so it's a little late to try and put that rabbit back in the hat, don't you think?" Harper pointed out.

Lili agreed. "What's the harm in calling him? You might have fun."

"If anyone needs some fun, it's you!" Harper added.

"Ha, ha," I replied sarcastically despite that fact that I knew she was right. "OK. Well, I'm gonna think about it." I got ready to sign off, having pulled into my driveway.

"Don't do anything I wouldn't do!" I could hear Lili smirking.

"Yeah," Harper chimed in. "That gives you just enough rope to hang yourself."

The evening dragged on with the lethargy of a turtle on Valium. I felt restless and ill at ease. Should I call him? Should I not? I had no idea what to do. On the one hand, I was still mourning the loss of my fiancé, and it was way too soon to be getting all stirred up! But on the other hand, I had asked Aaron for a sign and Garrett had appeared a minute later. Was that just a coincidence, or was it evidence that Aaron was indeed showing me the way back to the land of the living?

Maybe I should take a break from all this thinking, I told myself as I poured a glass of wine and hunkered down in front of the TV. As usual, nothing much was on, so I tuned to HSN to see what I could see. Maybe a bout of shopping would help to clear my mind! But after a few minutes of listening to a perky blonde sing the praises of her makeup line, I was bored. Shopping was no longer the thing that floated my boat. Garrett McLeod had taken the helm of that mighty ship, and, God help me, all I wanted to do was climb aboard and set sail.

Lucky for me, there was no wedding the next day. I slept in as late as I could, which was about eight o'clock, a fact that shocked me. There had been a time not that long ago when sleep was my best friend and I could easily luxuriate between the sheets until noon, even on Sundays.

Despite the fact that I'd been born and raised a good Christian girl, lately skipping church on Sunday mornings had become a bad habit. Somehow, I just could not get past the fact that the God I'd believed in since I could say the word had let my dear, sweet Aaron die so young and in such an awful way. And although I got an earful from my mother on a regular basis about how I'd let my faith lapse, I knew there was no lapsing about it; it was gone for good. But the absence of this Sunday tradition had left a gaping hole in the day, especially when I didn't have to work.

If it had been a rainy day, I might have been able to roll over, cover my head with a pillow, and fall back into a deep sleep. But the sun shined a little too brightly for that, so I got up and propelled myself downstairs to the kitchen, where the coffee—my

BFF of the morning—had already begun to brew. Filling the largest mug I could find, I grabbed the *New York Times* from its place in the front yard (somehow, the delivery guy never seemed to be able to hurl the thing onto the porch) and settled in on the back porch. But rather than relaxing me, this ritual, which Aaron and I had followed religiously for more Sundays than I could count, made me miss him with a vengeance. Still, I persisted in my reading, hoping the Arts and Leisure section would take my mind off the ache that had wedged itself into my solar plexus.

Somehow, my mind drifted from Aaron to Linc, and I wondered what he was doing on this bright and sunny morning. "Probably snuggling with Emmalyn," I thought out loud. And more than likely, they were doing so in some cabin or tent along the AT, where they were hiking to their hearts' content. As much as I envied the snuggling part, I did not envy the hiking part. My mind drifted back to the strange dream I'd had of Aaron and his dozens of ghostly hiker buddies. He was starting to move on, as was Linc. So what about me? What was I doing in the moving-on department other than fantasizing about Garrett? Maybe it was time to try and tackle Aaron's closet again; maybe that would help me begin my own journey.

As the sun crested the bank of trees that shaded the yard, I realized just how hot the day was going to be. I retraced my steps back to the cool confines of my kitchen, where I poured myself another mug of coffee and popped a piece of wheat bread into the toaster. Breakfast first, closet later, I thought, trying to put off the inevitable as long as I possibly could.

But the more coffee I drank, the more restless I became. I knew there was no way I could face packing up Aaron's clothes and personal belongings—not alone anyway. My mother would be headed to church by now, so she definitely was out. The organizational freak in my head reminded me that not only would there be sorting and packing involved in this enterprise, but I had no idea what I would do with all of Aaron's stuff once it was boxed.

After blending up a strawberry-peach smoothie, I carried it out to the porch, where the *New York Times* sat patiently waiting for my return. But waiting or not, the Sunday paper was not the least bit appealing. I wanted something more. "What is it you really want to do today, Jules?" I asked myself out loud. Call Garrett McLeod, my inner voice replied without missing a beat.

Wow! I scolded myself. Weren't you going to wait a few days? And hadn't you decided that it was best not to get involved with him at all?

Maybe I should call him now and see if he wants to meet for an afternoon coffee, I retorted, grabbing my phone from my pocket. What could be the harm? No matter what, I wouldn't accept an invitation to dinner, even if he asked. That was where I definitely had to draw the line. Just a quick coffee, and then I'm done, I told myself, retrieving his card from my other pocket.

Running my thumb across the raised letters that spelled out his name, I once again felt a surge of adrenaline rush through me. I took this as a sign; no time like the present, I assured myself, dialing his cell. It rang only twice before I heard his husky voice. "McLeod here," he said. I must have been silent for just a moment too long, because he spoke again. "Hello?"

"Garrett!" I blurted out a bit too enthusiastically.

"Is this who I think it is?" I could hear the smirk in his voice.

I couldn't help but break out in a shit-eating grin of my own. "Who do you think it is?" I got up and began to pace around the room.

"The only woman I'd hoped would call, Miss Julia Holmes," he teased. "What are you up to?"

"Oh this and that," I replied as nonchalantly as possible,

even though I was finding it hard to catch my breath. I hadn't done anything like this in years, and I was definitely out of practice. "I'm kind of at loose ends today. No weddings, and it's so beautiful . . ."

He took this as his cue. "Would you like to meet for lunch or a drink?"

Remembering the allegiance I'd sworn to boundary setting just moments before, I suggested we meet for coffee. What could be safer than that? "Fido at three?" I suggested the Hillsboro Village haunt that served up its own roasted beans.

"Sounds like a plan," he said in the sexiest voice I'd heard in eons. Thank the Lord we were just meeting for coffee.

The next couple of hours flew by as I readied myself for my date. My stomach was in knots as I ran scenario after scenario in my head, from the first hello to the first kiss. Oh, there would be kissing; of that I had no doubt. But even though I wanted to fly all the way to the moon with this handsome man, I vowed I would take things slow.

I tried not to think about Aaron and how he fit in the picture, but he kept popping into my head. I was about as far from over him as the North Pole is from its counterpart in the South, but there was no denying that Garrett McLeod had captured my imagination.

Maybe I should ask Aaron's permission, I decided as I headed toward the fireplace mantel, where his big and mini urns were stationed.

"It's only coffee . . ." I tried to sound reasonable. But Aaron and I both knew this wasn't only coffee. I waited a moment for another sign, but hearing not a peep from him—no rolling thunder or lightning strikes—I figured it would be OK if I left him for a while. "I'll see you later," I said confidently as I turned to go get dressed. He certainly wasn't going anywhere.

I must have tried on twenty different outfits, finally settling on a pair of khakis and a breezy little top, which looked effortless and pretty. The bedroom was another story however; it looked like a tornado had touched down there. But rather than lifting things and flying away with them, this tornado had just dropped its load and spun off. This in itself absolutely guaranteed that I would not be bringing Garrett home. I was determined to make this first date a chaste one, but the unruly state of my bedroom did give me extra insurance against allowing myself to get carried away.

The parking gods were kind to me that day, which is not always the case in that part of town. It was just before three o'clock as I made my way toward Fido. Up until that moment, I'd been able to convince myself that this was just another day and Garrett McLeod was just another guy. But as I rounded the corner, there he stood in front of the wooden-framed glass doors, a welcoming grin spread across his ruggedly chiseled face, and I melted like butter on a hot day.

"Good afternoon, Miss Julia," he intoned, bowing in my direction. "Don't you look lovely!"

I got chills just hearing him say my name, and my voice cracked a little as I greeted him in kind. "Thank you, Garrett. You look lovely too!" I giggled.

As usual, the place was packed, but we managed to snag one of the oversized wooden booths just inside the door. There he left me as he went off to stand in the seemingly endless line to order our drinks. Unfortunately, this gave me more time to think about the ramifications of what I was doing, which was not a good thing. So I did the only thing I could think of to calm myself down: I called Lili.

"Just be cool!" she told me in no uncertain terms. "Have fun! It's just coffee…Call me when it's over," she added excitedly before signing off.

No sooner had I stashed my phone in my purse than Garrett returned with our coffees and was sitting across from me. I began to feel like I wasn't all the way in my body as I flirted and giggled. My face was flushed, my heart was racing, and hundreds of butterflies were permanently camped out in the pit of my stomach, taking off and returning again.

But for the first time in months, my thoughts were of nobody but the man who sat across the table from me. In my mind's eye, I saw myself leaping across the short divide and having my way with him, but that would have been completely out of character for me. Public displays of affection were not something a well-brought-up woman would ever think about. Sure, OK, yes I was thinking about it, but good manners were just wound too tightly into my DNA for me to act on the thought.

RULE #22: *Never buck the rules unless you want to feel as lost as last year's Easter egg.*

Garrett was nothing but charming. As we made small talk, dissecting the wedding from the previous day, he told me some funny stories about the reception that had followed. "By the end of the night, the bride was on stage with the band, wearing a chain of glow sticks around her neck and singing at the top of her lungs." He laughed. "But by that point, pretty much everyone was doing the same. They were having way too much fun!"

"I always wonder which of my brides will go the distance," I said.

"Which brings me to a burning question." He leaned forward, looking me right in the eye. "Why is a beautiful, intelligent woman like you still single? I mean, have you never wanted to get married yourself? Or have you already taken the walk on the wild side and decided it wasn't your thing?"

There it was—the million-dollar question. And it made me realize that although the chemistry between us was undeniable, Garrett and I didn't know much about each another. So I just opened my mouth and let the story escape because really, there was no other way.

"I was engaged." I swept the straw around in my dwindling drink. "And actually, I was supposed to get married at Whitfield back in June. But Aaron—that was my fiancé—died suddenly, and so...I didn't get married after all." I looked him in the eye, trying to keep from losing it.

"Wow! I had no idea, Julia. I am so sorry," he said, reaching for my hand.

"It's been a rough few months. But I'm getting on with life, slowly but surely." I smiled at him. "So what about you?" I asked him, letting go of his hand and returning mine to my side of the table, where it belonged. "Why are you single?"

"Actually, I just broke up with a woman I've been seeing for almost three years," he shared. "So I guess I'm kind of on the rebound."

"Is that a good thing or a bad thing?"

"A very good thing, as far as I'm concerned." He shot that crooked grin in my direction. Then he went on to give me the CliffsNotes version of his failed romance, explaining that, in the end, they wanted different things from life. "The main thing was that she wanted kids and I didn't."

This gave me pause. I definitely wanted children, although I didn't plan on having them anytime soon. But I'd always pictured myself with a great husband and a small brood of kids, and I wondered if that was out of the question for him. It would certainly be a deal breaker for me if he was dead set against having a family.

"So does that mean you never want to have kids?"

"Oh no!" he stated. "I do want a family someday—just not right now."

I breathed a sigh of relief because I really liked this guy and wanted to see where the road would take us. "OK!" I took a long sip of iced coffee. "I'd say that's enough serious talk for now!"

"Agreed!" He laughed, clinking his glass against mine.

It was early evening by the time Garrett escorted me to my car. The sky was tinged with a deep-orange glow. The air, although still quite warm, had crisp overtones. "I had a wonderful time," I said, looking up at him.

"I'm really glad you called me," he said in a thick whisper. Leaning in, he ran his thumb across my bottom lip, parting it ever so slightly, and bent to kiss me. His lips tasted like late summer, warm and inviting, and I leaned into him, wrapping my fingers around his arms and drawing him in.

He pulled back and, cradling my face in his hands, began to kiss me again, this time more fervently and deeply.

"Thank you for the coffee," I managed to croak once I'd come up for air.

"We should definitely do this again." He grinned. "How about Friday night?"

"Perfect. I don't have a wedding that evening." I grinned right back.

"OK. It's a date! Call me tomorrow, and we'll make a plan." He leaned back in for one more sweet kiss. "You've got my number."

Oh boy, did I ever!

chapter twenty-two

I was flying high, and I liked the feeling just fine. I had more energy than I'd had in months and put it to good use—cleaning and doing yard work, catching up on some reading and phone calls, and generally taking each day as it came rushing by. But truth be told, I also spent a lot of time texting and facebooking Garrett. Every time I heard my phone go "ping!" I broke out in the biggest grin imaginable as a rush of joy swept over me like a welcome breeze on a stifling day.

What had begun as a phone call and subsequent texting session on Monday evening had become a thing. Ever since, we'd been engaging in what can only be described as our "cyber cocktail hour," wherein each of us would have an adult beverage and message back and forth. My favorite means of chatting with him during these times was private messaging on Facebook. I would say something charmingly pithy and hit send, seeing the words "delivered" and "read" pop up one after the other. A thought bubble devoid of text with little dots running across it would then appear. Below this would be the words "Garrett is typing," three little words that would send shivers up and down my spine, as if I could actually feel his fingers click-click-clicking across my skin. "Garrett is typing," I would reiterate through my grinning lips. I loved it.

Sometimes we actually chatted, which was wonderful, of course. Hearing the deep, sexy tones of his voice always gave me a thrill. But I found the messaging equally as alluring because it was like sending little love letters back and forth. And I could tell he found it as titillating as I did.

Of course, I'd kept Lili and Harper in the loop. After each chat with Garrett, I'd solicit their advice. In these moments, I felt like a teenager. But there were other moments, usually late at night, when the guilt would come barging in with the cacophony of a marching band. This would make me question my feelings for Garrett, often resulting in my vow to break things off. But by morning, the thrill of infatuation would be waiting there to greet me when I charged out of bed, and I would embrace the day with the excitement of my newfound attraction and the promise it held.

By Friday, I was psyched. Garrett picked me up at seven and, after bundling me into the front seat of his midnight-blue Ford F-150 pickup, we cruised down Interstate 40 at top speed. It was only a matter of minutes before we exited onto River Road—a winding expanse of blacktop that snakes along the banks of the Cumberland River, which, for the most part, is hidden from the road by thickets of trees and rolling hills.

Five minutes later, we pulled into a drive marked by a sign that read "The Commodore Yacht Club." I asked my companionable date where it was he was taking me, and he'd indicated that we were going on a picnic with a twist. I found this intriguing.

Enormous cabin cruisers lined the dock, which stretched the length of a good city block. As Garrett held the car door open for me, he smiled and gave me his hand.

"Don't get too excited," he said while helping me from my seat. "I do have a boat here, but it's quite a bit smaller than those." He pointed to the row of expensive toys tied up neatly in their slips, which were easily the size of a house. After passing a dozen of these big mammas, we finally came to a more modestly equipped boat, a four-seater with a tiny cabin, which he claimed as his own.

"Wow!" I exclaimed as he helped me down onto the deck. "This is so cool!"

"Glad you approve," he said, opening the large picnic basket he'd toted along.

Popping the top off two ice-cold beers, he started the engine and then backed us out of the slip and onto the smooth water of the inlet, passing the larger vessels we'd walked by a few minutes before. Although most of the boats were occupied, it seemed their occupants had no intentions of launching them. It was like these folks were just hanging out on their back decks, swigging cocktails and laughing, but here they had cool river breezes and the freedom to take off down the river whenever the feeling hit them.

"That's a weekend tradition." Garrett lifted his beer in salute to his neighbors as we slid by. "Most of these folks have had boats here for years, and they just hang out and party with each other while their boats are docked. It's like having a house in the country without the mowing."

"I've lived here my entire life, and I never would have guessed this was even here."

"I'm guessing your parents aren't boat people." He smiled, taking another swig of his beer.

"Nope. I come from a long line of water-averse people. My mom gets seasick just taking a bath!" I exaggerated.

Rounding a bend, Garrett pointed the boat straight ahead and pulled on the throttle, taking us from whoa to go in a matter of seconds, which sent my hair whipping in the wind with abandon. The breeze felt marvelous. I turned my face to the sun, which was perched just above the tree line, edging its way down for the night and taking the heat of the late September afternoon with it.

"The Cumberland is the best kept secret in Nashville," Garrett informed me as the beautiful scenery sped by.

The farther along we cruised, the more I could see how true this was. We passed only a couple other boats. I felt myself relax into my seat as Garrett offered me a second cold one, the golden light framing him from behind, as if he were some otherworldly creature. A small cove appeared around the next bend, and he steered us toward it, threw out the anchor, and took a seat at the back of the boat, where he invited me to join him. As I settled in next to him, I couldn't help but have a shiver of a déjà vu; this cove looked so similar to the one Aaron had brought us to in my dream. But I shook off the feeling; Aaron was not here now.

"This is heavenly," I sighed.

"I had a feeling you'd like it. Although I would have been more concerned if you'd told me you sprang from the loins of landlubbers!" He laughed. Reaching into the basket, which sat at his feet, he opened the top to reveal a wealth of containers nestled inside. "Hungry?" he asked as he set up a small table, throwing a red-and-white checkered cloth over the top.

"Famished," I said as I remembered how little I'd eaten all day. (Anticipation is the *best* appetite suppressant of them all.)

With that, he set out plates of assorted meats and cheeses, crackers, cornichons, olives, and plum tomatoes. And in the waning golden light of the setting sun, we feasted and laughed, sharing stories from our past, enjoying the moments that lolled on by with the current of the mighty Cumberland.

The sunset had begun in earnest, pink clouds streaked against a Maxfield Parrish sky. The temperature had begun to drop, but the cool dampness of it felt marvelous against my bare arms and legs. Reaching beneath his seat, Garrett extracted a small blanket, which he placed ceremoniously around my shoulders, as if he were covering me with a spectacular cape. "It gets chilly out here," he half-whispered, taking my face in his hands and kissing me deeply. He tasted like barley and olives, salt and honey. And I was hungry for him; hungrier than I wanted to be. We were alone, bathed in the afterglow of a late summer day. I felt like I could float away forever on the current of his touch, past the place where my heartache was firmly planted, past the landscape of my shattered dreams.

Taking me in his arms, he pulled me close, trailing the length of my neck with soft, feathery nothings that left me breathless and on fire. He pulled back, looking deeply into my eyes, and kissed me again. I was lost in the cascade of sweet whisperings as he told me how good I tasted and how beautiful I was. I soaked it in like a woman who had been lost in the desert, deprived of food and water, the very wellsprings of life—as indeed, I guess I had been. And we stayed that way for hours, under our own little acre of star-speckled sky, wrapped in each other's arms without a care in the world.

chapter twenty-three

We were dancing—twirling and twirling under a midnight-blue sky—and he held me like he'd never let me go. Off in the distance, an orchestra played. The scent of honeysuckle floated on the air. I felt intoxicated and breathless and so in love that I thought my heart might burst from the sheer perfection of it all.

The hilltop terrace where we danced was strung with a thousand lights, which rivaled the incandescence of the full moon, its reflection swimming like a pool of liquid mercury on the glassy surface of the lake below. The party was in full swing, laughter and boisterous conversation erupting in every quarter. As other couples spun by, I couldn't help but notice that there was a translucent quality to each of them, as if they were constructed of silk and gossamer. And although they moved and spoke, I found it odd that I could practically see right through them, and

I wondered why I'd never noticed that I could see through people before. But somehow, it didn't matter.

Aaron held me close. Although he, too, had an otherworldly look about him, he felt as real as he always had. Something told me this was just a dream, but I felt like I knew otherwise. I was visiting this place. I was dancing with Aaron at a grand fete, and we were together again in the moonlight.

"No matter what this is," I whispered, "I'm in this moment, here with you. And this moment is forever."

He smiled at me in the way he always did when I said something that delighted him—eyes twinkling, mouth slightly agape and caught in the beginnings of a laugh—and I leaned in to kiss him, a soft, dewy kiss. A rush of joy washed over me, bathing me in the knowledge that Aaron and I had come full circle in our dance together. I finally understood that it hadn't been cut short; it had come to its rightful end. And I knew that the love we'd held between us would live on forever, no matter what else came to pass.

I threw my head back and laughed and laughed as he twirled me around under that midnight-blue sky, holding me fast in his capable arms.

Out of nowhere, I began to hear a bell. It was clanging so ferociously that it drowned out the orchestra and the revelry of the crowd that still wove in and around us. I felt compelled to stop dancing, despite the fact that I wanted more than anything to ignore the insistent ringing, which was getting louder by the second. I flung my head this way and that looking for the source of the annoying ringing. But the pull of that sound was so much stronger than my desire not to hear it. And as I began to focus on it even more, the magical world around me started to melt away. And as it did, I found I was coming awake in my bed.

Turning to look at the clock, I realized it was already eight o'clock. I sat up with a jolt, trying to figure out where I was and why I had the feeling that I was terribly late for something. As I reached for the phone, the source of the annoying ringing stopped, and I saw that it had been my mother who'd roused me from the most perfect dream of all time. I wanted to be angry with her, but she had actually saved my butt. I had an early call at Whitfield and had forgotten to set my alarm the night before. Still in a bit of a fog, however, I lay back for a moment and tried to recapture the luscious dream from which I'd been woken too soon. But it was useless; there was no going back.

As I pushed back the covers and swung my legs over the side of the bed, my mind flashed to Garrett and our waterborne picnic. I could still taste his kisses, and I remembered the way my heart raced when he whispered my name. I thought about the dream I'd just had and how real Aaron had felt when I was dancing in his arms. But he wasn't real... not any more. And despite the fact that I would always love him, I needed to make a stab at loving someone else, didn't I?

The big question loomed large as I made my way to the shower and stepped into the pelting stream of hot, steamy water: is it too soon?

I'd asked myself this same question after Linc and I had shared that crazy kiss and I'd begun obsessing about him as if there had been something real between us.

After I'd toweled off and grabbed a cup of coffee, I retreated to the back porch to scroll through my missed calls. There had been quite a few. Lili and Harper had left messages wanting to get the dirt on my date, which was to be expected. But the last message certainly was not expected, and it made my heart beat wildly. Garrett had called!

His message was brief but sincere. I played it over and over again just so I could hear his deep, sexy voice telling me what a good time he'd had. "I can't wait to see you again," he said. "Are you working tonight? Call me."

Glancing at the clock again, I realized how late I was running. I quickly texted the girls to tell them I'd catch up with them later, promising details. But there was no way of escaping my mother. She wanted to be filled in on my second date with Garrett; she wouldn't stand for my keeping her out of the loop. Besides, I regularly confided in her and often trusted her judgment far more than I trusted my own.

"Memaw would have had a lot to say on this subject," she told me, referring to her dear departed mother, as I poured myself a second cup of coffee and leaned against the counter with the phone pressed to my ear. "Of course, if she'd had her way, you'd be draped in black from head to toe and unable to receive any gentleman callers for at least a year." We both laughed. "Now if you want my opinion . . ."

"You know I do!" I exclaimed.

"You just have to follow your heart. That's always the best barometer."

"You're no help at all!" I cried. "It's only been four months since Aaron died. Shouldn't I feel guilty because I like Garrett so much?"

"Sweetheart, you need to stop thinking about how long it's been and look at what's in front of you. Do you feel comfortable with this man?"

"I absolutely do. He makes me forget that I'm in mourning, which is a good thing—until I start analyzing it! Then I get totally confused and the guilt starts creeping in. I never saw myself with anyone other than Aaron and now . . . I just don't know how to proceed."

THE WEEKEND WEDDING ASSISTANT

"Very carefully," my mother said. "And one baby step at a time."

No sooner had I hung up than I began to pace around the kitchen like the house was on fire. I knew I was falling for Garrett too far, too fast. This man wiped away all traces of my past, as if he were the human equivalent of a Mr. Clean Magic Eraser, and I wanted to embrace this roller coaster ride of infatuation for all it was worth.

Since we'd met, barely a waking minute had gone by when I didn't think of some amusing remark he'd made or the feeling of his thumb as it trailed along my bottom lip just before he'd leaned in for that first kiss. The way he moved his hands when he was telling a funny story, his penchant for strong black coffee—nothing about him escaped me. And I couldn't help but fantasize about what it might mean to be his.

Really, I thought, what the hell am I waiting for? Life is a fragile thing, spun of wishes and impossible odds. And if I'd learned anything from Aaron's death, it had been that life is for the living, because once you're dead you're, well...dead.

So why wait? I asked the bedroom walls as I started to dress. Why make sensible choices? Where has that ever gotten me? I had planned my life to a tee: the perfect man, the perfect wedding, the perfect wife, the perfect life. But what I hadn't planned for was disaster.

RULE #16: *A disaster is called a "disaster" for a reason—there is no planning for it!*

Now, I know this sounds like I was trying to justify my overwhelming desire to jump Garrett McLeod's gorgeous bones, and if one of my friends had said this out loud, I wouldn't call her a liar. But I wouldn't call her a psychic either, because anyone with a pair of eyes could have seen this coming. This was my way of rationalizing the situation so I could move forward with as little guilt as possible.

We'd planned to hook up that evening, which, technically speaking, was our third date. And if I wanted to adhere to the third-date rule (which states that you must go on three dates before sleeping with a man), I was well within my rights to sleep with Garrett if I so chose. "It's settled," I told my reflection as I applied the last touch of my makeup. All systems are go! Now I just needed to decide where and when to launch the rocket.

chapter twenty-four

People come from miles around to get married at Whitfield Chapel. And when I say from miles around, I am talking about little bitty towns out in the sticks with names like Algood, Ducktown, and Bean Station. That Saturday, the bride and her fiancé were from Soddy-Daisy (I kid you not), and even I, a woman born and bred in the South, had a difficult time understanding a single word they said.

I think the bride was going for a classic statement for her big day—classic *Duck Dynasty* that is. Her colors were electric blue, screaming orange, and louder-than-loud fuchsia, and I must say I've never seen a bride use her color palette so unsparingly. I wouldn't have been surprised if she'd had a tramp stamp with the motto "More Is More" tattooed on her lower back in neon script.

The bridal gown and bridesmaid's dresses looked like a polyester factory had exploded and landed in the middle of a ruffle festival before covering each and every one of them in an explosion of sheen. This look, paired with the powder-blue tuxes sported by the groomsmen—who wore electric-blue boutonnieres—evoked a strong sentiment: senior prom circa 1972 wants their wardrobe back!

The chapel looked like a million glow sticks had given birth to a silk flower factory, as no corner of the place was left unadorned. Every archway, doorway, and door, not to mention the altar table, was festooned with a neon festival of fake flowers, making the place look like one of those over-the-top floats in the Rose Parade, dipped in redneck. Enormous white satin bows with acres of trailing white ribbons marked each and every pew, which made the aisle look like an artificial snowstorm had just blown in from East Jesus, and there were enough candles to fully illuminate the entire sanctuary even on the darkest night.

I was standing in the foyer at the front of the chapel—trying to make sense of it all and trying to quell the waves of nausea that were beginning to have their way with me—when one of the church ladies who'd transformed Whitfield into a carnival sideshow approached me. "Isn't it just something!" She beamed, clasping her hands over her heaving bosom and wiggling her ample derriere like a freshly caught bass.

"It's something all right!" I answered through clenched teeth.

Now I'm not about to stomp all over some bride's big day, especially when she hasn't had the foresight to hire a wedding planner, so of course, I kept my opinions to myself. But in my heart of hearts I wanted to take a Zippo lighter to every neon flower, ribbon and bow in the place. The only drawback to that plan was that I might have inadvertently burned down the entire Chapel in the process.

I was suddenly shaken from my daydreams by an onslaught of the largest and loudest pack of people I'd ever seen in one place. And it hit me that now I had a real fire to put out because Mama-and-them (pronounced Mama-an-'em) had descended on Whitfield Chapel and I knew my day had only just begun.

We in the South enjoy a rich matriarchal tradition wherein the women are the ones who really wear the pants in the family, and the men just pretend they're wearing them. Everybody is OK with this. The matriarch has the final word on everything from how the family spends their money to what they'll be eating for Sunday dinner. To everyone, including her husband, the matriarch is known as "Mama." This relegates everyone else in the entire family—which often includes uncles, aunts, cousins, and sometimes neighbors—to the position of "Them," which saves time when trying to remember dozens and dozens of names.

So let's say, for instance, you're hosting a barbeque in your backyard and a friend calls to ask if he can bring "Mama and 'em"? The polite answer would be "Of course. That would be nice." But this is not the time to be polite! This is the time you should not even be answering your phone. Because when you say yes to "Mama and 'em," you'll end up feeding not only Mama but also a village of "Thems," because, honey, these people travel in packs.

That Saturday, the "Mama" in question was an MOB in Naomi Judd's clothing. From the hair and makeup to the defiant jut of her chin, she had her Naomi impression down pat—that was, until she spoke. From the first syllable she uttered it was clear that even though she ruled the roost, a more discombobulated hen you'd never hope to find. Unfortunately, she was the sharpest tool in the family shed. The fact that she was the one in charge of a very large contingent of loud, unruly folks ("Them"), who were arriving in a mile-long line, was enough to scare a shadow off a wall.

An acquaintance with a camera was acting as the official

photographer. He did the best he could to gather the family together for pre-ceremony shots, but it was difficult because not only were the bride and groom not seeing each other before the wedding but also the bride and her entourage of poly-clad brides-maids was nowhere to be found. The groom and his groomsmen were clearly drunk, and the groom, who couldn't have been more than twenty, was a nervous wreck and sweating profusely. This is definitely not a good thing when you're wearing a powder-blue tux!

We were only forty-five minutes from lift-off, and all hell was breaking loose. The bride was still AWOL. Mama informed me that the bride and her entourage had been riding around in the limo "relaxing" (code for drinking). But unfortunately, she had been "relaxing" a little too long and had missed her window to enter the building unseen, as her guests were arriving in droves. I informed Mama that the recalcitrant bride could enter Beaumont Hall through a side door unseen, although this meant she'd have to walk right by the groom's room, which flustered Mama to no end. But I assured her that Buddy (the groom) and Sue Beth (the bride) would not collide and all would be well.

Finally, Sue Beth agreed to come on in. But just as she was about to enter the hall, out popped Buddy from his hiding place. Why he'd done this was unclear, but luckily, I was able to stop Sue Beth in her tracks before they actually came face-to-face. I ran back into the building to make sure Buddy had returned to his dressing room. But lo and behold, there he stood in the middle of the hallway, frozen in his tracks.

"Buddy, why don't you step back into the groom's room?" I asked him as nicely as I could. Buddy just stared at me like the proverbial blue-tux-wearing deer in the headlights.

"Buddy," I repeated, "Sue Beth needs to get by, and you can't see her yet. So let's get you back in your room."

Crickets. And a frozen deer.

Then I began to get forceful. "Buddy, you should get back in your room!" I raised my voice like I was speaking to a hearing-challenged child.

More crickets.

"Buddy, get back in your room now! Get in your room!" I shouted, giving him a shove through the doorway and firmly closing the door behind him.

I felt like I was on fire, but not in a good way. I'd never spoken to a groom like that before! And although I was a bit surprised by my outburst, I turned to see that everyone around me completely approved of my actions. Mama was standing outside with a tearful and sweaty Sue Beth, trying to shield her from prying eyes. It seems I had become her surrogate.

Hurling open the doors of Beaumont Hall, I came face-to-face with the most glassy-eyed bride I'd ever seen. Not only was she drunk, but clearly she was also stoned out of her mind on Valium or some such "relaxing" pill, which she had no doubt washed down with wine. Carefully guiding her down the hall to her dressing room, I suggested she try to pee and fix her lipstick, as her grand entrance was less than twenty minutes away, and then I left her to her own devices.

I felt for her; I really did. But my level of exasperation outweighed any generous impulses, and it took all the strength I could muster not to lose my temper—again. Really, I had no reason to feel this way. It was Sue Beth's wedding. My responsibilities went no further than opening the facilities and making sure nobody trashed the place. This bride hadn't hired me to make sure her day was seamless, so what did I care if she and her deer-in-the-headlights groom barely made it to the "I dos"?

There was absolutely no rhyme or reason for me to care, but I found that, for some reason, I did—a lot. And once again I wondered if I had finally found my calling. It was the only logical explanation! It felt good to care. And not only that, it felt good to know that I had the power to make or break this hapless bride's day.

Marching toward the groom's room with a renewed vigor, I knocked soundly on the door and then herded Buddy and his groomsmen to their proper place at the far side of the chapel. Once they were out of sight, I hurried to the bride's room to fetch her and the rest of the wedding party. They were already running ten minutes behind, and it was time to get this show on the road.

The "show," unfortunately, had different ideas, and still much primping to do. Not wanting to fluster Sue Beth any more than she already was, I stepped back. But after another five minutes, it became clear that these people needed a gigantic push.

"If you're going to go down the aisle, you need to go now!" I said, employing my best kindergarten teacher voice. To my surprise, each and every one looked at me as if they'd just been instructed to buddy up and walk in neat rows to a fire drill; and just like that, off they went toward the chapel.

After cueing the musicians and sending the parents down the aisle, I cued the men for their entrance and then sent the bridesmaids and the bride through the big wooden doors and down the aisle. I felt like a conductor leading my own personal symphony with precision and calm certitude. And as I watched the ceremony from the last pew, I felt a sense of satisfaction wash over me that I had never felt at any job I'd had in my life. As a real estate agent, I'd closed my share of big deals. And when I'd worked in retail, I'd always been a guiding light for my customers. But I'd never felt like I owned it the way I owned it now! This couple might not have gotten down the aisle if it hadn't been for me. But from the moment the music started, everything had gone off like clockwork. If you hadn't witnessed the chaos unfolding behind the scenes, you'd never have been the wiser!

"Mama and 'em" had finally departed, taking their acres of poly-ester and satin with them, and Whitfield was blissfully quiet once again. Having made my final rounds—checking for stray programs and Kleenex—I stood for a moment in the chapel, which sung with solitude and still vibrated with the fumes of the departed guests and the happy young couple that had promised forever.

Once upon a time, forever had been a promise I was sure I could keep; now it was a concept I dared not invite to the table. I thought about Garrett and the hope he engendered in my crum-pled heart, but I was under no illusion that he would, or could, replace Aaron as my life partner. As far as I was concerned, that ship had sailed.

Garrett was a port in the storm, an unexpected holiday from my confusing life, and one hell of a sexy man. I was intrigued. I was delighted, even. And what woman wouldn't give her eyeteeth to feel that, even if just for an afternoon? I liked him, but at the same time I felt like I had my head screwed on straight when it came to him. Somehow, the makeup of the relationship was very ordered in my mind. We were in different places in our lives. I was still confused and in mourning, and Garrett was...I don't know what. Honestly, I didn't know him well enough to know what his romantic aspirations were.

Once the doors were locked, the lights had been turned off, and everything was in its rightful place, I crossed the breezeway and returned to my office, where I plopped down in my chair. The moment of truth had arrived.

Garrett picked up on the second ring, obviously glad to hear from me. We chatted about this and that like the oldest of friends. I regaled him with stories of the *Duck Dynasty* wedding. He laughed in all the right places, which made me feel like he really got me.

"You must be beat." He sounded so sympathetic.

"You don't know the half of it!" I chuckled.

"Despite the fact that I told you everything."

He laughed his deep, infectious laugh. "So…there's no evening wedding tonight, right?"

"Thank the Lord!" I laughed.

"Well…I have a proposition for you."

"I'm listening," I said, hoping he didn't hear my breath catching in my throat.

"Why don't I bring over some dinner and take care of you. You deserve a little TLC after taking care of a loony bride all day."

What could I say but yes? "That sounds so wonderful." I let out a sigh.

"It's a date," he almost purred. And I was purring right along with him.

He arrived at seven o'clock, bearing Thai food and beer. I'd set the scene on my back porch, complete with candles and soft music, and we basked in one another's company and the cool evening breeze. September was one of my favorite months in Tennessee. The days were still warm but there's little to no humidity, and the late afternoon light takes on an auburn cast, which ushers in crisp, cool evenings.

The sun had set by the time we'd finished eating and moved to the wicker couch that sat at the far side of the porch. Grabbing two fresh beers from the cooler, we clinked bottles and snuggled into each other, his arm draped around my shoulder, my head resting on his.

We chatted about little nothings and laughed about almost everything. As the hours slipped by, so too did any reservations I'd had about moving forward. And as if he could read my mind, Garrett took me in his arms and began kissing me passionately. I was breathless, weightless, and suspended in time at the touch of his lips, and I returned his kisses with a volley of my own. We were heading down a road from which I was sure there was no return, and I had no intention of slowing down.

Pushing back a wild tendril, he held his fingers fast in my hair and studied the planes of my face, kissing each and every feature—forehead, eyelids, cheekbones—before pulling back to search my eyes. "Are you sure you're ready for this?"

"Oh yeah . . ." I said as I stood and offered him my hand.

He stood as close as he could and spooned me from behind. "Where are you taking me?" he feigned innocence, turning me around and kissing me deeply, his lips finding their way to the nape of my neck, where they teased and cajoled until I wanted to melt.

"To my bed, of course." I smiled up at him, turned, and then ran up the stairs. Garrett was hot on my heels.

We fell on top of the downy soft covers, rolling in each other's arms until we nearly tumbled right off the far side of the bed. I screamed; he laughed, as he kept me from falling. Then slowly, deliberately, he began to undress me, gazing down at me as patches of my skin emerged from beneath each button and snap. He took great pleasure in finding my most ticklish places and running his tongue in small circles around each one of them. He drove me into a frenzied state where my breathing began to match the pace of his own.

In turn, I removed his shirt with the same deliberate care, kissing every inch of his chest as each button opened beneath my fingers. And then, in one dexterous motion, he had removed my bra, and we were flesh to flesh and wrapped in each other's arms so tightly we could barely breathe. He took me in, his eyes fixing on mine as he slipped off my skirt and panties. It took but a second or two to free him from his jeans and boxers.

And then he began to kiss down the length of me until he was between my legs, parting my most secret places with his velvety tongue, driving me to a fevered pitch of nearly unimaginable excitement. I wanted him inside of me; he willingly obliged. Kissing me with all the passion I ever could have wanted, we rode the first waves of desire. We kept on like this for hours, moving from one position to another and then yet another. I thought he might never be done with me—and I hoped he never would.

Exhausted and spent, we finally ceased all movement and lay tangled up together, catching our breath and murmuring our mutual content. And then I was drifting away, the whooshing of the fan overhead casting me into a deep and dreamless sleep.

chapter twenty-five

I awoke to the sensation of someone kissing the back of my neck ever so gently. At first, I thought I was dreaming. But as I opened my eyes and rolled toward the lips that were setting me on fire, I came to the happy realization that it was Garrett having his way with me.

"What a lovely way to wake up," I murmured. Threading his fingers through my hair, he grinned mischievously and leaned in to kiss me. "You look like the cat that ate the canary." I laughed.

"Well, if the fur fits . . ." he quipped while continuing to dust my face and neck with little nibbles. It was intoxicating.

We made love for the better part of the morning as the steel-gray light grew brighter. Lying there afterward, I could hear the steady pitter-patter of rain tap-dancing just beyond the open window. The curtains were rippling in the cool morning breeze, and I pulled back the top sheet and let the air wash over me, smiling up at Garrett, who was slipping into his jeans. He looked so good both in and out of them that watching him dress gave me almost as much pleasure as I had experienced ripping them off in the frenzy of the previous evening.

"I wish you didn't have to go," I whined.

He walked over to the bed and sat beside me, twining his fingers through mine and kissing the back of my hand. "If I'd known you were going to have your way with me last night, I would have found a way to squirm out of Sunday dinner at my mother's house. But at this late date? There's no escaping."

Sunday dinner (the meal is actually served at lunchtime) is a ritual at most homes in the South. It is served right after church, usually at a person's mother's house, and consists of several kinds of meats, overcooked vegetables, potatoes, Jell-O salad, corn bread, biscuits, and several varieties of pies and cakes to round things out.

"You're preaching to the choir!" I smiled.

I offered to get up and make Garrett some coffee, but he refused my halfhearted attempt at hospitality. He could see I was happy right where I was.

"Don't move a muscle. I want to think of you just like this all day long." He leaned over to kiss me. "It'll give me something to aspire to this afternoon," he said with a laugh.

I listened as his steps threaded down the hall and then down the stairs, the rain keeping pace with his footfalls. Far away, I heard the front door open and close. I smiled to myself as I slid deep under the sheets, lulled by the rhythm of the steadily falling rain and the fact that Garrett McLeod had been here.

At first I thought it was the rumbling of distant thunder that woke me, but then I realized it was my stomach doing very noisy backflips. I'd gone back to sleep for several hours, and I was famished! Hopping out of bed, I felt lighter than I had in months, and I practically danced into the shower with a song in my heart and Garrett's name on my lips. Ah, the joy of new beginnings! Is there anything sweeter and more all-encompassing in the world?

After downing a strong cup of coffee and half a toasted bagel, I blended up my morning smoothie, complete with extra protein powder and chia seeds, and plopped down on the sofa to watch the rain, which continued to fall in sheets. In a way, I was glad Garrett had to leave earlier because I was able to take my emotional temperature much more easily when he wasn't around getting me all hot and bothered.

As ecstatic as I was about my newfound crush, when it came to Aaron I was still in grieving mode. And truth be told, I didn't think that feeling would ever go away. But what had gone away was the empty ache that had come to rest inside me, which had become such an integral part of my emotional makeup that I'd begun to take it for granted that it would always be there. At first, it had felt like an enormous boulder had come to settle in my gut; it was so deep and so wide that I'd been certain nothing could ever shake it loose. And then, little by little, as time had worked its magic, the ache had begun to shrink a centimeter at a time. But I'd had no real respite—until now. So despite what I might think intellectually about this new man, I had to admit it was freeing to feel good again.

As I downed my smoothie, I shared this with Lili—after running down the more important events of the past twenty-four hours, of course—and she was elated. Still, she had her questions.

"Sounds like you had quite the hot night, Jules!" she said. "So...there was no residual Aaron stuff?"

"What are you talking about?"

"No calling out his name in the heat of passion? No uncontrollable weeping, the 'I'm-freaking-out-because-I'm-a wiancée' thing in the throes of passion, where you dissolve into a puddle of tears and scare the new guy right out the door?"

I was grinning from ear to ear despite myself. "I assure you, there was nothing even remotely resembling a weeping widow in my bedroom last night! It was, well…perfection."

"Perfection? I see . . ."

I could picture the twinkle in Lili's eyes as she tried to goad me into admitting I was still an emotional mess. But the truth of it was, at that moment, I was anything but, despite the fact that any reasonable person might have bet otherwise.

I began winding my way up the stairs and back to the bedroom, where I threw myself dramatically onto the bed.

"I probably should have taken it slow. I know that," I began. "But I feel really great now that I've taken the leap, and I've come to the conclusion that having hot sex with Garrett McLeod was very cathartic for me."

"That is great, Jules. And I am over the moon for you! But do me a favor and take care of yourself, OK? You've been through a lot."

I wanted to argue, even though I knew she was right. But it felt so good to feel good that I wanted to bask in that emotion and nothing else. I felt like I could never feel awful again. And I decided that I would go with that.

"He's so friggin' hot!" I giggled.

"Yeah." She laughed. "And I am so friggin' jealous!"

chapter twenty-six

T he next few weeks flew by on wings made of hot sex and busyness, and I continued to feel like I was on the mend for real. Garrett and I saw each other every chance we got, which sometimes meant catching a meal here, a tryst there, as both of us were working like dogs. On a couple of afternoons, we set sail on the Cumberland, basking in the Indian summer sun and marveling at each other and the array of fall colors that made the hills look like they were as on fire as we were. But most of the time, we were like ships passing in the night—my weekends packed with weddings and his weekdays overbooked and crazy. But the challenge made the sweet taste of victory all the better.

I began to immerse myself in all things wedding, reading every how-to book I could get my hands on. Martha Stewart had several, many of them dating back to the '80s. But I'd come to realize that as far as weddings are concerned—despite the trends that come and go—you can't go wrong with tried-and-true; classic never goes out of style.

I found myself participating more and more in the weddings at Whitfield because, let's face it, nothing beats training in the trenches. If there was a wedding planner involved, I hung back, watching and learning, escorting latecomers down the side aisle, and helping with the doors for the bride's grand entrance when needed. I'd watch as the wedding planner fluffed the bride, straightening her train and veil, making sure every tendril of hair was in place. The music would start, and the planner would say, "When we open the doors, walk through and pause—take it all in. Now take a deep breath. You look gorgeous!"

From the guest's perspective, the doors opened as if by magic, revealing the radiant bride, standing there in all her glory. And as soon as she began her walk, we'd slowly close the doors behind her, although I couldn't help but linger a minute to watch from the back. It was one of my favorite parts, watching the bride's train floating behind her like a river of lace. It gave me goose bumps every time. And despite the fact that initially the act of getting these brides down the aisle had been like a knife to the heart, over time it began to heal me somehow. I guess seeing so many couples who'd found each other allowed me to still believe in love everlasting. And I needed that more than I knew.

Halloween was just a week away, and Garrett had asked me to a big costume party he attended every year. Normally, I was not a fan of this holiday; I hardly ever dressed up or went out. But staying home to hand out candy to the neighborhood kids was something I did look forward to. I loved to see the little ones dressed in all manner of costumes and hopped up on sugar. Part of me hated the thought of letting this ritual go, especially since it was the first Halloween without Aaron. He, also not a big fan of the day, had made the stay-at-home candy giveaway a thing of beauty. But Garrett's party started at nine o'clock, so I figured I could do both. The only problem was throwing a costume together. I knew I had some odds and ends stored in the guest room closet. Without giving it too much thought, I flipped on the light and stepped inside.

The scent of Aaron practically slapped me in the face. I hadn't set foot in there for a couple of months, and I felt dizzy and out of breath as I looked around surveying the contents of the little room.

Aaron's suits hung at attention, awaiting the moment when they would once again be called into service. It was as if they were expecting him back. His shoes, shirts, overcoat, and hiking gear lined the walls and shelves, a testament to the man who had once possessed these things and now had no use for them at all.

My wedding gown, stashed in its oversized white garment bag, stood out from the rest like a sore thumb. I felt compelled to walk over, unzip the bag, and run my fingers along the creamy-ivory silk of the bodice and the delicate lace and tiny pearls that covered it. I remembered what it felt like to wear this one-of-a-kind creation, from the weight of the train to the way it hugged every curve. I knew I should get rid of the dress—today. I could put it up on eBay or donate it to someone who didn't have the money for such a gown. I could burn it or rip it to shreds as a symbolic offering to the wedding gods. But I still couldn't bear the thought of parting with it.

Releasing the garment, I shoved it back in the bag, zipped it up, and pushed it as far back in the closet as it would go. Stepping back to cast my gaze over all of Aaron's things, I knew the time had come for closet closure and I knew that this time I could actually pull it off. However, this was a job I could not pull off on my own. The entire thing was too daunting on too many levels. First of all, I really had no idea what to do with all of this stuff—but I knew just the man who did. Before I could change my mind, I grabbed my phone and dialed.

The following afternoon, I heard Linc's familiar voice calling my name as he entered the house through the kitchen door. Grinning from ear to ear, he hugged me and gave me a big kiss on each cheek. "You look great, Jules!" he exclaimed, grabbing a bottle of water from the fridge and loosening the cap.

"So do you!" I grinned back at him. "It seems like forever since I've seen you."

"I know! Things have been crazy."

We plopped down at the table by the window, as if no time had passed. Both of us were involved with new people, and from the sound of it, things were getting serious between Linc and Emmalyn.

"She's so great." He smiled. "You know, we hiked almost every weekend this summer. It's getting a bit more sporadic with the fall weather though."

"Yeah, I've been keeping up with all that on Facebook. The pictures you've been posting are amazing."

"I'd love to say that we'll have completed the AT by May," he said, referring to the one-year anniversary of Aaron's death, "but that's impossible. Still, no matter what, I plan on being back at the top of Mount Katahdin to honor Aaron on the day." Linc's face took on a serious yet quizzical expression. "How would you like to climb that leg with us? I want to do a memorial up there for Aaron, and you should be there, Jules."

My heart froze in my chest for a moment as all the reasons why this sounded like a bad idea began to fly around in my head like a flock of uncaged carrier pigeons.

"Oh God, Linc. Besides the fact that I loathe hiking and can't think that far ahead, I just don't know what to say. I mean, I know I'll want to honor and remember Aaron on that day, but I'd rather just do it down here a little closer to sea level. Besides, I don't know if I could stand there…where he stood…where he fell. I just don't know . . ."

He put his hand on my arm and gave it a reassuring squeeze. "I understand. To tell you the truth, I don't know if I'll be able to handle it either. But it feels like the only way I'll ever get closure. You know what I mean?" He searched my eyes for complicity, smiling when he saw it there.

"Speaking of Aaron, I really appreciate you helping me with the closet." I stood, leading the way up the stairs. "It's such an overwhelming task."

"I see what you mean," he said as I opened the door and we stepped inside. "At least he was organized."

I nodded in agreement. "He was definitely that!"

Standing there with Linc made me feel all at once relaxed and nostalgic for the past. And then suddenly, I felt like the walls were closing in around me. Although the closet was actually quite large, I felt claustrophobic and short of breath, which was odd, seeing as how I'd spent so many hours shut up in there, grieving and crying. I didn't want Linc to notice, so I backed out of the door and told him I needed to get the boxes and bags I'd assembled for packing.

"Why don't you get started? And if there's anything of Aaron's you want, it's yours."

I wandered down the hall to the utility room, where I'd stored the packing materials I'd bought almost two months before. Bending over, I tried to catch my breath, telling myself over and over that I was going to be just fine. I was just getting rid of Aaron's stuff; it was no big deal, and it had to be done.

Gathering up the stack of boxes, I made my way back down the hall, a smile plastered on my face, and walked back in the guest room. I deposited the bundle of cardboard on top of the bed and turned to see Linc holding Aaron's bomber jacket and looking quizzically at me.

"How about this?" he said lifting it up toward me so I could see it completely.

"Actually, that's one of the only things I want to keep. I'm sorry," I said as I took the brown leather jacket and held it in my arms pressed up against my chest. Like an old friend I couldn't bear to say goodbye to, I thought about all the hours I'd spent cradling that jacket, my face buried in the lining, fingernails digging into the well-worn leather, sobbing and wishing time would hurry up and do its job on me.

"Damn!" He chuckled. "That was the only thing *I* wanted!"

I had to laugh, and this put me a bit more at ease as I turned to assemble the moving boxes and secure them with packing tape.

Linc came out of the closet with the first armful of clothes and began stacking them in different places.

"So we should put these in piles. Some of these suits are really expensive," he said, pointing to the top row of clothing that still hung in the closet. "You could sell them at FLIP, so I'd keep these hung up until you can get around to that. Lots of this can go to Goodwill, and there are a few things I'll take with me. But I think you should hold on to the hiking equipment...you never know," he teased.

"Ha ha," I said in a mocking tone. But Linc looked at me with a dead serious expression, so I relented. "OK. Even though I will never use any of that stuff, I'll keep it just to humor you. But it can't stay in here. I'll find a place for it in the garage."

"Fair enough." He smiled.

We returned to the task at hand, catching each other up on the comings and goings of our lives while we worked. I told him about Garrett and how happy he made me.

"I don't know if we're getting serious or anything," I said, feeling like I needed to justify my relationship to Linc as if he were a physical extension of Aaron. "But he's a good guy. I hope you'll get to meet him."

"I'm happy for you, Jules." Linc gave my hand a squeeze. "Emmalyn kind of saved me after Aaron died. She's so upbeat and full of energy. It made me want to match her zest for life."

"I know. Garrett has really hauled me out of my funk too. But I still feel kind of guilty about it all. Like maybe it's too soon or something."

Linc looked at me as he folded a shirt and placed it in an open box that sat on the bed. "Aaron would want you to be happy. I don't think he'd want you to spend your life in mourning, Jules."

"I know you're right," I said looking him in the eye.

He held may gaze for a moment and then quickly looked away, busying himself with folding one shirt after another, stacking them neatly in the box.

"You know," he said, a nostalgic smile playing on his lips, "I always envied Aaron for having the perfect life."

"Nobody has the perfect life, Linc." I folded a sweater and placed it near the top of the mounting pile of clothes.

Linc looked back up at me, as if he were taking the whole of me in with one glance. "He had you."

Our hands brushed as both of us deposited the last of the items that could possibly fit in that box. His touch ignited a spark in me, and I felt Linc lean in as if he were about to kiss me. Like a magnet whose poles are pointed in the wrong direction, I took a hurried step back and turned, hoping he hadn't noticed any of it. I began making noises about looking for the packing tape, as if creating a diversion could erase the moment that had just exploded between us.

I must have been imagining things, I told myself as I searched for the tape. Linc was in love with Emmalyn. He would never make a move on me while he was with her. "Here we go!" I shouted a little too enthusiastically, holding the tape aloft by the handle of its unwieldy dispenser, as if it were a trophy.

"Looks like we're finished here." He smiled as we sealed the last of the dozen boxes we had managed to pack.

Smiling back, I couldn't help but think how right he was.

chapter twenty-seven

Halloween screamed into sight before you could say "Trick or treat!" I found that I was excited about the holiday in a way I hadn't been since I was a kid. I'd selected the perfect costume, which I'd assembled myself. Despite the fact that I usually loathed going out on this night, I found Garrett's love of Halloween infectious. Next to Christmas, this was his favorite holiday.

He arrived at nine o'clock dressed as a Roman warrior—Mark Antony to be more precise—and man did he look hot!

"My chariot awaits!" he told me with a sweep of his arm when I answered the door. Taking in my costume, he furrowed his brow as if confused. "OK, I give. What are you?"

Dressed in a knee-length slip with a picture of the world's most famous psychoanalyst sewn on the front, I smiled as I ushered him inside. "I'm a Freudian slip!" I laughed.

"Clever!" He laughed in return. "Aren't you afraid you'll be a little chilly? It's gonna hit the low fifties tonight."

Donning an old tweed jacket I'd found in Aaron's closet, I assured him that I had it covered. "You're one to talk!" I said, indicating his bare legs and the skirt he was wearing beneath his metallic-looking breastplate.

"Won't be a problem," he said pointing to his helmet. "I have a hat!"

"OK, Mark Antony. Let's go!" I said as he ushered me to his truck.

Twenty minutes later, we arrived at a large house in Forest Hills, a section of Nashville famous for its McMansions and their wide expanses of manicured landscaping. His friends had custom built their home expressly for the purpose of entertaining. Despite the fact that it was barely nine thirty, the place was already packed with people dressed as every conceivable character.

"Wow!" I exclaimed, trying to be heard above the already raucous fray. "This is quite a place!"

Leading me by the hand, we headed toward the back of the house through clusters of partygoers who all greeted Garrett by name. Introducing me to at least a dozen people—whom I'd never recognize again in a million years, thanks to the masks and makeup that obliterated their normal features—the going got slower as the crowd got thicker and we wandered farther and farther from the entryway.

"Let's get a drink, and I'll introduce you to our hosts." He took me by the hand, ensuring I wouldn't get lost or trampled in the crowd. "That is, if I can find them!"

It was definitely a tequila night, so I ordered a margarita from the affable bartender, who was dressed like a barkeep from a 1920s-style speakeasy. Then Garrett and I roamed around the party for a while before we stumbled upon our hosts, who were dressed as John Lennon and Yoko Ono. "John and Yoko, this is Julia." Garrett smiled as I shook the hands of my look-alike hosts.

"If I didn't know any better, I'd swear you were the real thing!" I laughed.

"And you are?" Yoko tried to decipher my costume.

"A Freudian slip!" the John look-alike shouted in glee.

"Fery goot!" I said in my best German accent, lifting a pipe from the breast pocket of my jacket and pretending to puff on it. "This is an amazing house!"

"Would you like the fifty-cent tour?" Yoko asked me.

Drink firmly in one hand and Garrett's hand in the other, we spent the next ten minutes taking in the features of the rambling premises, complete with a secret room that housed a small movie theatre. I was certain you could fit five of my houses into the one we were touring, and I tried not to ooh and aah too many times lest I look like a total idiot. But I was definitely impressed—and struck with a roaring case of house envy.

Eventually, we circled back to the enormous eat-in kitchen. Standing boldly in the center of the room was an island that could comfortably seat twelve. At the moment, it was covered with appetizers and platters of cheeses, charcuterie, and other edibles and surrounded by a wall of costumed people.

"There's a buffet in the dining room as well." Yoko pointed to her right. "So glad you could make it, Julia!" She leaned in to give me a hug, something I wondered if the real Yoko would have done, and I returned her easy embrace with one of my own and thanked her for having me.

"Shall we?" Garrett said, placing his hand at the small of my back and guiding me through the ever-thickening throng that continued to pour through the door. We had just filled our plates and were looking for a place to perch when we rounded a corner and almost ran smack-dab into a woman dressed as Cleopatra, who looked none too pleased to see us. Well, to be fair, it was Garrett whom she was not too pleased about seeing; I didn't even know the woman. But that was about to change.

"Well, well, well. If it isn't Garrett McLeod," she scoffed. "Or should I say Mark Antony? I can't believe you wore that costume! Especially when you knew I would probably be here tonight!"

"Natalie!" Garrett looked as if he'd been hit by a bus. "Actually, if I'd known you were coming, I would have made other plans. I thought you were staying in Miami until the end of the year."

"Plans change, Garrett, as you know only too well! And what do we have here?" The queen of the Nile looked askance at me, as if trying to decipher just who I was and just what I was doing with this guy she was so pissed off at.

"I'm a Freudian slip!" I explained, clueless as to her true meaning.

"This is Julia Holmes," Garrett interjected. "Julia, this is Natalie Pressman."

I reached out to shake her hand, a gesture she found amusing for some reason. She blithely took my hand in hers, shaking it with the gusto of a dead fish, and said nothing. Then she turned to Garrett and sneered at him with more venom than the asp coiled around her beautiful jet-black hair. "Garrett, you have a lot of nerve! I really can't believe you wore that costume!" she repeated herself. "And showing up here with a date? That's low class. Even for you."

"Natalie, this isn't the time or the place!" He took a large swig of his drink, practically draining it in one fell swoop. "Well, what do you know?" he said, looking down into the empty glass. "Looks like I need another drink. Would you excuse us?" And with that, he turned and led me away from Cleopatra as fast as my feet could carry me.

I could feel her eyes boring a hole into us as we retreated to the other side of the house and turned to see if it was my imagination playing tricks. But sure enough, there she stood, arms crossed defiantly in front of her. I felt certain she could cut someone in two with her eyeballs alone if she had the mind to do so, her death ray of a stare was so powerful. She kind of freaked me out, and I said as much to Garrett.

"My God!" I said, pulling at the hem of my slip, which had caught on the netting of a passerby dressed like a fairy princess. "What in the hell was that about?"

"That was my ex," Garrett replied. Stopping dead in his tracks, he turned to look at me. His eyes were on fire, but I could see that he was trying to control his temper, a fact I was grateful for. "Maybe we ought to leave."

I started to protest, to tell him that she had no right to ruin our wonderful evening, but he was obviously crestfallen, embarrassed, and really pissed off—a combo platter I wasn't ready to deal with—so I agreed.

"I'm famished! Good thing I still have plenty of Halloween candy at my place," I tried to joke as the valet sped up the driveway in Garrett's truck. Garrett smiled while holding the door open for me, but the warm laughter I had come to expect from him had evidently gone walkabout. I wondered if the evening would continue to go steadily downhill. As we sped away into the chilly night, I wasn't so sure I wanted to find out.

We arrived at my house in no time flat. I offered to whip something up, figuring Garrett had to be as famished as I was. Despite the fact that we had loaded our plates at the buffet, his run-in with Natalie had proved not only to be a party destroyer but also the mother of all appetite suppressants; we had chucked our dinners into the trash just before we'd made our grand exit. As it happened, I'd made a big pot of chili earlier in the day.

Before you could say "Sorry we had to run into that bitchy ex of yours," I had set us up with dinner.

Focusing on the task in front of him, Garrett was anything but his usual charming self, and I struggled to fill in the silences with conversation about anything that wasn't Natalie Pressman. I had a feeling he probably wanted to say something about her—what a royal pain she was or, my worst fear, that he still cared for her and regretted ever letting her go. Granted, the woman had not shown her best side this evening, but I knew that had I been in her shoes I would have done precisely the same thing. I hated the fact that I could empathize with the woman who had ruined a really fun evening.

"This chili is great, Jules." Garrett glanced up from his nearly finished bowl and gave me a halfhearted smile. I knew it was the best he could do at that moment, and I was trying to believe he'd snap out of this funk any minute. But the sinking feeling in the pit of my stomach told another story. I smiled at him and rose to get him another beer, which he gladly accepted.

"I was thinking I should slip into something more comfortable." I laughed at my silly pun. Once again, I got a halfhearted smile but no rejoinder. As I cleared our bowls and set them in the sink, I turned to him and asked the million-dollar question, "Are you OK?"

In a moment, he'd gotten up and his arms were around me. And despite the fact that his breastplate was cutting into my shoulder, I gave him a squeeze to let him know I was here, that I was in his corner.

"Did you bring a change of clothes?" I murmured.

"I did." He pulled back to look at me. Kissing me softly, he let go and put his hand on the counter. "I hate to cut the evening short, but I think it would be better if I headed home."

"Better for whom?" I asked, the sinking feeling starting to rise into something resembling anger.

"For both of us," he said matter-of-factly, looking right into my eyes.

I couldn't believe my ears. "Is this because of Natalie?" I asked, a bit incredulous and hoping the answer would be a definitive no.

"Yes and no," he answered, as if this vague and shapeless reply would explain everything.

"What is that supposed to mean?"

He threw up his arms in exasperation. "It means that you don't have the market cornered when it comes to feeling confused about your ex," he said, his voice taking on an edge.

I gasped and took a big step back. Who is this guy standing in my kitchen in Roman warrior garb? I thought as tears filled my eyes.

"I'm sorry, Jules!" He reached out and wrapped his hand around my arm, drawing me toward him. "I didn't mean that! Seeing Natalie just really set me off. I don't know what else I can say."

There was nothing he could say. I felt like I'd just taken a sucker punch to the throat. As I fought back the urge to cry, I turned and marched into the living room.

He followed. "The last thing I was expecting was to see Natalie at that party tonight!" he shouted. "Do you think I would have taken you there if I'd known this was going to happen?"

"I don't know, Garrett."

"You know me better than that!" he shouted. "I adore you! I'd never intentionally do anything to hurt you. And I'm sorry about that cornering the market thing. That was just wrong." He stood as close as he could without touching me, his eyes filled with sincerity and regret. "I don't know what else to say . . ."

I wanted to tell him all was forgiven and forgotten, but I couldn't. Not quite yet. I had to ask him the question that had lined up at the back of my throat alongside the tears that were still poised to fall. "Are you still in love with her?"

He looked me right in the eye, and without missing a beat he answered, "No. I am not still in love with her."

"You're sure?" I asked again, a little less forcefully.

"Completely." He leaned in closer and took my face in his hands. Searching my eyes with his, he began kissing my forehead, my cheekbones, my lips...caressing, soft kisses that restored my faith in him. And I began to breathe again. I hadn't realized until that moment that I'd been holding my breath, waiting for the hammer of disappointment to fall.

We fell onto the couch and continued kissing, but as I went to loosen the straps on his costume and release him from the armor he was still wearing, he put his hand over mine and pulled back.

"I think I ought to go now." He smiled drowsily, as if we had just woken from a pleasant nap. "I am really beat, and I think it would be better if I slept in my own bed tonight. You understand, don't you?"

Are you freakin' kidding me? I wanted to scream! But rather than stir the pot, I nodded, trying to tamp down the feelings of panic and remorse that were beginning to bubble up. I managed to paste on a small smile. Standing up, I walked Garrett to the door, where he kissed me once more and thanked me for a wonderful evening.

"I'll call you tomorrow," he said over his shoulder as he walked out into the chilly October night.

I slunk back inside to sit alone with my feelings. Popping the top off an ice-cold beer, I slipped into a chair at the kitchen table and tried to tell myself that everything was going to be just fine, despite the fact that this had been the scariest Halloween of my life.

chapter twenty-eight

True to his word, Garrett did call the next day, but not until the early afternoon. By that point, I had worn a groove in my living room rug the size of the Grand Canyon. He apologized for the lateness of his call, explaining that his brother had had a fender bender that morning and needed help getting his car to the shop.

For once, there wasn't a single wedding booked at Whitfield, and we'd talked about spending the day together. After all, a free Saturday was rare for me. And although we hadn't made any specific plans, Garrett had been enthusiastic at the thought of having me to himself for an entire weekend. But that was yesterday.

"I was thinking I might just hang out with my brother and his wife today," he blithely explained. "They tell me I've been neglecting them lately, and I guess I kind of have. That's OK with you, isn't it?" he asked me, assuming I would say yes.

What could I say? I didn't want to behave like a willful child who hadn't gotten what she was expecting, throwing a temper tantrum until I got my way; well, actually, that was all I wanted to do. I wanted to ask him if this had anything to do with Natalie, but I couldn't bring myself to say her name because then I would sound like a suspicious wife, which is exactly how I felt—like he was cheating on me with feelings about his ex.

"I totally understand," I lied through gritted teeth. "Maybe we can have brunch tomorrow?"

"Sounds like a plan," he replied, signing off. "Call you later?"

"OK," I said, feeling like this was anything but OK. "Have fun!"

I hit "end" on my keypad, which I hoped was not a sign. But I put the thought out of my head as fast as it had entered, turning my attention to the rest of the day. However, despite my attempts to get busy with chores around the house, all I could think about was that call. Was that a brush-off "call you later" or the real deal? He had called as promised, but we'd had plans for the day and he'd blown me off. Who was to say whether or not he would do it again and keep doing so until he rode off into the sunset, never to be heard from again?

And if that happens, then what? I asked myself. I would lose my faith in the goodness of all mankind, that's what!

Is Garrett a bad boy in good guy's clothing? I wondered as I heated up some of Mama's lentil soup on the stove. If so, that would be really depressing because I've always been able to spot a bad boy at forty paces. "Have I lost this time-tested radar of mine?" I wondered aloud as I grabbed a bowl from the cabinet and filled it with the hot, fragrant soup. I'm still technically in mourning and off my game, I told myself, plopping down at the table. And if, just if, I had misjudged Garrett, I could always blame it on that! Plus, I reasoned, I'm probably out of practice at spotting "le bad boy," having been engaged to the most awesome man on earth and all that. But who is to say that Garrett is a bad boy? I wondered as I lifted the spoon to my lips. Up until now, he'd been so good—in every sense of the word!

After twenty minutes of playing this ridiculously one-sided guessing game, I realized that I just had to trust my gut. Garrett was a stand-up guy, a mensch, a good egg. He'd had a small emotional meltdown that I'd witnessed, and that had probably been an emasculating experience. I rose from the table and washed my lonely little bowl and spoon. So he had to go and lick his wounds in private; nobody needed to see that, least of all me! He would emerge from his funk, a victorious warrior like Mark Antony, only this time he would have washed his hands of Cleo-baby once and for all (unlike the original story, which didn't go quite that way).

I spent the rest of the day puttering around the house and yard, raking leaves and catching up on emails—the usual drudgery one does to fill up a suddenly empty Saturday. I tried to call my mom, Lili, and Harper, as well as half a dozen other friends, but no one was picking up, which further depressed me. Everyone was out there enjoying the day without me.

By four o'clock, my mind was spinning in circles that kept leading me back to one thought: "You said you could get involved with this guy and not get serious about him," I scolded myself aloud. "What the hell are you doing?" I had no idea how to answer the mother of all questions, so I decided a drink was in order.

I had just poured myself a second glass when the phone rang. I leaped up to answer, thinking that it might be Garrett. But the name that popped up on the screen was not Garrett's after all.

"Linc!" I answered on the third ring, a little too cheerfully. "Shouldn't you be freezing your ass off in the wilderness somewhere?"

I felt my shoulders relax the moment I heard his warm, easy laugh.

"Why freeze my ass off in a tent when I can do it right here?" he teased. He wasn't kidding. The temperature had dropped precipitously overnight. Although the morning weather had seemed promising, a half-frozen gray drizzle now held us hostage as the sun slunk away for the night.

"I know!" I commiserated with him. "Luckily, I have nowhere to be but home. No work this weekend. What's your excuse?"

"Em has a nasty cold, so we decided to skip this weekend's hike. She's at home passed out after downing a half bottle of NyQuil."

"That stuff is lethal!" I laughed.

"Anyway, I had time on my hands, which is never a good thing," he continued. "I was working on winterizing my house today, and then I got to thinking about your house. Thought I'd check in and make sure you had everything in hand over there. I know Aaron was a stickler for working flashlights and tuned-up cars!"

"You sound exactly like my parents!" I walked into the living room and plopped myself in front of the gas log fire, whose flames were dancing merrily.

Linc laughed again. "So butt out? Is that what you're saying here?"

"Uh…yeah!" I paused for a moment, wondering if I should ask his advice about Garrett. Before I could reason one way or another, the words just popped out of my mouth. "Can I ask your opinion about something?" I said, my brain taking a sharp U-turn.

"Sure."

"You know Garrett, the guy I've been seeing?"

"Never actually met him, but I admire his taste," he joked.

"I'm serious, Linc." I pouted just a little. "We've hit a speed bump."

"What kind of speed bump?"

"The 'he ran into his ex and got all bent out of shape' kind."

"Ouch! And I take it you were there to witness this little bump in the road?"

I got up to refill my glass, which I'd drained in record time. "I think he might still be in love with her."

"Breaking up is hard to do," Linc said, trying to lighten the mood.

"He swears he's over her, but he's acting weird. What should I do?" I asked, returning to my cozy spot by the fire.

"Give the dude his space."

"That's it? That's all you've got for me?"

"That's a lot!" he assured me. "He'll come around. I certainly would if I were him." I could hear him smiling through the phone.

Linc sounded so sure of this proclamation that I had to let the sentiment wash over me for a moment. I knew he was right and that I was probably blowing things out of proportion. But the afternoon had faded to dusk and Garrett still hadn't called, so as much as I wanted to relax and let the whole thing roll off my back, I was finding this to be a very difficult task.

"Are you gonna be all right?" Linc asked. "Need some company?"

Part of me wanted to say yes because I knew that no matter how I felt at that moment, seeing Linc would cheer me up. But the rain was really falling hard now, and I hated to drag him out on such a nasty night for a problem that was hardly life-threatening.

"You're sweet to offer, but I think I'm gonna have an early dinner and call it a night."

"OK. Well if you need any more sage advice, you know where to find me!"

I did know where to find him and thanked my lucky stars that I had a friend as loyal and caring as Linc.

"Always the lifesaver," I said with a smile.

"Yeah." He laughed. "But before you hang up, there is one other thing I wanted to tell you," he confessed.

"Oh! So this wasn't just about winterizing my car?" I teased.

"Of course that was my first reason for calling!" He bantered. "But as long as we're talking, I wanted to let you in on a little secret."

"Now I'm intrigued!"

"I've decided that Emmalyn is the one. I'm going to ask her to marry me!" I could almost hear him grinning. "I bought a big old diamond ring and everything."

You could have knocked me over with a feather; that was the last thing I'd expected him to say. But as my stomach leapfrogged its way into my throat, I did my best to hide my surprise. "Wow, Linc!" I said, my voice sounding a little too enthusiastic. "That is big news!"

"I know we haven't known each other for very long, but she makes me so happy, Jules," he continued as if asking for my blessing.

"I hope she says yes." I tried to sound normal despite the fact that I was still shocked by his announcement.

"So do I," he echoed my sentiment.

After we'd signed off, I began to run down the past few weeks of my life. I thought how much of a tinderbox it had become. And as I snuggled under the velvety warmth of the throw that had been draped on the back of the couch, I stared at the flames licking the sides of the logs that never burned down, and I let myself be hypnotized into a haze of nothingness.

chapter twenty-nine

Garrett finally called, waking me from a dead sleep at seven thirty the next morning.

"I know it's early"—the warm rumble of his morning voice wrapped itself around me like a cocoon—"but believe it or not, I've waited hours to call."

I was breathless. "I'm awake," I lied, an enormous yawn escaping my lips.

"I'm standing at your front door," he purred.

I was up like a shot as every ounce of adrenaline I had in my body coursed through me. I went from zero to sixty in three seconds. After flying down the stairs, I flung open the door and launched myself at him, wrapping my arms around his neck and kissing him with an urgency that probably left tracks on his lips.

As he backed me into the house, slamming the door behind him with his foot, I jumped up and wrapped my legs around him as well. He took three steps forward, and slamming me against the wall, he lifted my nightgown and began stroking my thighs with one hand while he held me fast with the other. We sidled toward the stairs, our lips never leaving each other except for the few seconds it took for me to pull his T-shirt clean off his body and for him to relieve me of everything but my panties.

We began to stumble up the stairs, falling every few steps, mauling each other where we lay and then picking ourselves back up and attempting to navigate the next few steps. I had a fleeting thought about the pain I was in and the fact that I would probably be bruised from stem to stern the next day, but I couldn't have cared less about that. I wanted him with a fierce energy I couldn't contain.

Finally reaching the landing, Garrett picked me up and carried me to the bedroom, where he placed me on the bed and leaped on top of me. His hands and fingers caressed every square inch of my flesh, his tongue trailing after his fingertips, finally coming to rest between my legs, parting me with a maddening combination of swirls and thrusts, making me cry out in ecstasy. I came over and over, clutching at the sheets as if holding on to them would prevent me from melting away completely.

And then he was inside of me, thrusting harder and harder, his eyes looking deeply into mine, the crooked smile I loved playing on his lips as he bent to kiss me again and again. I murmured how wonderful he was, how he fit just right, how perfect it was to make love with him. And finally, spent and winded, he fell to his side, arms still wrapped around me, feathery kisses landing on my neck and my breasts, his hands still caressing me with their gentle yet firm touch.

"All that before nine o'clock!" He laughed. "Hell, we could shower, eat breakfast, and still be on time for church!"

"Yeah, that's the last place we should go today," I joked. "We are such sinners!"

"Making love with you is church enough for me." He smiled.

And then his lips were on mine and we were off and running again.

We slept and made love, slept and made love until nearly noon, at which point we dragged ourselves down to the kitchen, ravaged and spent.

"I need some sustenance other than you!" He nibbled the back of my neck as I stood at the stove whipping up a cheese omelet, bacon, and biscuits.

When the food was ready to go, I took a big sip of my coffee, which tasted even better then it smelled, and then turned to kiss him. Grabbing some plates and cutlery, I had us set up and feasting before we could say "Yum!" I watched as he devoured his breakfast with the same relish he'd just used to devour me.

I thought about how sexy he looked when he ate and told him as much.

"You are so under my spell!" he laughed. Reaching for my hand and kissing it, he looked into my eyes. "I guess that makes us even."

"You sweet talker," I chided him, grinning from ear to ear.

"I wish I could stay all day, but I have a lot of work to catch up on," he explained as he lathered my back in the steamy shower we shared after breakfast.

"Ditto," I said as I let the flood of hot water cascade over me while returning the favor.

Squeaky clean and exhausted from lack of sleep and overexertion, I walked him to the door, kissing him gently and running my hand through his hair. "Thanks for the wake-up call," I purred.

"Any time you need one, I'm your man," he said, kissing me once more before he turned to go.

Oh, yes he was!

chapter thirty

Despite the barrage of gray-sky days and plummeting temperatures that marked our march into November, I woke every morning with a spring in my step because Garrett and I were going steady! It had taken several days for him to get over the October surprise that had cut him off at the knees, but he'd finally bounced back to the passionate, witty guy he'd been when we first met. But as curious as I was to the reason for this return to normalcy, I didn't have the guts to ask him about whether or not his recent funk had had anything to do with Natalie; that was a moot point anyway. He was happy in the here and now, and that was right where I needed him to be.

We saw each other every day and almost every night, and he had started keeping a few personal items at my house; not much—just a toothbrush, a razor, and a change of clothes—but it meant the world to me that he was marking his territory. It showed he was getting more serious about me, about us, which was good because whatever promises I'd made to my wiancée self about taking my time and playing it safe had, evidently, gone the way of the Swatch. I was falling hard and fast for Garrett McLeod.

It was a dreary Sunday, and I was wedding free. Garrett and I had lolled about in bed until midafternoon like a couple of heathens. Thanksgiving, my favorite holiday, was less than a week away, and this was the first we'd talked about how we'd be spending the long weekend to come.

"Don't kill me, Julia, but I'm not going to be around for Thanksgiving." He frowned at me as he sat up and leaned back against the pillows.

"What do you mean?" I sat up to face him.

"My family always spends Thanksgiving at our house in Sewanee."

"Oh . . ." I hung my head, trying to fight the stab of disappointment that swelled in my throat.

"Why don't you come with me?" he offered, reaching to rub my arm. "I mean, I know you've never met my folks, but I'm sure they'd be happy to have you."

This is silly! I told myself in an effort to tamp down my emotions. It's not like I don't have Thanksgiving plans of my own.

"That's sweet." I half-smiled. "But my mother has dibs on Thanksgiving, and she wouldn't hear of me not being there. Besides, it wouldn't be Thanksgiving without her turkey and dressing, not to mention her artery-clogging giblet gravy. And believe it or not, I have a couple of weddings that weekend. Unless I want to lose my job, I have to stay put."

"Cheer up!" Garrett implored as he pulled me into his arms. "I'll be around so much before I leave town, you'll be glad to get rid of me for a few days!"

"Impossible!" I let him cajole me back into a good mood as he peppered me with kisses.

Lili's annual stomach stretcher—the yearly pre-Thanksgiving potluck she held to get us in shape for the biggest gorgefest of the year—was that evening. I always looked forward to this party.

Garrett and I finally dragged ourselves out of bed and into the shower, and then we hurried to get dressed and on the road. As excited as I was to introduce Garrett to this annual bash, as well as to my cadre of friends, I'd also been dreading the party's approach because it had always marked the beginning of the holiday season for Aaron and me. Now it had become another milestone on the journey I was making without him.

I'd dragged my holiday decorations from the garage to the house a few days before, which had been quite the chore. I'd never realized how many things Aaron and I had accumulated over the years. As I began to unpack them, a tsunami of nostalgia swept over me, and I collapsed under the weight of missing him.

Realistically, I'm still bound to be feeling Aaron's absence, I told myself as I cried over each and every ornament I unwrapped. But at the same time, I thought, I have this great new guy in my life.

It amazed me that there was room in my heart to house so much sorrow and joy at the same time, and I realized that the square footage of love is a thing that can't be measured. I could compartmentalize my romantic feelings for Garrett and my agonizing grief over losing Aaron, effectively giving each their own heart-zones. As mystifying as this was to me, I was grateful for the fact that this was my reality.

By the time Garrett and I arrived at Lili's, the festivities were in full swing. She greeted him with a warm hug and then began introducing him around. Making our way to the bar, we found

Linc and Emmalyn standing there. After a series of hugs and introductions, the four of us grabbed our cocktails and headed for the buffet table, which was laden with every conceivable kind of food—everything but turkey and dressing, that is. Lili had one hard-and-fast rule when it came to her stomach stretchers: turkey was verboten. She asserted that we'd be eating more of the bird than we cared to for weeks to come. It would make its way into every potpie and tetrazzini you could sink your teeth into, not to mention sandwiches and just plain turkey and gravy with all the sides, which would be more than enough turkey for one season.

"So I hear you're a big hiker," Garrett addressed Linc, adding a spoonful of Harper's famous mac and cheese to his plate. Evidently, she and Jeff had had to bow out of the festivities because the twins were under the weather, but she'd made sure to drop off the casserole earlier in the day.

"Yeah!" Linc animatedly began describing his most recent exploits on the AT, which sounded both harrowing and exhausting to me. "You know, most of the original group who started this summer has disbanded. Dropped off, one by one," Linc addressed this part to me.

My heart twisted a little at the news, despite the fact that I loathed hiking and hadn't been a part of the group that had formed in tribute to Aaron.

"That's too bad!" I said. "What happened?"

"I just don't think they were prepared for how difficult some of the terrain would be. And as the temperatures started to decline, so did their enthusiasm."

"Honestly, it's hard, even for me and I'm in pretty good shape," Emmalyn chimed in.

Linc wound his arm around her proudly. "She is a trooper!" he said, looking at her with an adoring gaze before leaning over to kiss her. She beamed up at him and kissed him back.

"Well I admire the hell out of both of you!" Garrett told them. "It's quite a commitment to make."

"We're doing it for Aaron," Linc explained, and Garrett nodded to let him know that I'd filled him in on the details. "So what do you do, Garrett?"

"Photo journalist. That means I do a little of everything, from print to websites to portraits. I even do weddings now and again."

"Well you and Jules certainly have that in common." Linc smiled.

"Yeah, but I wouldn't want her job! I wouldn't have the patience!" Garrett laughed. Everybody laughed along with him.

Linc raised his glass in a toast to the coming holiday and all we had to be thankful for. We gave a rousing amen to that, clinked glasses, and made our way to a table, where we could dig in to our respective plates and mingle with the crowd, which was getting bigger by the minute. It was comforting to see so many dear friends in one place, and for this I was truly thankful; I'd missed them more than I'd realized. And seeing how Garrett fit so smoothly into the mix made me even more thankful than I had the right to be.

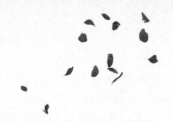

chapter thirty-one

He was standing at the head of a very long banquet table, carving the most beautiful bird I had ever seen. The scene looked like something out of a Norman Rockwell painting, so warm and inviting. The dining room table was a long, solid wooden affair with a lace tablecloth covering its wide expanse. Soft light emanated from a small crystal chandelier hung center stage, and it glinted off the large silver fork and knife that he held in his hands. And as he began to carve the turkey with the precision of one who'd done this forever and a day, I was impressed by his finesse and the way he effortlessly separated the delicate meat from the bone; it's something I do so admire in a man.

I walked toward him, marveling at the glistening guests who lined either side of the table, which was replete with large bowls and platters overflowing with mashed potatoes, roasted potatoes, fresh green beans, corn on the cob, dressing and gravy, cranberry sauce, peas and carrots, corn bread, a basket of fluffy yeast rolls, and at least a dozen pies of as many varieties.

At first, I didn't recognize any of those seated in this holiday tableau, and yet there was something so familiar about them. Upon closer inspection, I recognized the couple seated to Aaron's right as his parents. They looked exactly as they did in a framed photo that hung in our living room, down to the clothes they wore and the way they styled their hair! I gasped at the sight of them sitting there, looking so alive and happy—as did everyone else in the room, for that matter. I was sure I had stumbled upon a family Thanksgiving and that everyone seated at the table was a dearly departed relative. But that only made sense; Thanksgiving is always a family affair. I thought it must be a wonderful moment for Aaron and his folks, reunited after all those years apart.

Aaron laughed and joked with the crowd, who only had eyes for him. As he continued to carve—the perfectly even, thin slices of meat falling one on top of the other in a tall, graceful stack—I tried to catch his eye. But he was oblivious to my presence. I called out his name, certain he was just distracted by the task at hand.

"Aaron!" I shouted as loudly as I could. "Aaron, it's me!" But my voice fell away the minute it left my lips, as if it had no power to project into the room. I called out again, only to yield the same result. I was in Aaron's new world, as I had been so many times before, but this time he had no idea I was there.

I felt like some freaky voyeur who can see everything but is invisible to those she is watching, and I was shot through with the terror of knowing I could see Aaron but he couldn't see me. I rushed toward him and reached out to touch his shoulder, and my hand went right through him, as if he were merely a hologram made of sound waves and thin air. And I screamed—a long, bloodcurdling scream that could have been heard for miles had I been on earth; but in that warm and inviting room, not a sound could be heard beyond the voices of the crowd who couldn't hear me. This made me scream all the louder. I began running around the table, trying to get even one of the guests to notice me. But one after another they ignored me. Just like Aaron, they were unaware of my presence.

I woke to the sounds of the small cries I was emitting, which were not the bloodcurdling screams I'd been filling the room in my dream with seconds before, but rather more of a mewling wail. Sitting upright in my bed, I tried to shake the feeling of Aaron's presence, which still clung to me like a damp sheet.

I got up and padded down to the kitchen, which was lit only by the streetlight out front. As I stood there in the shadows, sipping water and staring out the window, I tried to push the cobwebs of the nightmare from my mind. I tried to convince myself that it had just been a bad dream, despite the fact that, as always, the whole thing had felt so incredibly real.

It's just the stress of the holidays, I told myself. Everything will be just fine. And oh, how I wanted to believe it.

A gentle snow had begun to fall, dusting the sidewalks and lawns of the neighborhood with a luminescent powder that caught the silver light of dawn as it peeked into view. The house was eerily quiet, and the silence weighed me down like an avalanche, making me want to retreat to my bed and sink back into a, hopefully, dreamless sleep.

It's Thanksgiving, I suddenly realized as I continued to stare at the scene outside my kitchen window. The thought made me feel empty and sad. Garrett had left town the day before, and Aaron would never be in town again to celebrate this or any other holiday with me. He was having Thanksgiving with the dearly departed who had surrounded him at that magically festive table, and I was alone at a table for one with nothing to feast on but memories.

chapter thirty-two

Thanksgiving came and went in a flurry of food, family, and football. Par for the course, all of the men in my family were glued to the TV most of the day while the womenfolk did most of the work feeding everyone and cleaning up afterward. But we had our fair share of football fun as well, rooting for our favorite teams and keeping track of the score.

Garrett and I had spoken that morning and I didn't expect to hear from him until the following day, but still I clung to the hope that he would miss me so much he'd call me again before nightfall. Unfortunately, he was true to his original word, which made me glad I'd decided to camp out at my parents' house for the night; going home would have felt like the loneliest thing I could do. Besides, it felt good to be pampered by my mother. I basked in the glory of having been missed by her. At least someone missed me!

By late Friday morning, I still hadn't heard from Garrett. When his cell rang right through to voice mail, I texted him but still got nothing. I thought this was odd but I figured he was tied up with his family doing whatever it is people do in Sewanee, so I let it go and went on with my day. I had a wedding that evening and needed to be at work by four o'clock, so I reluctantly dragged myself home to get dressed.

The bride was a beautiful young blonde who looked no older than thirteen, but I overheard a couple of her bridesmaids talking about their college graduation the spring before, so I figured she was a good decade older than my original guess. Her gown was a breathtaking sugary confection of tulle and satin, which made her look like a fairy princess come to life.

Her bridesmaids, draped in burgundy satin dresses with small capped sleeves, made their way down the aisle on the arms of the black-tuxedo-clad groomsmen. The glow of the chapel lights combined with the dozens of candles burning at the front of the church gave the room a magical incandescent glow that made me want to weep. Of course, I did my usual tearing up as I watched the bride glide down the aisle, but the entire effect was so mesmerizing that I added a serious case of goose bumps to my already emotional mix.

I wished Garrett was there to see the light and the way it made the bridal party glow as if they wore full-body halos. After the ceremony, I asked the photographer if she could send me a few random shots so I could show them to Garrett when he got home. Checking my phone for the hundred and fiftieth time, my stomach began to do serious flip-flops because he had yet to return any of my calls or texts.

By nine o'clock, I had wrapped things up at work and was headed for home. Freezing rain was predicted for Nashville. At that point I'd become nervous about the weather in Sewanee, which, situated in the mountains as it was, was supposed to be even more severe. What if Garrett had slid off the road and was lying in a ditch somewhere? I didn't want to call or text again lest I begin to look like a crazy stalker, but I was getting worried.

Stepping through my kitchen door, I heard my phone ringing in my pocket and dropped everything in my hands to make a grab for it. "Garrett," I said as calmly as I possibly could. "I'm so glad you called."

"I meant to call you hours ago, Julia, but my parents dragged me to a party at the neighbor's house and I lost track of time."

I was instantly relieved that he wasn't injured or dead. It hadn't occurred to me that his parents would have dragged him any place, as I had no idea they had friends up there.

"I was imagining the worst, what with the weather and all . . ."

"Sorry to worry you, babe! Truth is the roads are really bad here, so I may not make it out tomorrow as planned."

Disappointment sliced through me like a dull knife, but I took a breath and told him not to worry. "I'll see you when you get back. Be safe," I said signing off.

"Miss you, babe," he said. "You take care too."

Saturday came and went with the fanfare one would give a tepid glass of tea. The only wedding I had scheduled took place at one in the afternoon. Since it was a renewal of vows, it lacked the hoopla of a big first-time wedding. The couple in question had eloped two weeks after they'd met without saying a word to anyone; I guess they thought rational people would disapprove of the haste with which they'd rushed to the altar. But they obviously knew their own minds; they'd been married for four years now and had two beautiful children. I was touched by the love they had for each another, which proved that there is such a thing as love at first sight. When you know, you know. I'd certainly known with Aaron. But Garrett was proving to be another story, and a rather confusing one at that.

He'd called that morning to say he was staying another day, and I had a feeling that it wasn't just the weather that was keeping him there. I had nothing concrete to hang my suspicions on, but he sounded distant and distracted, which was a real 180 from the behavior he'd been exhibiting the past few weeks. I mean, the man had a change of underwear and toiletries at my house, for God's sake!

Was it me? Had I said something wrong? Left too many messages, been too clingy, too happy, too sure that I was beginning to fall in love with the man? Had I scared him off, or was I just imagining things?

Maybe the roads *were* too treacherous to chance just yet. Maybe his family had begged him to stay. The problem was, I could come up with a dozen reasons why he might be acting so strangely, but until I could see him face-to-face, I had no real way of knowing what was up with him.

"Maybe he's a jerk," Harper cut to the chase as she, Lili, and I ordered our second round of drinks at Union Common later that afternoon. "I know you don't want to hear it, Jules, but this whole thing has been moving pretty fast."

Lili sipped her wine, trying to act all noncommittal, but I wasn't buying it. "You've barely said a word," I scolded her.

"I want you to be happy…and you've been so happy, Jules. But I've gotta say, this is a puzzler. Doesn't pass the smell test, if you know what I mean." She frowned at me.

Harper used her front teeth to dislodge an olive from the toothpick that had been resting in her dirty martini and nodded her head. "Something's rotten in the state of Denmark," she said, waving the toothpick in the air before taking a sip of her drink.

I matched her sip and raised her one. "Thank you, Mrs. Shakespeare!"

"Just sayin' . . ." She dislodged another olive.

"Really, Jules." Lili reached out, grasped my forearm, and looked me in the eye. "I just don't want to see you get hurt. You know him best, but I think this guy is playing games with you."

Harper nodded in agreement and flagged the bartender for another round.

"So what should I do? Call him and ask him if there's anything wrong? Guys just love when we do that," I said, sullen and defensive.

Up until now, things had been going really well with Garrett and me. Maybe he was being weird or maybe he was just an unpredictable, moody guy; I couldn't say. But I had to give him the benefit of the doubt. He definitely deserved that, and I said as much to my well-meaning-yet-overprotective girlfriends.

"I think I should just quit stressing over this and take the wait-and-see approach," I decided aloud.

As our second round arrived, I lifted my glass in a toast. Harper and Lili nodded and told me that they'd support me no matter what, but I could tell that they were just being polite.

RULE #67: *The only people who can see what's happening in a relationship are the people in the relationship, but you should never discount the advice of your best friends; they have eyes too.*

chapter thirty-three

All of my chickens came home to roost late the following day when Garrett showed up at my door. But this time, rather than flinging myself all over him like a bad paint job the way I desperately wanted to, I met him with a casual hug at the door and then ushered him inside. He'd called when he was halfway here, and I could tell from the sound of his voice that he was tired and preoccupied. Still feeling uneasy about our tender footing, I decided to play it cool and let him take the lead.

He was genuinely happy to see me; almost relieved, it seemed. And as we sank down into the welcoming cushions of my sofa, he ran down the details of his weekend, which were plentiful.

One of his nephews had been injured in a sledding accident. His sister and her husband had gotten in a terrible fight over whether or not he should have been sledding in the first place. The other kids were noisily underfoot every single moment, except for a new baby who was suffering from colic and cried incessantly. I became exhausted just hearing about the exploits of this large, unruly brood, let alone living it. As he continued to paint the picture of madness that had ensued over the past weekend, I began to believe that the distance I'd felt between us had had nothing to do with me.

I lit the fire, fetched wine, put on my playlist, and settled in beside him, contented just to be there. Every doubt I'd harbored had sailed off into the sunset, and I wondered why I'd ever doubted him in the first place.

"I missed you," Garrett said, setting down his wine and turning to face me. He studied my face for a long moment, his lips parted as if in anticipation of a kiss, and he reached out and pushed a stray lock of hair off of my forehead. Brushing my lips with his, he teased my mouth with the tip of his tongue. I was entranced, mesmerized, transported to another dimension; yet somehow I'd found the presence of mind to set my wineglass on the coffee table before I became totally lost in his eyes, in his kisses, in the fortress of his embrace.

We stayed that way for some time, making out like a couple of teenagers while never making a move toward the bedroom or removing a stitch of clothing. Every now and then we'd come up for air. Laughing and thirsty, we'd take a sip of wine and then dive in again. He tasted like black cherries and heat. I was swept up in the moment, which I wished would never end. Unfortunately, all great moments have a sell-by date, and this one was about to reach its limit.

My stomach rumbled loud enough to be heard down the block, and I laughed. "Are you hungry?" I asked. "Evidently, I am! I have a ton of leftovers in the fridge." I started to get up and head to the kitchen.

Garrett reached for my hand. "Jules," he said, looking me in the eye, "would you hate me if I headed home? I have a long week ahead of me, and I need to unpack and get my ducks in a row."

I was taken aback, and I knew it showed. But before I could even process my feelings, I told him that of course I wouldn't hate him. What else was I supposed to say? "You've been away for the entire holiday weekend, and I thought you said you were glad to see me—what the fuck is wrong with you?" Nope. I had to be cool, even if I didn't feel cool. And his reasoning made perfect sense. He had just gotten back; of course he needed the evening to ready himself for the coming week. But the sting of rejection still persisted, despite my best attempts to reason it away. I figured I had two choices: suffer in silence or come off as a big whiny, needy baby. I chose the path of least resistance. (I wasn't that needy!) I walked him to the door, a smile plastered on my face, my stomach turning inside out with the emotions I dared not show.

"Thanks for the great welcome home," he said, kissing me sweetly and taking me in his arms. "I'll call you tomorrow," he said into my hair, grazing the top of my head with his chin.

As I watched him drive away from my spot in the front doorway, I couldn't help but feel that I had missed something. But on the face of things, that seemed absurd to me, so I brushed the thought away like so many crumbs on a table and made a beeline for the fridge.

chapter thirty-four

The season of Yule was upon us, and everything was rockin' and rollin' in my life. Garrett's strange behavior over the Thanksgiving weekend had evidently been nothing more than a blip on his emotional radar. He was back to being as attentive as ever, which was quite a relief.

I was enjoying the holidays as best I could, despite the fact that this was my first Christmas without Aaron. He'd been a big fan of Christmas; anything corny or old-fashioned—caroling, chopping down our own tree, stringing cranberry and popcorn garlands—was definitely his thing. We always sent out a gazillion Christmas cards featuring pictures of us doing adorable things. While most people were out being trampled to death in shopping malls on Black Friday, the day after Thanksgiving had always found us eating leftovers and addressing stacks and stacks of envelopes.

But that year, as much as I wanted to follow in Aaron's perfect footsteps, I really didn't have the heart for any of it. To send out cards meant having to do a "year-end wrap-up," which would have been awkward at best. "Season's Greetings from the Wiancée of Aaron DeMinthe" it would say. And the photos of Aaron and me, or worse, of me alone, would make everyone awfully sad, which is definitely not the feeling one hopes to engender with one's holiday cards. So I decided to opt out of the whole shebang, certain that not only would people understand, but they would probably be relieved. I thought of this as my way of being of service during the holidays; I would give the gift that keeps on giving—I'd alleviate awkward emotional moments between myself and everybody else.

The last wedding before Christmas fell on a Saturday. As the six o'clock ceremony time approached, a light snow began to fall, covering the chapel and Whitfield's grounds with a dusting of sparkly flakes that made the place look like it had been sprinkled with confectioner's sugar.

The bridesmaids wore forest-green velvet gowns with capped sleeves and ivory ballet flats. Their bouquets were made of white roses and holly, which matched the boutonnieres worn by the men. The bride was resplendent in an ivory silk gown that ended in a train as delicate as a butterfly's wings. Her bouquet of white and deep-red roses glowed in the candlelight of the chapel as she walked down the aisle toward her groom, who shone with the love of a million stars. I wept at the beauty of it all.

Garrett met me at Whitfield just as I was making my final rounds. He accompanied me as I shut off the lights in the chapel, one by one. In the dim light of the foyer, he took me in his arms and kissed me so softly, so sweetly that it took my breath away. Taking him by the hand, I led him up the darkened side aisle and through the side door. Outside, the snow continued to fall in large, puffy flakes, blanketing the grounds in several inches of fresh powder.

A hush had fallen on the city. We ran from the chapel into the brisk night and onto the enormous south lawn, which was carpeted with a pristine blanket of new-fallen snow. Lifting our faces to the sky, we tasted snowflakes on our tongues, gazing through the branches of the big, bare trees, which were silhou-etted against the silver-gray sky. They stood like wizened sentinels, the only witnesses to our unbounded joy. And we spun in circles, our arms outstretched and laughing at the sheer beauty of it all.

Then I took off and began to run, zigzagging back and forth, churning up the feathery snow with my footfalls, waving my arms and whooping it up like a country fan at a Garth Brooks concert. Chasing me across the great expanse of otherworldly white, Garrett caught me up in his arms, pulled me close, and began kissing me with full abandon. His cheeks and nose were icy cold, but his mouth was warm and inviting. Our breath escaped in clouds as I pulled back, laughing at the delight of nature's spec-tacle and the thrill of his passionate kisses.

"I love you, Julia," he whispered.

My heart was racing and my mind was dizzy from hearing those words—words I had been hoping he'd say. I smiled up at him and kissed him again. "I love you too, Garrett."

It was going to be a magical Christmas.

The snow continued to fall for the next few days, giving Nashville the rare gift of a white Christmas. Garrett and I celebrated the holiday on Christmas Eve, as both of us had family obligations the following day. I prepared a lovely dinner, which we shared by candlelight. Afterward, we exchanged gifts by the tree I'd finally managed to put up a few days before. He gave me a delicate gold necklace with a teardrop-shaped amethyst hanging from the chain. Amethyst was my birthstone, a fact I'd mentioned in passing, so that shot him straight to one hundred on the thoughtfulometer. I felt like I was falling more in love with him by the second. I, in turn, had found a good-looking black leather motorcycle jacket for him, which he adored. It made him look so macho and handsome, I told him I never wanted him to take it off.

As a matter of fact, we made love that evening in front of the fire with him still wrapped in the soft, dappled leather until he finally cast it off and slid it under my head as a kind of pillow. I loved the feel of the leather next to my skin, which made me feel a little bit wicked and made the sex a little bit hotter.

Christmas morning came way too soon. Garrett apologized as he slipped out of my bed to head home and shower; he was expected at his parents' house by nine o'clock.

"Even that was a compromise." He smiled down at me as I snuggled under the comforter. "I'll try to get away later." He leaned in to kiss me. "But chances are I won't see you until tomorrow."

I frowned, but just a little bit. After all, I didn't want to spoil Christmas, especially after the lovely evening we'd had. And despite the fact that I didn't want to let him go, I too had to get up, shower, and dress in order to get to my parents' house for a long day of Christmas activities.

"Merry Christmas, Garrett. I love you." I kissed him again.

"Love you too, babe." He stood to go. "Merry Christmas."

As I heard his car pull out of the driveway, my thoughts turned to Linc and his proposal to Emmalyn. I knew he was going to pop the question that evening, after the day had wound down and she wouldn't be expecting any other gifts from him. He'd mentioned something about taking her to his house and pulling a small, delicately wrapped package out from under his

Christmas tree. He'd tell her he had one more gift for her, and then, on bended knee, he'd ask her to be his wife. I couldn't think of anything more romantic.

It was funny, but I no longer felt those little pangs of jealousy when I thought of Linc proposing to Emmalyn. I guess Garrett declaring his love had banished my romantic feelings for Linc and brought back the sisterly kind of affection I'd always had for him. This led me to thoughts of Aaron, and I burrowed down a little deeper under the covers and just lay there, holding his memory tight.

How was it possible that I could be falling for someone new when I still loved Aaron with all my heart and soul? Would those feelings ever go away, or would they continue to ride in tandem with my feelings for Garrett? I had no way of knowing; only time would tell. But as I asked myself this untenable question, I felt a single tear slide down my cheek. I closed my eyes and slipped into a dreamless sleep, far away from the Christmas morning at hand.

A few hours later I was at my parents' house, opening gifts and eating an enormous pancake breakfast. All in all, it was a quiet day, and I knew my mother had planned it that way. She knew that I'd be missing Aaron terribly, despite the fact that having Garrett in my life was a balm for my still-fresh wounds. I had packed an overnight bag, just as I had for Thanksgiving; being alone in my house on this day of all days would have broken my heart.

After breakfast, I retired to my old room—now a scrapbooking room—for a little respite. As I lay there staring at the wallpaper that had listened to all my girlish dreams and plans, I found myself confessing again. I'm living between two worlds,

I told the rosebuds and vines. I'd come to realize that living the double life of a wiancée and a wanton woman was a heady, yet confusing cocktail. I had no idea where my life was going. All I knew for sure was that, as I desecrated the memory of my fiancé by having hot sex with another man not six months after said fiancé had died, and on Christmas Eve no less, I was definitely driving the bus to hell! *Beep, beep.*

A few neighbors graced us with their presence at Christmas dinner that afternoon, along with a smattering of uncles, aunts, and cousins. They all knew me well enough to know I didn't want them to make a fuss, and things almost felt like they were back to normal. I drank a little more than the daily recommended dosage, but then, so did everyone else. And rather than becoming maudlin, as I had suspected I might, I was the life of the party. There was a lot of laughter all around.

I didn't hear from Garrett the rest of the day. Even though I hadn't expected to, once everyone had gone home, I felt empty and a little sad. I longed to hear his voice if for no other reason than to fill the yawning canyon of grief that was starting to open up in the pit of my stomach.

My mother, in her infinite wisdom, suggested watching a movie. She selected *The Holiday*, one of my favorite romantic comedies of all time. The problem was that I cried through much it, which I suppose was cathartic, but still, it's not the way you want to spend Christmas night. Even the happy parts—especially the happy parts—made the inner ache rear its ugly head again and again. I was glad that my mother was the only witness to this cryfest. I snuggled up against her like I had when I was a little girl. She even went so far as to put me to bed, tucking me in and sitting with me until I was close to drifting off to sleep. I don't know what I would have done without her.

"You did remarkably well today," my mother assured me,

stroking my hair away from my forehead. "It can't have been easy for you, sweetheart."

I smiled up at her, so thankful that she understood me better than anyone else on earth. "Garrett said he loves me," I told her.

"Do you love him too?"

"I do. But not as much as I loved Aaron. Do you think that will ever change? Do you think it's true that love grows over time?"

She thought about this for a moment. "I think that love changes over time and sometimes it grows," she said. "But I think that the kind of love you and Aaron shared is a rare thing. Some people never get the chance to experience a love like that. Maybe you shouldn't expect that what you and Garrett have will be the same. That doesn't mean it can't be a fulfilling relationship."

I nodded and sat up to give her a big hug. "You are so wise." I pulled back to look at her and gave her a kiss on the cheek.

"That's why I'm your mother." She smiled, smoothing the covers over me as I lay back down. "Merry Christmas, darlin'." She kissed me and turned out the bedside lamp. "Sweet dreams."

We were in a sleigh, and the vast expanse of crystal-white snow stretched around us as far as the eye could see. The sun shone brilliantly in a vivid blue sky, and the frigid air whipped across my face as we moved in one fluid motion like we were flying inches above the ground. Aaron was at my side, commanding the two dappled silver horses, which ferried us along at an incredible speed. Tucked under an enormous fur throw, I felt as if I was living out a scene from *Doctor Zhivago*—one of my favorite movies of all time (I know, that is pathetically sappy, but there it is!)—and I began to hear "Lara's Theme" playing.

Early on in our relationship, maybe the third or fourth date, I had dragged Aaron to see a rare showing of this iconic film on the big screen. He had teased me for days afterward about the fact that I cried through most of the film. So being here with him inside a movie I adored was thrilling beyond belief, and I remarked on this fact.

"You always said I gave you the most imaginative Christmas presents." He turned to me and smiled. "Thought I'd go out with a bang!"

For some reason, I found this uproariously funny, and I threw my arms around his neck and hugged him with more joy than I could ever remember feeling. It was perfection to be here with him like this. I wanted to keep the feeling close, like a shadow you can actually hold on to—the never-ending echo of a sublime moment that holds within it the essence of happiness and never becomes diluted, despite the passage of time.

"It's the best present ever," I said as we sped away into the light of a golden, endless sunrise. "The best."

I woke the next morning with a feeling of complete satisfaction that was mixed with an air of anticipation I could barely contain. The sky outside was a pale gunmetal gray that was threatening snow, and I could hear the wind whipping past the frost-covered windows. As I propped myself up in bed and rested against the pillows, I invited the delicious feeling of my *Doctor Zhivago* dream to play over again. I could almost feel the bracing chill of the wind on my face and the shelter of Aaron's arms wrapped tightly around me, keeping the cold at bay. I felt like the world was my oyster as I got dressed in the pale light of the burgeoning morning. As if I had nothing to lose.

That's my real gift from Aaron, I thought. We were barely a week away from a brand-new year, one I'd been dreading because it meant going ahead without him in my life. But suddenly, I felt like it might be a good year after all, one filled with promise and hope rather than the plodding trajectory of misery that had dogged me for much of this one. I wanted to break into song as I tiptoed down the stairs, but I knew I'd wake my parents, who were still peacefully dreaming. So instead, I headed out the door, singing "Lara's Theme" loudly in my head and basking in the glory that was my happy heart.

chapter thirty-five

The rain was coming down in a relentless stream that cast a gray pall on the day. The early morning's fluffy white snow had become a slushy, slippery mess. I found driving was hazardous at best, so I took the few blocks from my parents' house to mine as slowly as I could. As I pulled up to my house, I saw Garrett's truck parked out front and my heart began to race uncontrollably. It was still quite early, and I was thrilled at the thought that he was there waiting for me. He must have missed me as much as I missed him, I thought. As I pulled into the garage, I could see him running up the driveway, head down, ducking and trying to skirt the pelting rain as best he could without the aid of an umbrella.

I leaped out of the car and ran to greet him. "Garrett! I'm so glad to see you!"

He put his hands on my arms and pulled me to him, being careful to keep a bit of distance between us, lest he get me sopping wet, but I didn't care! I leaned against him, savoring his kisses, which tasted like coffee. But I could tell something was bothering him, and I leaned back to take in his expression.

From the dark circles under his eyes, I could see that he'd hardly slept. He looked like he'd aged a year since the last time I saw him, and he wore an expression that reminded me of Linc the night he had come to tell me about Aaron's terrible accident.

I hurried to unlock the kitchen door. Leading him inside, I turned to face him. "What's wrong?" I asked, trying not to sound as alarmed as I suddenly felt. "Did somebody die?"

As he hung his coat on the rack by the door, he shook his head and walked into the kitchen. After pouring each of us a mug of hot coffee (preprogrammed coffee maker to the rescue!), I joined him at the kitchen table, where he'd sunk into one of the chairs.

I reached my hand out to cover his free one and looked at him as he took a few sips of his coffee.

"I don't know how to say this . . ." he began in a halting voice, eyes downcast.

Now he was scaring me. "What? What is it?"

He looked up, searching my eyes as if for a reprieve. "Do you remember Thanksgiving?"

Of course I remembered Thanksgiving. It was just four weeks ago! Had he lost his ever-loving mind? "What do you mean? What I had to eat? What the weather was like?"

"No. I mean, do you remember me telling you about the party my parents dragged me to in Sewanee?"

"Yeah . . ." I hesitated.

"Well, I ran into Natalie there and—"

"Hold it. You ran into Natalie . . . your ex, Natalie?"

"Yeah. Actually, funny story! Nat and I originally met in Sewanee. Her parents have a house up there just next door to ours."

"Uh-huh . . ." So far, I didn't see the humor.

"So, anyway, her family was there too, which is odd because they usually don't go up there for Thanksgiving. But there they were. And there she was, and there I was . . ."

"So are you telling me that you murdered her, hid her body, and now you need to go on the lam? Because the last time you saw Natalie"—I said her name as sarcastically as I could—"you certainly wanted to kill her!"

"Well, not exactly. I was really surprised to see her, and naturally we got into it immediately . . ."

"Naturally."

"And so I told her we should take it outside because everyone was starting to stare. So we did. And I guess our tempers gave way to some kind of twisted passion-play, because all of a sudden we were kissing and then she dragged me into the garage and we did it."

I leaped from my seat, knocking my chair to the floor and spilling coffee in the process as I stormed out of the kitchen and began pacing around the living room.

Garrett was on his feet and coming after me, pleading for me to settle down and listen to what he had to say. But I was too stinking mad to settle down! What was I, an overexcited puppy or something? Settle down? Was he freakin' kidding me?

I kept pacing and shaking my head, and Garrett just stood there, helpless to stop me, watching and continuing to try to calm me down. "If you would just let me explain," he pleaded. "Please, Julia."

Hearing my name on his lips shot a torpedo of conflicting emotions clear through me. I had fallen so hard for this guy, and now I had fallen flat on my face. I had no idea how to pick myself up or what to say once I'd been righted.

"Julia, please," he said in a desperate, raspy whisper, reaching out his arms to me.

I froze midstep and allowed myself to look at him. His face was twisted into a macabre kind of a mask; pain, vulnerability, and shame fought for territory there, and the sadness in his eyes was palpable. He looked disheveled, his hair clinging to his head in a damp mop and his clothes a haphazard, wrinkled mess, as if he'd slept in them all night. I felt sorry for him, and at the same time I was so mad I could spit nails! I dropped to the sofa, my legs curled under me, and grabbed a large cushion, holding it to my chest as if it would hold my insides in place, because they were threatening to explode right out of me.

Garrett sat down beside me, close enough to touch but not quite, and he bowed his head as if praying for the courage to continue on with what he had to say. He took in a breath, let it out, and looked me in the eye.

"I am so sorry, Julia," he began. "I know I broke your trust. And I don't know if you can find it in your heart to forgive me. Believe me when I tell you, I never meant for anything to happen. I can't even explain it!"

"I think you've explained it pretty well. I mean, you painted a clear enough picture!"

He was quiet for a moment, as if he were trying to come up with another line of defense. "I want you to know that it was just that one time. I haven't seen her or spoken to her since then."

"Uh-huh . . ."

"Except for yesterday . . ."

I was up and out of my seat in a shot. Throwing the pillow at him and missing, I began to pace again, coming to a stop opposite him. Good thing for him there was an apothecary coffee table standing between us, because all I wanted to do at that moment was leap at him and beat him senseless—or shoot him, despite the fact that I didn't own a gun. But standing there facing Garrett, all of a sudden I knew that anything was possible.

RULE #18: *Just because you don't own a gun doesn't mean you can't wish you did.*

"On Christmas? You spoke to her on Christmas? I didn't even get to talk to you on Christmas!" I bellowed.

"Well, to be fair, I did wake up with you in my arms on Christmas . . ." he started to defend his position.

"Are you freakin' kidding me?"

"OK, OK. I get your point. But she just showed up and said she had to talk to me. What could I do? Slam the door in her face?" He got up, stepping around the coffee table until we were face-to-face. "It was Christmas," he said in a quiet, pleading way, as if that should be explanation enough.

"I can't listen to this." I turned to walk away, but he grabbed my arm and pivoted me back so we were a hair's breadth apart.

"She came to tell me that she's pregnant." He let my arm drop and just stood there waiting for my reaction. I was frozen in place, not yet lucid enough to be bowled over by the audacity of his last statement. I was dumbfounded and speechless. But that didn't last very long.

I shook my head as if trying to clear cobwebs. "And it's yours?"

"Evidently," he said a bit too contritely, as if he'd had absolutely nothing to do with her condition.

"And she wants to keep it?" It was a terrible question, but one I had to ask. He gave no answer, so I figured this meant yes. "Well, that's just perfect!" My voice began to rise precipitously.

I marched back to the kitchen and poured myself a fresh cup of coffee, obviously not offering Garrett the same.

"I can't believe this, Garrett!" I turned to look at him as he hung back in the doorway, leaning against the frame like a teenager who'd just received a stern reprimand.

"You told me you love me." I felt the tears welling up in my eyes. I will not cry, I will not cry! I told myself, digging my finger-nails into the palm of my hand.

He stepped forward, a plaintive look in his eyes, his arms reaching out to hold me. "I do!"

"You have a funny way of showing it!" I said, holding my palm up toward him like a cop stopping traffic.

He froze in his tracks, still holding his arms out to me in a beseeching manner. "I don't know what to do here! I am so in love with you that it hurts. But I have to think about the fact that I'm going to be a father . . ."

The last phrase stung as if he had poured salt in an open wound, but it also snapped me out of my emotional death spiral. "And what do you expect me to do? Make this decision for you?"

"That's not exactly what I'm saying here."

"Really. What is it you are saying? Exactly."

"I just need time to think," he said, as if he were trying to figure out how much gratuity to tip an errant waiter.

"Well, why don't you go and start your thinking right now?" I said, grabbing his damp coat from the hook and throwing it at him. He looked like he wanted to say something more, but I opened the door and swept my hand toward it.

Through the window across the room, I could see that the rain had abated and the sun was trying to peek through the densely packed clouds in one small corner of the sky. It was a perfect metaphor for my life.

"And let me be perfectly clear." I looked him dead in the eye. "When you're doing this deep thinking of yours—be sure to leave me out of the equation."

I felt him brush past me, and then he turned and looked at me with a kind of sad expression reminiscent of those paint-ings of the children with the overly large, overly mournful eyes. "Goodbye, Julia," he murmured. And then, just like the morn-ing's rain, he was gone.

I slammed the door behind him and finally allowed the wellspring of tears I'd been holding back to overflow their banks with a vengeance. And somehow, I felt like those thunderous tears had taken the place of the storm.

chapter thirty-six

I wept and I wailed; I cursed and I cried. The remainder of the day found me buried up to my neck in self-pity, wallowing about in it like a pig in mud. I lit the fire in my living room. It gave me some comfort against the weather, which was raging not only outside my house but inside my head as well. And as I pulled the cork from a bottle of malbec and settled in on the sofa with both the bottle and a glass in front of me, I began to think things through. The fight and subsequent breakup with Garrett ran over and over in my head like a hamster on a wheel. The more I tried to make sense of the situation, the less sense it made.

Garrett had gotten Cleopatra pregnant! I sure hadn't seen that coming! Looking back on his odd behavior during the Halloween party and Thanksgiving weekend and the fact that he hadn't wanted to make love to me upon his return, which was so out of character for him—suddenly everything made perfect sense. I mean, I knew my bullshit detector was a little rusty but, Lord!

Red flags had been waving at me since day one, and I hadn't seen them! Those fucking flags had been so big I could have spotted them from outer space if I hadn't been such a blind, lovesick fool!

I'd dated my share of guys before falling for Aaron. There were bad boys and sweet guys, go-getters and slackers, but I could always tell if they were telling me the truth. I had never suffered fools lightly. But now? Not only had I suffered the mother of all fools, but I'd served my heart up to him on a silver platter while sporting white kid gloves and an earnest smile. I'd welcomed Garrett to come stomping into my life with his bravado and charm and that sexy smile of his. And that would have been OK if I'd seen him for what he was. But I had done nothing of the kind, and it made me ill.

I hadn't trusted my gut. And as I thought about all those times when Garrett's behavior had been strange—when he'd been distant where he had once been devoted, his absence on two major holidays, which he'd said was family related—I wanted to lose what was left of my mind! Yeah, it had been family related all right, but more like "in a family way" related!

Had Natalie planned the whole thing? Seduced him when she knew she was fertile? And hadn't Garrett ever heard of a fucking condom, for Christ's sake? He'd certainly been packing every time we'd hooked up. Maybe, I continued my pointless conjecture, on some subconscious level he wanted this to happen.

Despite the fact that I'd felt so sure I knew him, I'd obviously had no idea what made Garrett tick. He'd shown me the Garrett McLeod he had wanted me to see. He had played me! But if I was going to be honest with myself, I'd had nagging doubts about him, but I'd put the onus on myself because I'd wanted to believe that the person I was falling for was the real deal.

I guess I needed to feel like my life hadn't ended with Aaron's death. I needed to believe that someone would love me again, as deeply and completely as Aaron had. I'd wanted Garrett to fit that bill so badly that I'd ignored the little voice in my head that was warning me to back away from the man!

RULE #52: *Never, under any circumstances, ignore that little voice in your head. It's your own personal Emergency Alert System screaming "This is not a drill! I repeat, this is NOT a drill!" You'd better damn well listen!*

But in the end, we believe what we want to believe; we see what we want to see. If anybody should have been dressed as Cleopatra on Halloween it should have been me because, Lord knows, I was the true Queen of Denial.

I got up and dragged my sorry ass to the kitchen just as the light of the grayest day on record made its final curtsy. Filling a plate with leftovers, I nuked it and padded my way back to the sofa. After refilling my wineglass and perching my plate on my lap, I turned on the Blu-ray player to watch *The Holiday* again. When I'd been head over heels in love with Garrett (twelve hours ago) and watched it with my mother, I'd cried at the happy ending because I could identify with the characters who'd found beautiful, perfect love. But as I watched that final scene, where the happily-ever-after happens, I saw everything a different way: I wasn't getting *my* happy ending, and they were! It was just heart-wrenching, and I cried like the sad sack I was.

Midway through my fourth glass of wine, my body finally decided to give up the ghost, and I gave in to the bone-crushing weariness I'd been working toward all day. I'll just rest here for a minute, I told myself.

Eight hours and an incredibly long trail of dried drool later, I woke to the sound of birds singing and immediately regretted passing out on the sofa in a drunken, overfed stupor. Not only did I have a headache the size of Detroit, but my head felt like it had been screwed on the wrong way. I couldn't turn it to the left without being met with a searing, shooting pain that emanated down my neck and into my shoulder. I tried to get up but failed. It took every ounce of strength I had left in my poor, wrung-out body to propel me up and onto my feet, whereupon I made a beeline for the kitchen and that blessed first cup of coffee.

It was 6:00 a.m. on the nose when my phone rang, and I knew it had to be my mother. Nobody else I know would dare call me at such an ungodly hour.

"I just got your message from last night. Are you all right? Do you need me to come over there?"

Had I called my mother in the middle of last night's bender and left a crazy message? I didn't remember doing that. Or did I? Bits and pieces were coming back to me like flashbacks in a horror movie.

"I hope I didn't wake you." I cringed as the memory of my sobbing message resurfaced in my hazy brain.

"I didn't even hear the phone ring. You know me—once I'm out, I'm out. Now, sweetheart, if you need me to come over there I can be dressed and in the car in five minutes."

As tempting as that sounded, I just wanted to go back to bed, for real this time, and bury my head under the covers. "I'm OK. Really," I lied.

"Well you sounded awfully upset in your message, although you were blubbering so hard I could barely understand you. Something about Garrett and someone being pregnant…Is there something you want to share with me, sweetie?"

"I haven't gotten myself knocked up, I promise you. Knocked down, certainly! But not knocked up."

"Well, that's a relief," she said, trying to sound as if she'd always had utter confidence in my safe-sex practices. "So then . . . if you're not pregnant, who is?"

"Garrett's ex-girlfriend, Natalie. Actually, I guess that's not her status anymore. I guess she's his current girlfriend and I'm the ex." I burst into tears, spilling coffee all over myself in the process, and sank down at the kitchen table with my head resting in the palm of my hand.

Naturally, my mother gasped and tut-tutted in all the right places as I continued to run the horrible story by her, which made me feel a little less like an ass.

"Oh, sweetheart. I hate to hear you like this. I really should come over there!"

"No, Mama, really. I just need to get some rest. It was a rough night," I said, drying both my eyes and my runny nose on the sleeve of my shirt.

"If you need anything, you know where we are. We're just a holler away."

"Thanks," I whispered.

We signed off. And after I had turned off the fire and the TV, I stumbled up the stairs. The house felt so small all of a sudden, like there wasn't room for me and all of my emotions too. I felt like the walls were closing in. "Not a good sign," I said out loud. I was taking a trip to panic-attack-city, a place I hadn't visited in eons and where I never wished to go again. "That's it!" I screamed. "I have officially become certifiable and have taken my place on the Island of Misfit Toys!" I just hoped that someday soon, somebody would vote me off.

chapter thirty-seven

New Year's Eve arrived before you could count backward from ten. As I looked back on the week that had slammed me into a wall of pain, I was amazed that I'd made it through intact. But after Garrett had ripped off the emotional Band-Aid, a.k.a. his deep-and-abiding-love, despite the fact that he'd left me raw and wanting I had rebounded fairly quickly. I had survived Aaron's death; I could certainly survive a little hiccup like Garrett's betrayal. This realization gave me the strength to move on.

Both Lili and Harper had been out of town since Christmas, and I'd been able to fill them in only briefly on the crashing and burning of my fling with Garrett. I still marveled at the fact that I'd seen this guy coming and had done nothing to block his path. In fact, I had waved the dude in and invited him to take a front-row seat at the pageant of my crazy life, which made me just one thing: crazy. Yep, I was cray-cray, or as they say in France, très-cray (they don't really say that in France).

"What an SOB!" Harper declared when she and Lili dropped by earlier that day.

"At least he didn't get *you* preggers," Lili added as they followed me to our seats by the fire, where I'd set us up with hot cider and cookies. "You would have been tied to him for the rest of your life!"

"Tell me about it," Harper joked, poking fun at herself.

I couldn't help but laugh at my narrow escape, and it felt good to introduce a moment of levity into the conversation. "I should have trusted my gut," I said, my eyes searching their faces for a reprieve.

"It's what we do," Lili said. "Women, I mean. We always think we're the ones who are at fault when things get weird in a relationship. You just behaved the way you're hardwired to behave, Jules. We've all been there," she said, helping herself to her third Christmas cookie.

"But that's the thing—I've never been here before. No one has ever broken up with me. Died? Sure. But I've always been the one to call it quits!" I shoved a cookie unceremoniously into my mouth.

"You were bound to get a bad egg eventually," Lili said, trying to make me feel better. "But it's good you found out now, before you got in too deep."

"Yeah!" Harper chimed in. "You could have ended up like me." She pointed to her belly, grinning like a magpie.

I'd noticed she'd put on a few pounds and it did look like her tummy was protruding a bit, but I'd thought she'd just over-indulged during the holidays. Of course, I'd never said a word about it. But now I couldn't help but stare.

"Oh, Harper!" I jumped out of my chair and grabbed her up in a big bear hug. "I am so happy for you!"

"When did you find out? How far along are you? Is it a boy or a girl?" Lili began pelting her with questions as she, too, rushed in for a hug.

"I'm about three months along, and we've known for two. But it's bad luck to talk about it until the second trimester—that's what you always hear anyway. And I have no idea what the sex is. It's too early to tell, and I want to be surprised. Of course, we're hoping for a girl. I could use an ally at my house!" She laughed.

I was so happy for Harper that I forgot my own troubles for a little while. But I'd also forgotten the time, and when I glanced at the clock I realized I had under an hour to get ready for work. Naturally, there was a New Year's Eve wedding. Thankfully, the wedding would be over by ten at the latest and I'd be free to roam about the countryside. But what good was that?

I had no plans for ringing in the New Year, so I looked at the rest of my day as a downhill slide. First, there would be a wedding, which would remind me of how alone I was. Then there would be New Year's Eve festivities, which would be going on without me since I didn't have a date, once again reinforcing how alone I was.

"You should still come to the Threadgill's party tonight, date or no date," Lili urged.

"You should," Harper echoed her sentiments. "It'll be fun!"

"I'll see," I lied, ushering them out the door so I could get ready. "But if I don't see you, happy New Year, girls!" I hugged them both in turn.

"Happy New Year, Jules!" They sang out in unison as they retreated down the walk in the fading afternoon light.

It was bitterly cold that evening, but the velvety night sky was blanketed with silvery stars that twinkled like a thousand tiny eyes. The chapel was awash in candlelight, and the walls veritably glowed with the magic of it. Dozens of pillar candles of various sizes were placed on the altar table, and four large twelve-branch candelabras banked the table on either side. But the huge spray of white flowers that stood five feet tall at the center of the long wooden table was the evening's crowning glory.

The bridesmaids were decked out in formal black dresses, which were strapless and very structured. Each carried a small bouquet of white roses in her gloved hands. The groomsmen who escorted them down the aisle were clad in white tie and tails. As far as I was concerned, when it comes to men in evening wear, there's simply nothing more heart-stopping than seeing a man dressed in white tie. As I pinned on each of the gentlemen's boutonnieres, I remarked upon how handsome each of them looked. You could see by the way they carried themselves that they were just as beguiled with their look as I was.

When I caught my first glimpse of the flower girl, I gasped; it was like looking in the mirror at my five-year-old self. She was the same age I'd been when I was in Aunt Bitsy's wedding, and she looked like a princess, her long, beautiful silk and lace dress mimicking that of the bride. She wore a wreath of tiny white roses atop her head, and the white satin ribbons that hung from the back of the headpiece fell against her golden-red hair, which hung in ringlets cascading down her back. In her small hands, she carried a white velvet basket filled to the brim with red satin rose petals. My eyes filled with tears at the very sight of her.

"You look so beautiful!" I told her as I knelt down to greet her. "I'll bet you're going to be the best flower girl we've ever had here!"

She beamed at me. "I'm going to throw the petals," she said in a hushed tone.

"You're so lucky!" I stood and smiled at her mother, who was standing by her side, proud as punch.

"She's so beautiful," I told her.

"She's been practicing her part for days," she said and smiled.

It was time for the bride to go down, as we say in the business. As everyone in the wedding party lined up to go down with her, she emerged from the dressing room. A statuesque blonde, she stood at least five feet eleven in her heels, and every inch of her was polished and coiffed to perfection. Her ivory gown hugged every one of her unstoppable-yet-slender curves mermaid-style to just below her knees, and then it draped majestically to the floor, pooling into a four-foot train that would follow her down the aisle like a river of liquid glass. Hand beading graced the entire length of the gown, which was spun of delicate ivory lace and laid atop silk. The way the dress moved with her was its most remarkable feature; it looked as if it was alive. It seemed to breathe in and out with every step she took.

Her lustrous hair hung in a long band of curls, which fell softly around her shoulders. She wore a cathedral-length, hand-made lace veil that has been in her family for over 150 years—her crowning glory. She carried a bouquet of white hydrangeas and red roses, and that pop of red made her stand out in a subtle but overwhelming way. As she stood at the back of the sanctuary, awaiting her big reveal, her music began. The guests, who were also dressed in formal evening wear, rose to face the doors through which she would walk at any moment. She leaned over to kiss her father on the cheek and whispered something only he could hear.

"I'm so proud of you," he whispered back, returning her kiss and trying not to lose control of the tears that were banked at the edge of his eyelashes.

And then it was her moment. Just above our heads, a girls' choir began to sing a cappella. As we opened the doors and the bride and her father stepped through, her beauty and the sheer happiness she was holding in her heart came bursting forth with the radiance of a thousand suns, and there were audible gasps from the onlookers.

I began to cry softly, tears escaping my eyes before I could even think to put a stop to them, but I tried not to make a sound lest I draw attention to myself. Grace Kennedy—wedding planner extraordinaire—and her assistant had just finished closing the doors. She turned to me, put her hand on my shoulder, and smiled. She was all welled up too.

"Wasn't she just the most exquisite bride?" She wiped her tears away with the back of her hand.

Rather than admit that my tears were not just brought on by the romance of the moment but moreover by the weight of my aching heart, I said, "She was amazing." I reached up to wipe my own tears away. "I should start carrying a hankie with me!" I joked. "I always tear up when we send them down."

They'd said their "I dos" and the happy couple was on their way to their reception, where they and two hundred of their closest friends and family would toast in the New Year. Beginning a new life with someone you couldn't live without seemed like a wonderful way to begin a new year, and I wondered if I would ever be lucky enough to feel that way again or if I had missed my chance for happiness.

I turned off the lights, locked the chapel doors, and then returned to Beaumont Hall. Sinking into the chair at my desk, I looked at the clock—9:45, it read. Maybe I should go to the Threadgill's party, I thought. I could go just as I was; after all, I had dressed up for tonight's wedding. But I had neither the energy nor the inclination to go to a New Year's party on my own, even though I'd probably know everyone in the room. The trouble was, strangers or not, all the people at the party would be coupled up, ready to kiss at midnight—and most likely beyond midnight.

RULE #20: *When you're already lonely, you don't need a reminder of how alone you are. That would be like being reminded that you have a dental appointment while you're sitting in the chair with a drill in your mouth.*

I put my head in my hands and let the tears that I'd been fighting for hours fall. I had never felt so alone or so lost. This was truly the grand finale to a less-than-stellar holiday season if ever there was one.

I heard footsteps approaching my door. Thinking it must be the wedding planner returning to retrieve some mislaid item, I stood up and ran my palms over my face, trying to erase the tracks of my tears.

"Grace, is that you?" I called out.

"Who's Grace?" I heard a familiar voice say. Bless the stars above and all that is holy, if it wasn't Lincoln Douglas walking into my office! Once again, he'd ridden to my rescue.

chapter thirty-eight

"What are you doing here?" Those were the first words out of my mouth—not "Hi, Linc!" or "Happy New Year!" or anything that reflected how glad I was to see his tall, lanky frame hovering in the doorway.

"I was just driving by and saw the lights, so I thought I'd check and see if you were here."

"Where's Emmalyn? Did you leave her in the car? If you did, I certainly hope you left the window cracked," I said before I thought through the words escaping my lips. "Sorry...that was rude." I smiled apologetically.

"Don't worry about it." He smiled back for just a second before dipping his head. "Honestly, I don't know where she is." He allowed himself to meet my eyes. "Don't care, really."

"Did I miss something here? I thought you were gonna slip that awesome rock on her teensy finger and make her yours."

"She turned me down—in a sweet way, mind you. But she turned me down flat." He walked across the room and slumped into one of the ornate chairs facing my desk, which we used for bridal consultations. He looked as out of place as a duck in a swimming pool. "It's been a brutal week."

I told him I could relate because I had been unceremoniously dumped on Boxing Day, which was totally appropriate as all I'd wanted to do was punch Garrett McLeod's lights out. "Guess I was just too much of a lady," I joked.

"All that breeding came in handy"—he laughed along with me—"for him!"

"So here we are, two jilted people, all alone on the biggest date night of the year," I said, as if I had just announced our plane would be departing on schedule. "What now?"

"I know a friendly spot with loads of good champagne on ice," he said.

"You mean the Threadgill's party?"

"No. I mean my house. Would you like to join me for a drink or two? I'm not in the mood for a crowd of happy people."

"Sure. I'd rather be alone with you than all by myself any day!" I smiled.

Slipping on my coat and grabbing my purse in one hand, I took his proffered arm in the other, and off we trudged together, into the last night of a very long year.

Two hours and just as many bottles of champagne later, midnight was almost at hand. We'd turned on the TV to watch fireworks from around the world. Now the climax of the evening had begun, the moment we'd all been waiting for: the dropping of the guitar over downtown Nashville. Not to be outdone by the Big Apple's Times Square ball drop, Nashville had out-country'd the biggest party of the year by squeezing 150,000 drunken revelers into a large park known as The Mall where a plethora of country music stars rocked in the new year with music, fireworks and an ungodly tonnage of confetti.

Only a few years before, these festivities had been held downtown on Lower Broadway's "Honky Tonk Highway" which consists of five blocks choked with dozens of live-music venues that runs from 5th Ave. to 1st Ave. There on 5th, squatting like an enormous, out-of-place ottoman, sits the Bridgestone Arena and it's futuristic-looking radio tower that stretches high above its bell-shaped roof. At the stroke of midnight, an enormous guitar festooned with lights, and perched atop the tower (our answer to the Times Square Ball) would swoop down to the roof to the delight of the thousands of screaming New Year's revelers. It was a spectacular thing to behold! Unfortunately, the crush of spectators had grown so large over the years that the festivities had been relocated to The Mall. But as far as I was concerned, the new digs were a bit anticlimactic, so watching from the comfort of Linc's living room suited me just fine. And as the crowds standing in the frigid night air cheered in real time, so did Linc and I.

"Five, four, thee, two, one!" the MC shouted for all he was worth as we counted right along with him at the top of our lungs.

"Happy New Year!" we shouted joyfully at one another as we met in a seemingly innocent and customary kiss. But then something happened that wasn't customary. Despite the crowd noise screaming from the big screen, the room had become unspeakably quiet. It was just the two of us standing there. Linc leaned in to kiss me again, his lips sweet and welcoming, his arms wrapping around my waist and pulling me close. He leaned back and took me in. Like a tourist studying a rare and beautiful painting they've only glimpsed in books, he looked at me in amazement.

"Oh, Julia," he whispered so close I could taste his words. "Thank God!"

He pulled me into a tight embrace, his kisses echoing the thrums of desire that raced through my limbs, my kisses returning his in a never-ending volley. We stood there for some time; it could have been minutes or hours, I don't know. But I was entranced with him and he with me, and all we wanted to do was kiss and kiss and hold each other tight.

He led me to the bedroom. Regardless that not a stitch of clothing had come off, I felt like I stood naked before him. As we made our way toward the bed, lips still entangled and limbs entwined, we began to undress each other with abandon. We were dancing to music that would have been inaudible to anyone but the two of us. He played me like a virtuoso, and I willingly resonated under his touch. He kissed me with obvious delight and caressed my breasts until I was tingling with desire and my knees had given way. We fell into his bed then, still kissing, still caressing each another without ceasing. He knew my body better than I knew it myself, and I let him lead me to inexorable heights of ecstasy, only to come down and rise to them again. Time stood still; the future had no weight and the past was a distant memory as we tumbled in a free fall, in the moment, together. Nothing had ever felt more right.

"Julia," he repeated. "Thank God! Thank God," he whispered, searching my eyes as if I were the only thing in this world worth living for.

Exhausted and sated, we would drift off for short periods of time, wrapped up in each other's arms like kittens. Then we'd stumble to each other again—half awake, half in a dream—and make love again, the steady rhythms of our breath rising and falling in tandem until we had sated ourselves once more.

I woke to the smell of bacon and eggs as Linc set a tray on the bed. "Woman cannot live by champagne alone!" He smirked from beneath his hooded eyes and tousled hair. "Mimosas, anyone?" he said holding a flute aloft before settling in beside me.

I took a sip of the citrusy, bubbly concoction and sighed with great appreciation before clinking my flute against his and digging into the scrambled eggs, bacon, and toast and jam that had appeared as if by magic. He followed suit as we shared the plate of ambrosia otherwise known as breakfast.

"This is delicious," I said, my mouth full of half-chewed food. Linc laughed at my hilarious display of bad manners, spitting bits of toast in my general direction, which made me laugh all the harder.

Dawn was just coming on, and the sky began to reveal the pearly gray hue of an overcast day. Linc got up to move the tray and all traces of breakfast from our warm and cozy bed. As he trotted back shivering, I held back the covers and patted his side of the bed with an inviting come-hither leer. He leaped in beside me, seeking warmth for his ice-cold feet, which made me shriek out loud.

"Don't you believe in slippers?" I laughed as he wound his arms around me. "I'm freezing now!"

"Let's just see if we can warm you up!" he whispered in a gruff and suggestive manner. And what could I do but let him have his way with me (for the seventh time)?

The first sounds of morning came alive outside the windows, heralding a brand spanking New Year. As I nestled into the crook of Linc's arm, which felt like it had been made especially for me, I snuggled close, hugging him as tightly as I could. I wanted to stay awake, but the long arm of sleep was pulling me down and I had no choice but to give in to its weight.

"I love you, Julia," Linc whispered as I sank under the water of my unconscious mind. And as I drifted off, I let the magic of the moment carry me away.

chapter thirty-nine

The overly loud ringing of my phone snapped me awake several hours later, although I couldn't have told you the time had my life depended on it. Still wrapped around Linc, as I had been when we drifted off for the last time, I smacked his jaw with my head as I shot up from the depths of a very deep sleep.

"Ouch!" he yelled as his head snapped back, hitting the headboard with a fierce thud.

"Sorry," I half-whispered, my voice gravelly with sleep and dry mouth. "I think that was my phone. I don't remember carrying it in here last night."

"I brought it in to charge when I brought up the breakfast tray. Worst decision of my life," he tried to joke as he stroked his jaw in search of a possible fracture.

Swinging my feet over the side of the bed, I winced at the soreness between my legs. My head didn't feel all that great either. Punishment for last night's frivolities, I reckoned with a sleepy smile as I reached for my phone to see who'd called.

"Oh no!" I jumped to my feet, trying to steady myself; this was not an easy task.

"What's wrong?" Linc sat up, a look of concern spread across his face.

"That was my mother!" I dropped the phone like it was on fire.

"So?" Linc's expression went from concerned to mystified.

Bending to retrieve the discarded phone, I saw the time and lost it. "Holy shit! It's after one!"

"And . . ."

"And I was supposed to be at my mother's an hour ago. She invited me for lunch." I hobbled toward the bathroom. "Just gonna freshen up before I call her back," I said, disappearing around the corner.

"Can't you tell her you're not gonna make it?" Linc called after me. "I thought we'd spend the day together."

Peeing was another exercise in pain. After I had accomplished that feat, I splashed some water on my face and hobbled back to perch on the edge of the bed.

"I'll just call her back real quick," I informed Linc without answering his question.

"Where are you?" my mother cried as if I'd been missing for weeks and presumed dead. "When you didn't show up, I sent your father to check on you and he said your car isn't there!"

"No need to worry, Mama," I said, looking down at my feet. "I crashed at Lili's last night. I didn't want to take any chances driving on New Year's Eve. Guess we overslept," I continued my bald-faced lie.

"Well, as long as you're OK . . ." She seemed to have calmed down a bit.

"Let me just go home and grab a shower, and I'll be there in a jiff," I assured her as I began to roam around the room in search of my panties and bra. Hanging up, I donned my undies and then went in search of my dress.

"I guess you heard that," I said, slithering into the wrinkled garment and staring at Linc.

"Couldn't help but hear that," he said in a less-than-happy tone. Jumping out of bed, he grabbed the top sheet and wrapped it around his torso, ever the gentleman. "Lili's? Really? Why didn't you just tell her you were here?" He rounded the bed and stood in front of me, worry and anger crisscrossing his face.

"I couldn't just blurt it out!" I said defensively. "What would she think? I just broke up with Garrett. She'd think I was some kind of a slut!"

"You're not serious!"

"She's my mother, Linc!"

"Exactly!" he said, starting to raise his voice.

"I just lied to my mother!" I responded in kind, the blood rushing in my ears.

"And that makes you feel bad," he said, taking it down a notch as he gave my arm an understanding squeeze.

"No, it doesn't make me feel bad!" I took a step back, effectively shaking him loose, my voice continuing to career upward. "It makes me feel stupid! Do you think she won't figure this out and realize I lied to her?"

I turned away and began searching in earnest for my boots, which I found discarded in the corner. Hopping up and down on one foot, I began trying to put one of them on without sitting back down; forward momentum was everything at that moment.

"Julia, you need to slow down! Everything will be fine if you just take a breath!"

"What is it you want from me?" I asked as I continued to struggle with my boots.

"I thought I made that perfectly clear last night," he said, taking my hand to steady me and looking at me with the earnestness of a newborn calf.

I stared at him for a few seconds, not knowing what to say. Part of me wanted to throw my arms around him and stay there forever, to hold the real world at bay. But somehow that didn't seem like an option. I leaned in and planted a gentle but firm kiss on his lips.

"I'll call you later," I promised, giving his hand a reassuring squeeze before turning to go.

"Julia!" Linc followed me to the top of the stairs and called after me.

"I'm so sorry!" I tossed one last apology over my shoulder as I headed out the door.

I should have felt giddy after the night I'd spent doing unspeakably luscious things with Linc; but on the contrary, I was just a bag of mixed emotions who knew how to drive a car. And as I wound my way down deserted, snow-covered side streets toward home, I flashed on the night I met Linc. Remembering how attracted I'd been to him before Aaron had made his move, I wondered if this was fate finally taking its turn. I replayed the night we'd just shared, the perfection of our bodies, minds, and hearts opening to one another in a world of our own making. In the heat of passion, everything had seemed so clear, as if my life had finally come into focus.

But the cold light of day had cast a shadow on the entire situation, and now everything was as clear as mud. I was dumbfounded by the fact that one little phone call from my mother could make me question the night I'd spent with Linc. But it had. And the farther away I drove from his house, the closer I came to losing my lunch.

Screeching up to my house, I leaped out from the driver's seat and immediately slipped on a patch of black ice. I caught myself as simultaneously my stomach gave it the old heave-ho all over the hood of my car. "Great!" I screamed at the top of my lungs as I righted myself and stumbled up the front walk.

A hot shower and change of clothes did about as much to spruce me up as putting lipstick on a pig might have done. When I walked through the door of my parents' house, I could tell by their shocked expressions that I looked like the hot mess I felt like; this did little to improve my mood.

My daddy chalked my appearance up to a nasty hangover. After plying me with his surefire remedy for what ailed me— more alcohol—and joining me in his second (or was it his third?) round, he proclaimed that the color was coming back into my cheeks. He seemed satisfied with his ministrations.

My mother plied me with food, of course. She wouldn't hear of me not partaking of her collard greens and black-eyed peas, which were the traditional New Year's dishes rumored to bring prosperity and luck to all who ate them. Who was I to say no to that? I needed all the luck I could get.

But as the afternoon wore on, so did my thoughts. I was so confused, I couldn't have found my ass with my hands in my back pocket. What am I doing? I scolded myself. My night with Linc had been a dream come true in so many ways, but regardless of that, I definitely wasn't ready for that kind of dream. If my dalliance with Garrett had proved anything, it had proved that!

Aaron had been gone for only eight months. I was finally beginning to get my bearings. And now, here I was hopping into bed with Linc like some sex-crazed maniac! I loved Linc and I needed him in my life, but I was still a thin veneer of my former self. And I was no good to him like this, not really. I needed to find myself again, to rebuild my identity. Until I accomplished that, I would be worthless to Linc and, ultimately, to myself. I hoped I could make him understand how I felt; Lord knows, I barely did.

It was all I could do to get through lunch. Making my excuses, I texted Linc to let him know I was on my way. Bracing myself for the chill of the evening air, I headed back to his house, my heart heavy with determination. I had to put the brakes on this thing between us before it went any further and one of us got hurt—that one being Linc, of course.

Linc was waiting by the door with open arms as I rushed in out of the frigid air. I could tell I'd roused him from a nap; he was tousled and unshaven, and he looked like a five-year-old with a five-o'clock shadow. We held each other for a moment, and I could feel the tension in his body, the uncertainty crouching there just beneath the surface of his skin.

"How was lunch?" he asked, trying to make small talk as he released me and turned toward the living room.

"It was the usual." I half-smiled. "I brought you some collards and black-eyed peas." I extracted a bag from my oversized purse.

"Thanks," he said as we slunk down on the sofa. "I need all the luck I can get!"

"I was just saying the same thing." I half-smiled again.

And then the ball was in my court. It was a ball I had no wish to lob over the net, yet I had no choice but to serve it up and hope it landed inbounds. "Linc, you know that I love you . . ."

"Uh oh." He smirked. "That's never a good place to start a conversation."

"Please . . . you have to let me get through this." I looked him dead in the eye.

"Fair enough."

"I love you, and I could fall in love with you so easily! But it would be for all the wrong reasons, and that wouldn't be fair to you."

"Why don't you let me be the judge of that?"

"I can't, Linc." I shook my head. "Last night *was* amazing, and you're beyond amazing! But it's too soon for me. I keep looking to you for the second coming of Aaron, but there's never going to be one. And I need to make peace with that!"

He stood, arms folded, and glared down at me. "I'm grieving too, Jules! And if anyone can understand what you're going through right now it's me. Can't you see that we need each other? That we belong together?"

I didn't know what to say, so I just stared at him and said absolutely nothing. Crossing to the fireplace, he threw another log on the fire and began stoking it fiercely with a large andiron.

"Last night was amazing, but this is not just about last night," he said and then turned to face me, his eyes burning brightly. "I've loved you for longer than you can imagine, and I—"

"Linc don't!" I cried, shooting up from my seat. I couldn't bear to hear another word! Making the decision to walk away from him had been hard enough; hearing Linc declare his love for me wasn't going to make it any easier. If I let him finish his thought, I might never have the strength to disengage, and where would that leave us? Maybe we'd be all right for a week or even a month, but eventually the ghosts of my unfinished business with Aaron would rear their ugly heads and come between us. And that would definitely break Linc's heart. So better to break it now, I reasoned.

"I know how you feel. I know how we both feel. But our timing is lousy, and there's just no changing that," I declared.

"How can you be so sure, Julia?" he pleaded, tears welling in his eyes.

"I'm not," I whispered, shaking my head. "Maybe things could go back to the way they were?" This time I was the one with the newborn calf's eyes.

I could see him visibly wince. "I don't think I have the strength for that." He turned back to the fire and began stoking it purposefully.

"I guess that's my cue to go," I said, gathering my things. "Let me know if you change your mind," I said in the most hopeful tone I could muster.

"You'll be the first one I call," he said without turning to face me.

Every step I took from Linc's living room toward my car was fueled by a deep-seated doubt and the urge to turn, run to him, and take back every word; it was almost more than I could do to make it out the door. And as I drove off into the night, a crippled and heartbroken wreck, I felt like I'd lost an appendage. And I wondered how in the world I was ever going to manage without him.

chapter forty

Days turned into weeks as I marched steadily forward with halfhearted resolve. I replayed that last conversation with Linc over and over, as if it would change things. Some days I felt about as useful as a screen door on a submarine. But on those days, I just kept my head down and kept on moving until the sun had set and I had a reasonable excuse to crawl into my bed.

By March the half-frozen ground in my backyard had begun to give way to brave little crocuses that raised their colorful heads in spite of the cool weather. They made quite a show of it until they were wiped out by a freak snowstorm; I knew exactly how they felt.

I did the only thing I knew to do: I threw myself into work. And after running into Grace of Graceful Weddings one Friday evening, I asked her to take me on board as an assistant—and she agreed. Under her tutelage, I learned how to develop a timeline for the ceremony and reception, how to speak fluent Mother-of-the-Bride, and how to sew a bridesmaid into a dress that had unexpectedly burst at the seams.

Every wedding was a new, heady experience for me because, just like fingerprints, no two brides or weddings are alike. And getting to juggle an entirely new set of circumstances and people under the guise of a tried-and-true regimen was nothing if not a fascinating challenge that I welcomed with open arms. It felt marvelous to be so good at something; I had never dreamed I would love a job so much.

Mostly, I kept my head down outside of work. I was still getting together with Lili and Harper for quick lunches or drinks, but I avoided all of Linc's regular haunts lest we have an awkward encounter. I missed him more than I could stand to admit, and most days I wondered if I had made the right decision. He'd texted me a few days after that painful New Year's Day conversation, asking me to reconsider, but I told him I just couldn't do that. There had been nothing but radio silence from him after that. I figured he had finally given up on me. The thought made me feel hollow inside, like my heart was doomed to rattle around in my chest for the rest of eternity. But I had no choice other than to learn to live with the restlessness, and I shelved it alongside my grief for Aaron, which was still clutching at the edges of my heart.

I couldn't bring myself to confide in anyone about the night Linc and I had shared. To breathe a word of it out loud felt as if it would shatter the fragile and beautiful moment we'd shared. And if there was anything I didn't need, it was to damage the memory of that night in any way, shape, or form. It was all I had left of him.

Every couple that I saw down the aisle made me believe that

my decision had been the right one despite the fact that I continued to second-guess myself every chance I got.

Maybe I should have stayed with him and given us a chance, I'd reason. But in the end, I always came to the same conclusion: it could never have worked out for us, not when I was standing on such shaky ground, so why even give it a shot?

This is what I get for breaking Linc's heart, I told myself when I was caught up in the spiral of self-pity that often visited me in the dead of the night. You should feel like shit! I would berate myself. Look what you've done to Linc! But then the voice of reason would chime in with its well-hewn mantra—you did the right thing, you did the right thing, you did the right thing—until I'd finally give in to sleep.

And then, out of nowhere, it was April 1. Spring had finally wrested control from the last of the winter frosts. I still felt like a fool, which was appropriate considering the date, but I felt less and less sad, so at least there was some progress being made.

When I wasn't working at Whitfield, I was working other weddings with Grace, learning my craft and developing a style all my own.

"How can you be so calm?" brides would often ask me on their big day when everyone's nerves were aflutter.

"I'm not getting married today." I would smile as if we were sharing an inside joke.

It had been nearly a year since Aaron had died. So much had happened to me since then. Sometimes it felt like a hundred years since he'd passed, and sometimes it seemed like it had happened yesterday. But however I measured the passage of time on any given day, I could see that it was doing its job because my perspective had finally begun to change.

I'd certainly had a part to play in the difficulties I'd faced in the aftermath of Aaron's death. I'd aggrandized him so thoroughly in the days and weeks after he died that I had essentially propelled him to sainthood in my mind. I never deigned to think about the niggling habits of his that had driven me crazy when he was alive, like the fact that he consistently left his wet towels lying on the bathroom floor and never put the cap back on the toothpaste tube. He also had the annoying habit of being ready ten minutes early for everything, which made it appear that I was running ten minutes behind. And he drank straight from the orange juice container despite the fact that he knew how much it grossed me out. All of these little details, the ones that had made him human, slowly started coming back to me. Of course, all of these faults paled in comparison to his biggest faux pas of all: the man had hauled off and died on me!

RULE #78: *Try not to blame your fiancé for his death, even if it was his own fault. It will only enrage you and make the creases between your brows so much deeper.*

But like it or not, Aaron's death had been a catalyst for me, although there's no way I could have seen that at the time. I was finally coming into my own. Despite the fact that I was still alone and often quite lonely, I knew I was on the right track; I'd finally found a career that I was good at. The only other thing I had a natural talent for was eating my way through a bag of Pepperidge Farm cookies in under an hour. And the last time I checked, nobody was hiring for that.

So there I was on a Friday afternoon, busily setting up for the two thirty rehearsal, when I heard the front door of the chapel opening. I swung around to tell the interloper that the rehearsal didn't begin for another thirty minutes and he'd have to come back, but the words didn't have a chance to form on my tongue. I let out a gasp of recognition as Linc made his way from the back of the chapel to where I stood at the foot of the dais. My heart lurched at the sight of him.

"Hello, Julia." He smiled, looking up at me.

"What are you doing here?" I asked, breathless with anticipation.

Walking up the steps, he came to rest in front of me; now I was the one who was looking up.

"I've come to talk with you. And if you don't like what I have to say, I'll go away and never darken your door again."

"That's a bit dramatic," I began.

He pressed his finger to my lips to quiet me, which made my pulse quicken all the more. "Just listen, OK?"

I nodded. He lowered his finger and looked me in the eye. This did nothing to still my heartbeat.

"Do you remember the first time we met?" Linc asked.

"What does that have to do with anything?" I challenged him. Where was he going with this?

"Just answer the question," he said a bit impatiently.

"Sure I do. It was at that symphony fundraiser. That was the night I met Aaron."

"Correct. But there's something I don't think you know about that night—I was the one who noticed you first. When I saw you walk through the door in that clingy little black dress of yours, I was knocked into yesterday. I wanted to meet you so badly. But of course, our boy Aaron beat me to the punch...and the rest, as they say, is history."

Now he really had my attention. "You wanted to meet me? I never knew that...And you remember what I was wearing?"

"I swear," he said, crossing his heart like some Boy Scout. "But like I said, Aaron beat me to it. When I pointed you out, he said 'Now there's a woman worth crossing a room for!' And let's face it, what woman in her right mind wouldn't have wanted Aaron to cross a room just to talk to her? I saw the way you two connected, and I knew that was that. You'd never be mine. But I did get the benefit of being his best friend so I got to be around you all the time, and that was better than nothing."

"But you've had several girlfriends over the years," I stuttered, shocked to be hearing this unexpected confession. "You proposed to Emmalyn . . ."

"I did," he admitted, sliding his hands into the front pockets of his jeans. "But none of them were you."

"Why didn't you ever tell me this before?" I searched his eyes.

"I was planning to spill the beans on New Year's, but you blew that plan all to hell when you cast me aside."

I was stunned. How was it possible that both of us had felt the same way on the first night we met and yet neither of us had ever had the guts to say the words out loud? But now was my chance!

Taking a step toward him, I started to explain the feelings I'd been carrying in a secret compartment of my heart all these years. "That's amazing Linc because I—"

"Wait, Julia. There's more." He stopped me dead in my tracks. "After you walked out on me, I figured it was time I did some soul-searching. I kept thinking about us and our near misses, and I tried to put everything in perspective. You broke my heart that night. I thought the hand of fate had finally brought us together. But then I realized you were right. As much as I loved you from the first moment I laid eyes on you, you were Aaron's and you always will be. But I've missed you so much these past few months," he continued. "And I finally came to the conclusion that we should return to the way we were—best of friends who have each other's backs. There's nothing more important than that."

Wait. What? No, no! This was the part where I was supposed to tell Linc how I'd loved him at first sight too! But with this proclamation of his, he'd made that impossible. I felt like I'd been sucker punched. What was I supposed to say now? I was speechless.

"That's what you want too, isn't it?" Linc seemed confused by my silence. "It's what you said you wanted the last time I saw you."

"Of course it is," I lied with all the conviction I could muster.

"Good!" Linc leaned in to seal the deal, grabbing me up in an enthusiastic hug.

Still, as I crushed in against him, I couldn't help but feel disappointment cresting like a giant wave over both of us, washing away all hope that we'd ever find our way back to each other. It felt like I was losing him all over again, and I ached with the memory of the perfect night we'd shared. But I had to put a brave face on it. Pulling back, I did just that.

"So I have this idea." Linc took me by the hand and escorted me to the first pew, where he slid in beside me. "You know how I said I plan to be at the top of Mount Katahdin on the anniversary of Aaron's death to honor him?"

"Yeah . . ." I said, panic starting to seize me by the throat.

"Well, I think you and I should climb up there together."

"Climb to the top of a mountain."

"Yes."

"You and me."

"Mm-hmm."

Once again, I was speechless.

"Everyone from the original hiking group has dropped out, which means it'll just be me up there. I know you had reservations about going, but I just can't face it alone. I need you to be there with me, Jules. I realize you're not a big fan of hiking, or sweating, or working out in any way, but you can do this! It will just be a day hike, and we have almost two months to get you in shape. I'll help you train for it."

"Me. Climb to the top of a mountain," I said, repeating myself like a blithering idiot.

"It'll be fun," he said, squeezing my hand emphatically.

It was all I could do to get through the rehearsal without losing what was left of my mind. As I waited for the wedding party to hurry up and get the hell out of Whitfield, I ran the conversation with Linc in my head at least a dozen times.

Finally, I was able to head out the door, and I found myself driving straight to Lili's without bothering to call or text to let her know I'd be dropping in. Of course, she was happy to see me, unexpected or not. Plopping myself down at her kitchen table, she poured me a hefty glass of wine as I began to spill the beans. All of them.

"I can't believe you kept these juicy details from me all this time!" she finally interjected as I paused to take a breath.

"I know!" I took a large sip from my glass. Spilling so many beans was thirsty work. "At first I just wanted to cling to the memory of the whole thing. And then I felt like such a first-class idiot I just couldn't bring myself to talk about it."

"I get that," she empathized as she refilled my dwindling glass. "But why in the name of all that is holy didn't you tell Linc the truth today? You know, the part about feeling the same way he did the night you met and the fact that you are kind of in love with him?"

"I just couldn't!" I stood and began to pace the confines of her small kitchen, which meant I was going in circles (so what else was new?). "I was about to tell him everything, but then he told me how he was over the whole romance thing and had decided we should just be friends after all!"

"You know he didn't mean it," Lili assured me, leaning back in her seat as she watched me continue to pace.

"Do I?" I sunk back into my chair and looked at her.

"I guess time will tell," she replied noncommittally. "So what are you going to do about the whole hiking thing? Are you actually going to climb to the top of that mountain?"

"I feel like I don't have a choice, especially since I gave Linc my word."

"Well, all I've got to say is more power to you." Lili raised her glass in a salute. "I definitely want pictures."

chapter forty-one

The view was so breathtaking, I couldn't help but gasp with delight. Hills and valleys stretched out as far as the eye could see. A majestic river ran through the canyon below, mirroring the perfection of an azure-blue sky.

"I can see why people climb up here," I said. But as the words escaped my lips, I suddenly realized that I had no idea how I had gotten to the top of the mountain. I had no memory of ascending it.

To my left, I could hear jubilant voices coming from the valley floor. As I turned to investigate, I could see Aaron approaching, followed by the same group of hikers I had seen with him before.

"Aaron!" I shouted, bouncing up in the air and waving my arms.

He came running toward me—bounding really, as the ground up here had a spongy texture to it and gave more easily than any surface I'd ever stood upon.

"Juila!" He caught me up in a hug, lifting me into the air as if I weighed nothing. "So! You're a hiker now. Quite a view from the top of the world, isn't it?"

"Is that where we are?" I asked him, staring at his eyes, the blue of which matched the sky exactly.

"That's where you're going—with Linc. To the top of the world, right?" he smiled at me, laying his hand on my shoulder.

"We wanted to say goodbye to you. And Linc thinks this is the best way . . ." I trailed off, feeling like this was an awfully odd conversation to be having.

"I think it's a great idea! Looks like you've got the shoes for it," he said, pointing down to the pair of hiking boots I was sporting. "It's a long way to the top of that mountain. Just one thing, Julia"—Aaron lowered his voice, as if he were about to share state secrets with me—"don't fall off!"

He began to laugh as if he had just cracked the best joke of all time, but I didn't find it amusing at all!

"That is *so* not funny!" I shouted as the ground began to rumble. And I was falling, the sound of Aaron's hearty laughter trailing behind me through the ether.

Then I was awake. Glancing over at the clock, which read 2:35, I realized it had been just twelve short hours since Linc had proposed that we hike to the top of that godforsaken mountain. He'd refused to leave the chapel until I'd agreed to go, but coming awake from that dream I realized I was shaken to my core with fear. And as I attempted to get back to sleep, I tried to think of anything but falling.

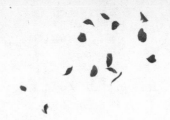

chapter forty-two

True to his word, Linc showed up bright and early the next morning to get me started on our trek to the top of the world...and closure. Unable to get back to sleep after that crazy dream, I'd pulled an all-nighter in front of the computer researching the best ways to get in shape for this exercise in insanity, and I looked like I felt—exhausted and overwhelmed. Googling "How to prepare for a strenuous hike," I was met with an encyclopedic range of options. Diving in apprehensively, it wasn't long before I had gotten sucked into the vortex of the hiking world.

Hiking is just walking, one website (my hands-down favorite) announced. I could easily get in shape by walking daily and building up to longer and more strenuous hikes, eventually adding a pack, it told me. But that would take four months, and I had less than half that time, so that was a nonstarter.

Strength training was widely recommended, but most of the terminology associated with that form of exercise was foreign to me. One site featured photos of this buff, muscular woman doing everything from lunges to push-ups, which I found totally intimidating. Forearm and side planks looked excruciatingly difficult, and I suddenly longed for the days when all I knew about planks was that they were great for grilling salmon, especially if they were made of cedar.

Crunches, hip bridges, climbing Jacob's ladder (you don't want to know)—the list went on and on and on. By the time the sun had peaked over the horizon, so too had my enthusiasm for Linc and his crazy idea. Nursing my fourth cup of coffee, I realized I'd done it again. I'd said yes to a thing I'd never set out to do, and now there was no turning back.

Taking the job at Whitfield had been my way of losing my shit after Aaron died, and hiking to the top of some godforsaken mountain to scatter his ashes in the exact spot from which he'd plummeted to his death was evidently going to be my way of getting on with my life—that is, if I didn't die first. But these choices, like them or not, were the bookends to my grief. And deep inside I knew that somewhere, somehow, Aaron was leading me on this journey toward closure. Despite my fear and loathing of the impending hike, I knew it was something I had to do.

Linc joined me for coffee before venturing out to the garage where, true to my word, I had stashed all of Aaron's hiking gear. Unearthing a sturdy day pack, collapsible walking stick, water bottles, a tarp, and innumerable other pieces of necessary gear, we devised a setup for me that would—after I added the things I'd need to buy in my own size, like rain gear and other layers of clothing—weigh about fifteen pounds. Linc would carry most of our water and food. He reassured me that he was going to get me into shape in time.

Next we hit REI, the mecca of outdoorsy people the world over. There I found not only the right clothes for the hike but also the exact same boots I'd been wearing in both of my hiking dreams. And although this really freaked the shit out of me, it also felt like, once again, Aaron was giving me a sign. So naturally, I bought them.

Radnor Lake was our final destination of the day. There I donned my new boots and tried them out on the Lake Trail, which had few hills and wound around the reservoir for a little over two miles. "That was doable," I told Linc as we arrived back at my car.

But when we returned to Radnor the next morning, he chose a trail that snaked up and over a formidable ridge. Although I completed it without breaking any bones, I'd stumbled more than once on the switchbacks. By the time we'd finished, my muscles were screaming for mercy and I felt like I was bruised from the inside out. I was certain I was never gonna make it through the day, let alone to the top of Mount Katahdin!

Each and every morning, rain or shine, Linc pushed me to new heights, literally, as we tackled tougher and tougher trails in a half dozen parks. After a couple of weeks, I was in a little less pain, which wasn't saying much.

In addition to my morning hikes, I accompanied Lili to yoga classes or spinning classes most evenings. I missed the days when the only time I broke a sweat was when walking from my air-conditioned house to my air-conditioned car on a hot summer afternoon. And I cursed Aaron on a regular basis for dying in such an inconvenient spot.

Ibuprofen and long, hot baths became my best friends. As my training continued, so too did my hatred of exercise. I was committed to doing this for Aaron, but I was never going to acquire a taste for hiking or working out in any way, shape, or form, that was for damn sure! I couldn't wait for Aaron's death-day to come and go so I could get back to my former life as a layabout.

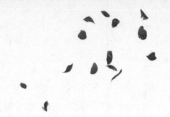

chapter forty-three

I t was the last Saturday in May, and the moment of truth had arrived. I've been training for this, I told myself as I strapped on my pack and stared at the trailhead where Linc and I would begin our ascent. The air was a bit brisk, but the sun was shining for all it was worth—so very different from the weather on this date just one year before.

Linc came up beside me, eyeing the bulging pack on my back with a bit of concern. "That looks kind of heavy. Are you sure there's nothing in there I can carry to lighten your load?"

"We've been through this, Linc," I said firmly. "I need to carry my own weight, both physically and metaphorically." I paused so he could take my meaning. "And besides, I've been walking, running, doing squats, and God knows what else with this damn pack on my back for weeks, so if there's a time for me to prove that I'm ready for this, it is now!"

"That's my girl!"

"No time like the present," I said, repeating myself on purpose while taking the first step.

The beginning of the trail was easy to maneuver. Despite the fact that it wound up and around small hills and switchbacks, the climb was steady and manageable.

"Nothing to it," I assured Linc when we stopped to drink some water and take in the first of the dozens of glorious vistas we would see that day.

The trees were dressed in their brightest spring green, and wildflowers burst forth in myriad colors that carpeted the fields and valleys below, which got smaller and farther away the higher we climbed. We had started walking at the crack of dawn. Linc figured that it would take us several hours each way, including taking breaks for water and food. He'd also packed a flashlight, flares, a tarp and stakes for a makeshift tent, and a small emergency first aid kit that had everything from Band-Aids to snake antivenom. He was prepared for any eventuality, unlike the last time he was on this trail.

The trails and its offshoots were marked with rustic wooden signs, like the kind you would have seen at the entrance to an old Western town or at sleepaway camp. When we crested the top of Pamola Peak, we came to stand in front of a trail marker that read "Saddle Trail." The vista was remarkable, stretching as far as the eye could see. In a moment of déjà vu, I realized that I had been here before. This was where I'd been standing in my dreams with Aaron. A chill ran down my spine, and I had to shake my head a little to make sure that I truly was awake and seeing what I thought I saw.

"Magnificent, isn't it?" Linc stepped beside me and took my hand in his. "I remember how ecstatic Aaron was that day. I suggested we stop here to plant the flag and call it a day. The winds were whipping through here good, and we'd been told not to cross the Knife Edge between Pamola and Baxter Peaks because the trail is only three feet wide for three-tenths of a mile."

"Did you really have to remind me of that fact?" I tried to joke.

Linc dropped my hand and reached for his water bottle, taking a big swig before handing it to me.

"Somehow, the winds died down long enough for us to get across the damn thing. I guess the top of the mountain was waiting for him." He stopped and looked down at his feet and then looked over at me, tears hanging at the edge of his lower lashes.

Seeing Linc start to lose it made me join right in, and we dropped our packs and hugged each other as tightly as we could for several minutes, if for no other reason than to affirm the fact that we were still strong, alive, flesh-and-blood beings despite the fact that Aaron was none of these things.

"He was so stubborn." Linc pulled back to look at me, wiping his face with the sleeve of his shirt.

I pulled a Kleenex package from my pocket (or as we call them in the business, Sniffs) and handed him a couple before taking one for myself.

"Always be prepared," I said like the Girl Scout I'd been once upon a time, blowing my nose like a trumpeter playing "Reveille."

The reality of what we were doing hit me like a two-by-four. As if he'd read my mind, Linc lifted my pack from where it lay on the ground and, without a word, helped me into it, as if he were a gentleman helping a lady on with her winter coat. It was such an intimate move and yet so noninvasive, and this seemingly small gesture spoke volumes. We were in this together, and he was and always would be a dear friend who would stay right by my side. He hoisted his own pack on his back and took me by the hand, leading the way toward our final ascent. I knew in that moment that there was no turning back for either of us.

I'm not going to recount the details of the treacherous steps I took along Knife Edge, but I will say this: it was grueling, it was terrifying, and if I never had to traverse that .3 miles of narrow, stomach-churning terrain again, it would be too soon! But we were resolute in our push to reach the top of Mount Katahdin, buoyed by the fact that we had already come so far and by the sheer inexplicable beauty of the expansive view. From up there the world seemed to go on forever. Once again, it made me think of those dreams I'd had of Aaron. He lived in a grand expanse, just like the one I was looking at now. But rather than being a part of this earthly station, he was floating above it all, somewhere in the ether, in a place just out of my grasp. He had gone back to his beginnings. He was stardust. He was infinite. And he would always be with me, deep inside my heart.

The sun was straight overhead when we finally reached the summit of that big, beautiful mountain. I breathed a sigh of relief and tried not to think about the trek back down. Dropping his pack, Linc pulled out the big urn containing the bulk of Aaron's ashes. I'd decided to keep the mini urn on the mantel; maybe someday I'd be ready to part with all of him, but now was not that time.

"Do you want to say a few words?" he asked.

"You first," I said, dropping my pack next to his.

Linc thought for a minute, swallowed hard, and began. "Aaron, you were like a brother to me. I miss you every day, and I don't think I'll ever stop. Rest in peace, old buddy."

"Life will never be the same without you, Aaron," I added. "I'll always love you."

And with that, Linc walked to the edge of the cliff and upended the urn, sending Aaron's charred remains over the edge, where they flew out on the currents of the wind. The ashes swirled around us for a moment, as if they had borne wings and knew what they were aiming for, and then they fell away down the side of the mountain to parts unknown, chasing Aaron to his final resting place.

And then it was my turn. Bending down, I unzipped my pack as far as it would go, reached in, and dug deep. With my fingers splayed out, I wrapped my hand firmly around the thing I had brought to commemorate this moment. With a yank of my arm, I lifted my beautiful wedding gown out of the pack with a flourish.

"Oh my God!" Linc cried out. "That's what you were carrying? No wonder your pack looked so enormous."

I walked to the same spot where Linc had just stood, trying to think of something appropriate to say. "This is for you, Aaron!" I yelled to the heavens at the top of my lungs. I stepped back a few feet and spun a couple of times, like a javelin thrower warming up for the pitch, and then I let that damn dress fly, a bellow of release and finality escaping my lips as I felt the dress sail from my grasp.

Up and out and over the edge it went, catching an updraft for a moment and then sinking, only to be caught by another burst of wind. It twirled and danced out there as if it had a life of its own; and in a way, I suppose it did. And then it fell, catching on a branch halfway down the mountain, where it hung for a few minutes before being propelled by another gust of wind, which hurled it up for a second and then down, down, down into the canyon below.

After Aaron had died, I'd spent countless hours with that dress—admiring it, cursing it, trying to figure out what in the world to do with it. I'd thought about wearing it as a Halloween costume, but in the end I'd decided that that would have been way too frightening and, let's face it, a bit pathetic. I would have been the belle of the ball in that thing, maybe even Bride of the Year. That gown was supposed to have been my crowning glory, the pièce de résistance, the centerpiece of our big day. Aaron was supposed to have watched me walking toward him, radiant and perfect in my gorgeous confectionary, tears in his eyes and his heart full to bursting with love. But he'd never gotten a chance to see me in it. That was one of my biggest regrets because, in the end, it had really all been for him: the dress, the music, the vows I'd planned to say. I wanted to show him how much he meant to me, how much I loved him, to celebrate us, to share our good fortune with everyone we held near and dear. And that gown, that symbol of our happily-ever-after, had done nothing but haunt me ever since he'd left me alone and confused and wishing I had died right along with him.

That damn dress had been a constant reminder of everything I'd lost—not just the wedding and the love of my life, but the future I had planned and everything I was, everything I thought I would become. All of that had been inextricably wrapped up in Aaron. And then all of a sudden there had been no Aaron, and for a long, long time, I'd felt like there was no me either.

As I watched my gown dancing like a prima ballerina out there on the wind, I realized what a burden it had become in the end, which was the exact opposite of what I had intended it to be. And until I'd decided to climb this great, big, awful, spectacular mountain—a task I absolutely did NOT enjoy—I'd had no idea what to do with the giant white intrusion. But as I'd flung that dress, as I'd run my fingers along the lacy contours of its magnificent shape for the last time and released it, so too had I released the hurt, anger, betrayal, and feelings of abandonment that had been sewn up with it this last year. And with this final gesture, the disappointment, the what-ifs, the "woulda, shoulda, couldas," and the unrelenting pain had finally been put to rest— here, where the man I'd built my whole life around had taken his last breath.

A piece of my heart sailed on the wind that day along with the gown that I would never wear. But it was a piece that belonged to Aaron, and it didn't have a place in my life anymore. I'd grown to realize that you never run out of love no matter how much of it you give or how much you lose, because your heart is bigger than anything you could ever imagine it could be. Casting off that piece of my heart and letting it fly free was like sending a blessing out into the ether. And maybe Aaron was waiting there to catch it as it sailed on by and he would hold it close forever. I could only hope as much.

And then, there was nothing but silence; my screams were just an echo in my head. I'd never realized how absolutely still it was at the top of the world, where I could hear nothing save my labored breathing and the beating of my heart thrumming in my ears. I turned to look at Linc, who stood stock-still, his mouth agape, the only witness to the flinging of my wedding gown and the release of all the shattered hopes and dreams that had been wrapped up within the confines of its lacy expanse. Running the few feet that separated us, I flung myself into him, wrapping my arms around him and hugging him for all I was worth.

"I need to tell you something!" I shouted as I released him and stepped back. Taking him by both hands, I began my confession about how I'd noticed him on that first night too. How I'd been wishing he had been the one who crossed the room to meet me, and that, although I had loved Aaron with all my might, in some distant corner of my heart I had always loved him too.

"Why didn't you tell me this before?" he echoed the question I'd asked myself a thousand times.

"Timing…" was the only thing I could come up with. "But none of that matters now."

And then I had a brilliant idea. "Linc"—I smiled up at his beautiful face—"will you marry me?"

"Will I ever!" he shouted without missing a beat. And picking me up as if I weighed nothing, he swung me in circles, laughing with an explosion of pure joy. "So...I'm guessing you'll want a small wedding?" He grinned.

I grinned right back.

chapter forty-four

'm in the wrong life, and I don't know how I got here. But all
I can say is thank the good Lord that I am!

Today, I stand where I belong, where I wanted to stand
all along, in the place where I have helped dozens walk before
me. Today, I am the bride. My attendants and flower girl have
already gone down the aisle, and I am the one being fluffed and
fussed over behind the confines of those big oak doors. My father
is at my side, my arm entwined securely in his. And as my signa-
ture music begins, he turns to me with a wink and a nod and,
without missing a beat, he whispers, "OK, sweetheart, here we
go. Take two!" I can't help but laugh.

As the doors open and I step through them, I am beaming
with more than just the excitement of the moment. I am beaming with love for every brick and stone, every pane of glass, for
every pew, every beam and rafter in this beautiful chapel that has

been both sanctuary and schoolroom for me. I am beaming with love for each and every person who is standing, facing me as I walk down the aisle, because each and every one of them has seen me through the darkest days of my life. And they're here now to share in the light that was there, all along, at the end of a very long tunnel.

I am beaming with love for the man who only has eyes for me. As I glide down this glorious aisle to stand by his side, where I will promise to love him forever, he steps down from the dais to meet me, offers me his hand, and escorts me to the spot where we will exchange our vows.

My saga of sorrow and defeat and of rising from the ashes to begin my life anew has come to a close. Today marks the first day of the rest of my life—a life I never expected but that I wouldn't trade for anything in the world. And I stand here today, a true believer in one thing:

RULE #101: *Miracles can happen. Miracles do happen! And more often than not, they ride in on the coattails of second chances.*

Acknowledgements

My first inclination is to thank every single person I've ever known in my entire life. But that's a lot of people and I hate it when the orchestra plays me off. So if you don't see your name listed here, and think it should be, I owe you a glass of bubbly.

A full-throated shout-out goes to my manager, Carey Nelson Burch: I absolutely would not be here without you! Thanks for believing in me through the lean years and for all the Kumbayas.

Todd Bottorff thanks so much for inviting me to be a part of the Turner family.

Stephanie Beard Bowman, thanks for saying "I do" to this book. It means the world.

Heather Howell thank you for helping me get this novel all the way down the aisle.

Kathleen Timberlake your enthusiasm is so contagious it makes me want to buy my own book.

Katherine Haake I am awed by your editing prowess. I never knew how much I didn't know about commas.

Carolyn Gauthier, no truer sister could I have in this world. Your picture will always be on my piano.

Kevin Gladstone, you are my hero. I love you Brother-boo.

Steven Gladstone, you definitely inspired some of the dream sequences in this book. It was a little spooky, bro. RIP.

To my dad, Gene Gladstone thanks for passing on your irreverent sense of humor and flawless understanding of what makes people tick. I wish you were here to see this.

To Dave "Dude" Carew, my first reader, editor-in-chief and favorite plus-one, thanks for always getting the joke.

Mary Helen Clark, your impeccable eye and sense of style gave this novel a fighting chance.

Jennie Fields, thank you for insisting I take a hatchet to the prologue and for the precious tin of Lady Grey tea.

Billie Joyce, Patricia Conroy, and Michelle Wright thanks for enthusiastically listening to snippets of early drafts. You inspire me every day.

Kellen, Kelsey, and Sapphira, thanks for all the joy you bring to my life.

Thanks go to Rick Fisher for being a long-time reader and fan. I love you cuz.

Genesis, thanks for being brave enough to read this book when it was a jumble of loose-leaf pages and for encouraging me to keep writing. You're always in my heart.

To Women Who Write, and our fearless leader Melanie Klinck, I offer endless thanks for seeing the potential in the bare-root-tree of this novel and believing it could blossom.

Heartfelt love goes out to Michael, Nancy, Greer, Blythe, and Satchel Daly. When I think of home I think of you. I never laugh harder, longer or louder than when I'm in your company.

A million hugs and kisses go out to the Tribe: My California Family. You are the heart and soul of it. We are the lucky ones.

To Lynn Brown-Bird, Majors Harris, Ray Pardo, thanks for always picking up the phone.

Humor Writer's Anonymous thanks for teaching me how to deliver a punchline and when to pull a punch.

To my Coco's family, many thanks for all the love and support, and for the cannoli's.

Jill Stiber, I can't remember a time in my life when you weren't beside me fighting the good fight. Let's keep doing that forever, kiddo.

Rosie Flores we never gave up on believing. This is our year.

Linda Marks, thanks for talking me off the ledge on more than one occasion.

Special thanks to Meghan Gwaltney, my partner in the crazy world of weddings. We've seen it all and lived to tell the tale.

A million thanks to my Nashville Family. You make me want to stay in the South and that in itself is a miracle.

Lynnie Lou Furtado, you've believed in me since our "cabinet food" days and that's a mighty long time. Thanks for keeping me going.

Julie Alexander and Brian Gordon thanks for the New York digs. You're beautiful.

Suzanne McCallen, I thank you for giving me some really cool spaces to write and for the hours I got to spend doing water aerobics with you in your pool and dreaming of this.

And to every bride I've gotten down the aisle, thank you for letting me be a part of your Big Day. And for all the stories.